# Praise for Frederick Schofield's

# *A Run to Hell*

"This exciting tale grabs you from the first page . . . packed with secrets, intrigue, and adventure—something for everyone.

—*Book Dealers World*

"Schofield is fun. He's entertaining. A storyteller."

—*The Press of Atlantic City*

"Tom Clancy and John Grisham fans will REALLY love this one! Fiction and fact are mixed so well that I cannot tell where the truth ends and lies begin. HIGHLY RECOMMENDED READING."

—*Huntress Book Reviews*

"It's the way the mob stuff really ran."

—*Fat "Joey A" Altimare*, longtime alleged and prison-pedigreed Philly mob member

"A spellbinder."

—*The Tampa Tribune*

"A great mix of fact and fiction, thriller and history."

—*Naples Daily News*

"*A Run to Hell* mixes a Grisham-style law story with the intrigue of organized crime, with a romantic subplot."

—*Ambience Magazine*

"*A Run to Hell* jabs like a pitchfork to your heart."

—Don Cannon, *WOGL-FM*, Philadelphia

"Recommended reading."

—*Royalty.nu,* The World of Royalty

"Captivating stories."

—*Writer's Life Magazine*

**Find more critical reviews, learn about the author, and discover the "stories behind the stories" in videos, magazine articles, news stories, music, and more at . . .**

**Frederick-Schofield.com**

Also available

by

Frederick Schofield

In Print, LARGE Print, Audio and E-Book

# A Run to Hell

**Second Edition with Epilogue**



ISBN: 978-1-7347024-7-7

Library of Congress Catalog Card Number: 1-73470-247-8

Published by Beach Books Publishing, LLC
Email: Publisher@BeachBooksPublishing.com
Web Address: BeachBooksPublishing.com

Titles for year-around pleasure reading.

Warehoused by Ingram

Available in print, large print, e-book, and audio book.

Printed in the United States of America

Frederick Schofield's

# A Run To Hell

## Second Edition with Epilogue

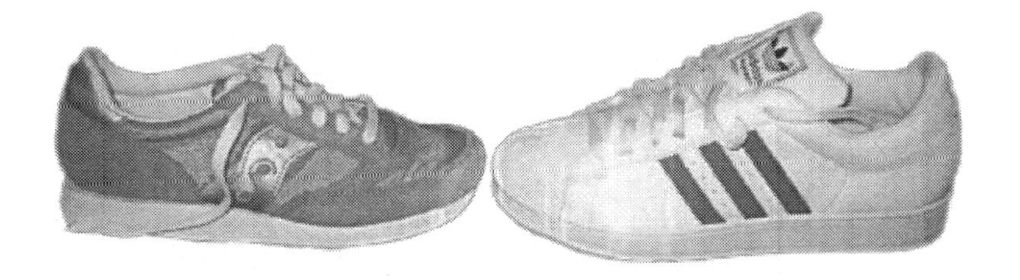

BEACH BOOKS PUBLISHING, LLC

# Frederick

---

# Schofield

# A Run

# To Hell

*For Antonio "Quick Fish" DeBona*

# About the Author

SAVOR A DREAM. In it, legal thriller king John Grisham mates with romance genre queen Nora Roberts. Later that night—because it's only a dream—she wraps with mob master Mario Puzo or is it thriller titan Tom Clancy? Anyway, the child they spawn creates easy reads: entertainment that's perfect for any beach, hearth, or comfort zone.

Frederick Schofield delivers those tales. The former trial lawyer, who colorfully prosecuted and defended, is a U.S. Marine combat veteran. He shares a wealth of tales in light reads that are flavored with intrigue, mystery, suspense, a smidge of romance, and a dash of humor.

ITALIAN
MARKET
SPICE CO., INC.

# Part I

# Chapter One

# There Are No Sweet Goodbyes

WIND CUT DOWN THE STREET like a sharpened axe. Its lonely lament was all to be heard that late wintry night. Draped between telephone poles on opposite sides of the narrow commercial avenue, a banner proclaimed, "Happy New Year 1985!" Hanging beyond the holiday, it found freedom when a gust sent it swirling to the roadway.

Lee Gunther routed his Corvette around it. Shops in the Philadelphia Italian market section were dark, streets deserted. His eyes combed for the alley where they'd meet until he jammed brakes to peer into it.

*Too dangerous*, he thought. *Don't go*.

He had no choice. Breeze from the alleyway beckoned. It whipped as he entered, and still whisked when he stopped at the door bearing worn signage for "Ottaviano Fine Meats."

"Maybe I'll be their morning special," he wheezed.

With engine churning heat and doors locked, he waited for Frankie "No Throat" Cinelli. Lee ran his hand over blond hair, pulled back tight in a ponytail. His tailor-made suit was his battle armor. Long hair and a polished look gave the lawyer the appearance of a rebel who'd fight for clients. His slight limp was rarely detectable yet caused the tall and lanky lawyer to think twice before leaping—a credo that manifested more than physically: Lee scrutinized courtroom adversaries before striking.

He jolted as something bustled. Racing from the shadows, a rat jitterbugged as if cold concrete stung its feet. It leaped into a drainage sewer with tail waving adieu.

*Why*, Lee wondered, *did I agree to meet here?*

If a mob client couldn't see him in his office, he'd connect in a crowd filled place like Harlow's nightclub on Bank Street. Bars were safe havens to meet clientele and contacts, who were sometimes dangerous, even to him as a respected criminal defender. Besides, the thirty-five-year-old bachelor enjoyed mixing business with pleasure.

He had waited at Harlow's, but Frankie sent a message to instead meet behind the butchery. Nursing misgivings, Lee clutched a thick file that the mob wanted so badly, the one he'd received ten days earlier from a friend just buried. Perhaps because he and Frankie had developed an enduring relationship, the Philly mob captain had warned him that their rendezvous was the only thing sparing Lee from his own funeral.

"Frankie," Lee mused.

At fifty-one, the guy maintained boyish looks that had earned him the moniker "No Throat" on South Philly streets. Frankie had shared the story. It came in deference to his slight stature, curly black hair, ice-blue eyes, and facial features so like young Frank Sinatra—the way the crooner looked as a skinny kid from Hoboken, not the older, toupee-topped version. Cinelli's inability to carry a tune gave him the name: Frankie had no throat. His long career of malfeasances had begun as a paper hanger.

"What's a paper hanger?" Lee had said, when Frankie first came to him.

Frankie stared.

"I know you're *kinda* new to this, but don't they teach you anything in law school, Counselor?

Frankie paused, as if stupefied by the ignorance he faced.

"A paper hanger passes bad paper," he explained. You know, clearing bad checks and working kiting scams.

"Bank fraud," Lee offered.

"That's the criminal charge but it doesn't have to come to that. Here's what happened. I deposited a thirty-seven-thousand-dollar check and worked the float time.

"The float—"

"My bank cleared the check and I cashed out before they realized funds weren't in the payer's checking account."

"How did that happen?"

"This is Banking 101."

Lee understood. He sensed the man's reluctance to reveal all his trade secrets on an initial meeting. Moreover, Lee didn't need to learn Banking 102. If he were aware of any irregularity, rather than being an attorney representing a client, he could be an accessory to a crime. That was something never taught in law school, now stored in his mental arsenal.

"Their error embarrassed me," Frankie moaned. "I relied on pin-striped-banker-suit guys to hand me cash after they said the check cleared and I spent the money. It's impossible to repay them. So, they can file charges and get nothing back from me . . . or I can borrow a couple bucks from relatives."

"In exchange for a signed release," Lee offered, "so they can't sue or prosecute."

"Naturally, the whole fuckin' thing is their fault. They cleared the check. I didn't. I'll toss 'em a couple bucks to settle and pay your fee as my business expense. That makes me, as their customer, the victim of their carelessness."

Frankie slid an envelope across Lee's desk and offered: "Here's a few gee-whizzes."

Now, it was Lee's turn to stare.

"Your fee, Counselor. A gee-whiz is a grand in cash and this is how family business usually pays."

From that day, Frankie counted upon Lee's talents to keep his butt out of jail, whenever malefactions caught up to him. Frankie reciprocated by referring clients needing effective representation.

Like many mob wise guys, Frankie branched into drug trafficking. Knowledge of offshore banking perfectly suited him to launder his crime family drug money in the Cayman Islands and Panama where banking secrecy laws benefitted drug dealers. The countries were used as laundromats to clean and store billions.

Frankie was taking another business trip to Panama in the morning. Something there, he said, something besides business always drew him back. Still, the hood seemed uneasy—as if fearing he wouldn't return from the place. The country was a land of tyrants and its current dictator genuinely frightened him.

*What's so sinister about General Manuel Noriega,* Lee wondered, *that conjures fear in a man who embraces murder in his Mafia credo?*

Lee had no idea. Yet, more than anyone alive, he knew why Frankie was so eager to meet him before taking that trip. Each document in the file folder that Lee held implicated the Philadelphia crime family—and Frankie No Throat particularly—in the deaths of Grace Kelly Grimaldi and her popular city councilman brother.

*Mutual affinity brings me here,* Lee thought, *but if I'm wrong in assessing our relationship . . . I'm dead.*

An explosive burst from a mallet pounding glass filled his eardrums. Crystalline fragments whizzed. Hands thrust through the shattered driver side window and yanked Lee to frost covered concrete, where fists pummeled, and shoe leather stomped him. Agony fused with terror as Lee realized he was being beaten to death.

Above the lawyer, icy eyes peered then a boney hand reached through the broken window for the folder. Jagged glass lacerated flesh in the overly anxious grasp, causing a boogeyman shaded in darkness to suck severed man meat like a hungry carnivore.

He slammed the file on the Corvette hood, ripped out papers with his good hand, then dropped them into a metal trash container beside the car. Blood stained sharkskin pants as his hand dove into his pocket for a wooden match. He struck it against his teeth, dropped it, and watched an affidavit burst into flames. One at a time, he burned investigation reports from the European police network Interpol, Philadelphia Police reports, documents bearing the royal seal of Monaco, hospital records, and photographs: a snapshot of a porcelain princess charring brightest.

Lee's mind entered that surreal realm where conscious and unconscious worlds collide. While evidence crackled in flames, a solid blow to Lee's head launched a vivid mental montage. It all played out in his mind: a car somersaulting down a steep ravine as a woman's screams filled his ears. Then, a boot crushed Lee's skull, jettisoning him to a deserted street. Gunshot rang, then a bleeding man wormed on pavement. As Lee took another pounding, a sea of lustrous bouquets beside coffins burst in a kaleidoscopic vision.

He wondered if the moans he heard were part of a surreal dream or his own, then spied a silhouette standing before high-rising flames. With a shadowy wave of the man's hand, the beating ceased. Time arrived for death's cold kiss to smack his lips.

*My God,* Lee thought, *now they'll finish this with a bullet or a blade.*

He ached to escape with a body too broken. Still only a silhouette, Lee watched the shadowy figure lower to one knee, then pull his hand from his mouth. Blood spurted like a fountain.

"You're disappearing," he said.

Lee couldn't discern the man's face through eyes swollen to slits, yet he recognized the voice that carried no tune.

Frankie watched his lawyer twitch, then expelled breath that steamed in frigid air.

"This is your warning shot," the mob *capo* said. "We gave one to your friend, but the councilman didn't take the hint. If you don't want the boys planting you next to him, leave town and never look back."

Lee groaned like a diseased goat. Bile seeped from the corners of his mouth. Frankie admired the way his younger friend endured pain: embers still sparked in those assaulted eyes, perhaps too brightly.

"You're good, Counselor. Good as they come in drug work. Start over in Miami. It's the Super Bowl of major crime. Dealers import their shit from Central America to South Florida shores and outlands, then distribute nationwide. They've turned Miami into a place where drug money papers walls and players race 'round every corner, dealing drugs, death and disorder. You know, the stuff that feeds lawyers. I'll even send you some office traffic. Just leave on the next flight out and never say Kelly again."

Frankie wondered if Lee could keep a lid on what he knew. The only way to be certain was to give the lawyer a permanent reminder.

"You've got pain-in-the-ass ideals, Lee. You don't know where to draw the line, helping friends or asking them for help. Sometimes friendship shouldn't be put to the test."

Frankie paused to lick his wound, then continued.

"Maybe that's what's held us together—maybe we're alike. One thing's for certain, though. If you reopen this investigation, 'the boys from downtown'," as Philly Mafiosi refer to one another, "will kill you."

Frankie shook his head. He had known Lee since the younger man was in high school. The kid never suspected, not even for an instant, that he had a benefactor. Still, sometimes guardian angels must do devilish deeds. He planted a kiss on Lee's forehead, stuck a one-way plane ticket in Lee's mouth, then whispered so only the younger man would hear.

"The Boss wanted me to whack you. I convinced him to let you live. Get out, while you can."

Frankie nodded to his men, who were shifting weight from one leg to another, battling the chill. An impish assistant hustled behind the fiery trash can. Expelling the oomph of a brawny leprechaun, he carried a cinder block over his head, and set it down. Another man gingerly raised Lee's leg to rest upon it.

Disgusted by what he had to do next, Frankie turned his face upward and spoke to heaven.

"There are no sweet goodbyes."

He raised his foot high and smashed down on Lee's kneecap. Snapping cartilage, cracking bone, and Lee's woeful groan filled their ears. Frankie wondered if someday he'd have to whack him . . . as his lawyer focused on the raging fire.

Lee longed for unconsciousness to steal his agony but something in the flames riveted him. Burning in the heart of the inferno was the face of an elderly man who had a small and heavily furrowed brow. Deep creases etched auburn cheeks and framed the corners of his mouth. Dark, bottomless pools filled his eye sockets, leaving no room for the whites of the eyes. In a soft and lyric chant, he called to Lee, hypnotizing as intoning:

Run to Hell
Fast as you can.

Run to Hell
And meet the man.

Run to Hell
But have Godspeed.

Run from Hell,
It's what you'll need.

The mouth twisted, teeth reaching through dissolving lips, nose distending like a protruding tusk. The metamorphosis compelled Lee to lower his eyelids. Then, a power surge of pain electrified his body and a blown fuse stole his senses.

Frankie studied the unconscious lawyer, knowing they were both bound for bumpy rides. The Philadelphia crime family was sending him to deal with Panamanian dictator Manuel Noriega, who shared intimacy with torture and death. Frankie knew what that meant to Lee. The mob wanted the lawyer dead and if Frankie died, the lawyer would stop breathing, too. As Frankie's gaze turned from Lee's broken body to his own wounded hand, he realized something else with stone certainty.

*Our lifelines intertwine*, he mulled, *in a way that proves a bullet fired twenty years ago can still kill.*

## Chapter Two

# Dead Off 95

SOME FOUR YEARS LATER, JANUARY 14, 1989 to be exact, FBI Special Agents DiPoala and Marx baked. Parked under noonday sun, from the only vantage point they could muster for the stakeout, their eyes focused on a private dock situated behind a cluster of Miami Beach waterfront homes. Their Bureau car, a stripped Chrysler, hardly blended into a neighborhood where Benzes, Porches and Cadoos cruised, but neither did the red Pontiac Trans Am parked at the dock. They called in its plate number and learned it was tagged to Luis Gomez, a dope dealer with a rep nasty enough to pique their interest. Temperature in their sedan, where they sat with the engine off and windows rolled down, took its toll.

If raisins groaned while sun drying, Marx was mimicking their tune. The veteran agent opened buttons on a starched-white shirt, then scratched his clammy scalp through bristles on a flat top 'do. He bore the no-nonsense image of an army drill instructor, the kind of man who habitually broke shoelaces by pulling the strings too tight.

"At least there's a breeze off the water," his bespectacled partner said. The younger man, who was eager for Bureau advancement, did the driving, and relished scutwork.

Marx turned to him.

"Are you lending me that twenty bucks or what?"

DiPoala pushed himself back from the steering wheel and dug for his wallet.

"Your wife is really keeping you to that budget, isn't she?"

"Credit cards buried us," Marx groaned. "I'm short on cash until we catch up."

The younger man tugged a fat billfold buried in his pocket.

"Man," Marx wheezed when he saw its size. "What do you keep in there?"

"Pictures of my little girl mostly. Want to see?"

Marx shook his head.

"No thanks, proud pop. Wait 'til you have three of 'em and they move into your only bathroom for their teen years. I haven't done a meaningful dump at home in a decade."

DiPoala smiled. He wiped his horn-rimmed eyeglasses with a tissue and held them up to sunlight, checking for smears. Then, he set them atop a pug nose that pointed toward a sixty-foot Sea Ray yacht.

The huge cabin cruiser had brought them there. Though registered to a recognized Panamanian banking conglomerate, the agents knew what business was really conducted on the pleasure craft. They were engaged in a routine drug investigation that had produced few surprises, thus far, and was likely to generate none that day. They studied the Sea Ray, their eyes darting from gleaming white decks to black-tinted windows, while their backs sweat against vinyl seats.

On the dock, a pelican craned its long neck, poking its beak under a wing before settling down to nap. Marx prepared to doze, too. He flipped onto his side and positioned his head on a sticky headrest.

"I'm taking five," he drawled through a yawn. "Nothing's happenin' aboard that thing."

In the cabin cruiser master berth, two men breathed hard. Gun smoke twisted through silencers on their semiautomatic pistols. Naked targets sprawled lifeless on a king-sized bed. The gunmen studied the potbellied white man. His receding hairline had retreated farther when their firepower had ripped apart his skull. His ebony bedmate possessed beguiling endowments drawing their attention. They had caught her mounted on the fatso and peppered her back with bullet holes. Her broad bottom was untouched and raised high in death's awkward repose.

The Dark Angel surveyed the yacht fineries, admiring mahogany-paneled walls. Above them a ceiling mural displayed Rubenesque beauties bathing with lusty-eyed cherubs.

*Such grandeur*, he thought.

He had grown up too poor to have once considered finding himself in those lush surroundings—except as a lackey. Brown skinned with Anglo features, coarse black hair greased back, the compactly built man viewed the pasty fatso with resentment. He was the kind that had looked down on Angel in boyhood.

As he studied the dead man's woman, the corners of his thin lips lifted. Angel knew what to do. He opened his belt and lowered his trousers.

Gomez stood beside him. The tall and spindly man shook as if firing his pistol had a reverberating aftereffect. He touched the gun barrel, then instantly withdrew his hand from hot steel. As Angel approached the woman, Gomez blandly observed: "She's dead."

"But still warm," Angel remarked, while caressing commodious cheeks.

"Wake up," Agent DiPoala called. He smacked his partner's shoulder and adjusted his eyeglasses, straining for a better look.

Marx squinted to focus in glaring sunshine. His eyes followed DiPoala's finger that pointed to the docks. Two men emerging from the yacht casually strolled toward the Trans Am.

"Check him out," DiPoala said, "the little guy."

Marx was nonplused.

"Never saw him."

"No one in the Bureau has—not here, not in the flesh." DiPoala's voice elevated an octave. "First time he's been spotted in this country. It's Rodolfo Angel, Noriega's Dark Angel."

"You're spending too much time studying mug shots. Can't be . . . or is it?"

"That's him, all right," DiPoala declared.

"A colonel in Panama's Battalions of Dignity? What's he doing in Miami with a mid-level dope dealer?"

"They say he supplies serious muscle for Noriega's drug connections."

Both agents knew that and more. Angel was the right-hand man of Panamanian dictator Manuel Noriega, his drug kingpin overseeing cocaine distribution, his personal henchman and cold-blooded killer. Angel had snaked his way into favor with the dictator as an eager-to-please member of Noriega's Battalions of Dignity, the internal security force that infiltrated every level of Panama society. Members of the force settled unrest by torturing and killing proponents of political opposition. The Dark Angel was a natural killing machine who, like his boss, had been morally scarred from birth.

The agents watched Angel settle into the Trans Am. Gomez jumped behind its steering wheel and the car pulled away.

Marx grimaced as he said, "You know our MO."

DiPoala nodded.

"Tail 'em," Marx directed.

A quaver in the veteran's voice let the younger agent know their next moves wouldn't be routine, causing him to share the tremor as Marx declared, "I'll call in who've we ID'd, and where we're headed."

DiPoala started the sedan as Marx picked up their radio handset. They followed slowly through Miami Beach streets until the Trans Am found the causeway linking them to the City of Miami. When the red car picked up speed, DiPoala pumped his gas pedal. Their Chrysler accelerated with a surge of hesitation.

"Move," DiPoala urged it.

Somehow, they maintained pace as the speeding vehicles crossed the expansive waterway. To their right and left pleasure crafts bobbed atop turquoise waters. Suddenly, the Trans Am took off with a jet burst. It barreled up the Route 95 on ramp.

"They know we're onto them!" DiPoala shouted to his partner. "Give Papa our location. We're in pursuit."

"In a bucar?" Marx moaned.

He picked up the handset and called, "This is alpha one-niner. Papa, we've been burned. We're jumping the Miami causeway onto ninety-five northbound."

Ahead of them, the Trans Am raced. It was fast and hot—everything their bucar was not. Bureau cars aren't built for speed because FBI agents, unlike police officers on patrol, rarely engage in high speed pursuits. Neither their car nor the agents were up to the job. Armed with Smith & Wesson .38 caliber revolvers, which held six shots, the agents knew the men they tagged outgunned them.

A call came back over the radio: "This is Papa. Go in alpha one-niner."

Marx screamed to DiPoala, "Go in? Those bastards will be armed like a combat patrol."

"Where's the shotgun?" DiPoala yelled over engine roar.

"Where regulations say it belongs—locked in the trunk," Marx called back. "Unloaded, I think. We weren't expecting this shit on a routine stakeout."

DiPoala spun the wheel to avoid tail-ending a tractor-trailer. Interstate Route 95 in Miami was bustling at the height of the winter season. Suddenly, the agent wondered if they should've pursued the Trans Am at all. Bureau policy is to outman and outmaneuver the other side by planning ahead and choosing the time and place of an arrest. Still, the Dark Angel was too big a fish to let go. There weren't many chances to reach into Noriega's inner circle. The dictator was a major law enforcement target and picking up the Dark Angel was worth any risk.

The Trans Am cut across three lanes of Route 95 traffic. Its tail clipped an old Dodge. Hubcaps flew. One sailed into the bucar windshield as DiPoala swerved. He saw the red car zip to an exit ramp for a North Miami neighborhood. Marx radioed the move as DiPoala charged toward the exit ramp doing ninety miles per hour.

On the ramp, the Trans Am didn't slow. Instead, it picked up speed and plowed into the rear of a car blocking it, letting them know that Gomez was a pro. The impact hurled the car ahead out of the way and the Trans Am turned right onto a neighborhood street, beginning to put distance between itself and the bucar.

"We'll never catch them!" Marx observed.

DiPoala instantly responded, "I know a short cut."

He swerved right and their Chrysler barreled through a barrier and off the exit ramp. It plummeted to the ground with a series of thuds as springs and shocks absorbed the jolt. DiPoala cut across a vacant lot to take advantage of the angle on the Trans Am right turn. He floored their Chrysler and accelerated toward the Trans Am broadside.

Marx shouted, "You're ramming them?"

He dropped his pistol and covered his head with his arms, bracing for collision.

The crash came like a cannon burst. Steel ripped into steel. Tires screeched. The Chrysler overturned and skidded on its roof, sparks flying, until it smashed into a parked car.

DiPoala looked toward his partner. Marx returned a disoriented gaze. They were upside down, strapped into the car by their seat belts, dizzy and stunned. DiPoala scoured for the Trans Am but his eyeglasses had sailed off his head and he couldn't see farther than ten feet. Everything else blurred.

Marx pulled himself out of the car through an open window, then screamed, "Where's my Smith and Wesson?" He dove back into the car for it.

DiPoala pulled himself from their car, still looking for his eyeglasses.

"Two men coming fast," Marx screamed, "heavily armed!"

"Grab the shotgun in the trunk," called DiPoala.

"Don't have the trunk key."

DiPoala couldn't see to find it.

Gomez carried a Colt AR-15 assault rifle. Angel toted a Ruger mini-14 semiautomatic carbine. The Ruger had a thirty-round clip and its bullets traveled with enough velocity to penetrate a car door. The two Panamanians fired rapidly.

Agent Marx leveled his .38 and squeezed off six quick rounds.

"Goddamn!" he shouted. "Six rounds and you *haveta* reload, one bullet at a time."

He ducked and feverishly reloaded behind the Chrysler.

DiPoala reached around the front bumper and fired at the two fuzzy forms approaching. Heavy firepower forced him to slink back behind the car. Suddenly, he felt the sensation of a thousand bee stings, and realized he'd been shot. DiPoala howled as he saw that the round had chopped out a chunk of palm. His shooting hand was useless.

The Dark Angel signaled his colleague to pause and reload. They dropped their near empty ammunition clips. Instantly and effortlessly, they shoved full clips into their weapons. Smiling to each other, the shooters strolled to the overturned Chrysler. Gomez pumped rounds from his assault rifle into the car to keep the agents' heads low. Angel just walked. He whistled as if on a casual Sunday stroll down Avenida Central in Panama City, the capital. How often he'd enjoyed traversing the bustling commercial street, music streaming from cantinas, always plunging him into a mood of Latin American ambiance. Suddenly, music played in his head. How good it sounded.

Angel signaled Gomez to cease firing. With a broad grin, he spotted the two agents on the ground and sensed their emotions. Their fear whetted his appetite for blood. Music in his brain resounded, conga drums pounding a frenetic beat. He came close enough to smell their terror and realized time had come to kill.

Marx leaped up with his pistol cocked and Angel casually pumped ten rounds into the agent, who writhed across the roadway with the impact of each bullet.

Gomez walked to DiPoala. The younger man lay perfectly still as Gomez pulled out the agent's thick wallet and flipped through it. Jittery hands caused photographs of a toddler to fall like autumn leaves.

"*Mierda*," he cussed, shit.

His heel forced the kid's face to kiss concrete. At the wallet bottom, Gomez found what he sought, pulling out an ID card.

"They're feds," he said, "fucking FBI."

Angel watched DiPoala play dead. Standing over the agent, he spoke softly.

"If you give up, if you lie to die, you die."

A siren howled. Angel stuck his nose into the air as if he could smell the approaching vehicle.

"That's backup for these guys or local cops on their way," Gomez said, his hands still trembling.

Congas in Angel's head beat loudly as he taunted Agent DiPoala.

"If you give up, if you lie to die, you die."

DiPoala's eyes were bleary. The lids began to close, then opened wide and wider still as he raised his left hand, lamely dangling the pistol, finally gripping it more steadily. When he extended his arm to firing position, Angel nonchalantly released four rounds, shattering DiPoala's left hand to bits. The pistol flew with fingertips still on its grip. The agent howled in agony, then lay still and moaned.

Angel looked down and told him, "I must leave you, Amigo."

He fired the rest of his clip into DiPoala's body. At such close range, the heavy fire power made the agent's body dance. Angel laughed in glee. Music from Avenida Central still blared in his mind, so he, too, did a dance, the Noga Kope folk dance of the Kuna people.

Gomez watched, as if transfixed, jaw agape, while sirens screamed louder from approaching police cars, then louder still. Sweat beads flowed down his brow.

"Run for the car," he shouted.

Angel heard its engine start. Tire rubber burned as Gomez pulled the car up and jammed its brakes. Yet, Angel heard something else, congas still beating passionate rhythms that moved his soul. The Dark Angel danced with greater fervor over the fallen agents.

Gomez called through an open car window, "Get in or I'll have to leave you here, man!"

Angel knew he was too important a friend of Noriega to be left behind. He danced until the congas stopped beating, then looked around. Residents of the neighborhood were hiding. Smoke was still clearing when Angel saw the first police car pull into view.

He shouted for all the world to hear.

"If you give up, if you lie to die, you die!"

'Then, he jumped into the Trans Am and laughed gleefully.

"I long for *musica* on the streets of home, *Amigo*," he sang out.

The red car sped out of sight as police cars converged. With his work in Miami done, Angel was ready to board the small, private plane that would take him home. Noriega's men left death marks that had become the dictator's signature—like a calling card from Hell.

Someday, the Bureau would use such incidents to lobby for higher powered handguns with 35-round clips to issue all field agents, all except those agents. They were dead off 95.

# Chapter Three

# Deal or Do Time

LEE STEPPED INTO THE FBI MIAMI FIELD OFFICE alone, wondering what they wanted from him and how they intended to get it. Moving quickly, the slight limp in his left leg wasn't detectable. His confident stride concealed emotion though he entered the building with genuine trepidation. Lee knew he shouldn't meet them. He knew he shouldn't go without legal counsel. Yet most of all, he knew he had no choice.

He had learned that Frankie No Throat was right about Miami. Truly, it was the Super Bowl of major crime. Illegal drug distribution, which impacted the nation, and accompanying nefarious activities roosted in that corner of the Sunshine State. The local Bureau office had so much work, its agents turned down many cases other field offices would seize. In Miami, even a million-dollar drug bust is no big deal.

*Why are they interested in me?* Lee thought.

Why were they pursuing income tax evasion charges against him that stemmed from years he represented mob figures in Philadelphia? The allegations weren't new, but charges had never been pressed. Four years earlier, in 1985, when he abruptly moved to South Florida, Lee had left his Philly law practice in his former partner's hands. Neither he nor Alfonse had heard a peep since then. Moreover, Lee had always been Mister Outside, handling courtrooms, while Alphonse countered as Mister Inside, managing the firm and tending to their financial accounts.

Rules for the impromptu talk were simple. It would happen off the record. Lee was to come alone, without counsel. They would present a onetime plea offer he could accept or reject. If Lee rejected the deal, charges would be immediately presented to indict him before a federal grand jury. That wasn't how they usually played the game. Something was more than mildly amiss, and Lee didn't know what or why.

Under the cyclops eye of a video monitor, Lee approached a young woman, who sat behind bulletproof glass. He slid his attorney ID card through a metal drawer to the receptionist.

"I'm here for a ten o'clock meeting," he said.

The young woman smiled warmly. Lee remained lean and ruggedly handsome. He had trimmed his long blond hair since his Philadelphia days. The ponytail was gone, yet, with a permanent tan Lee almost looked like a California surfer. At thirty-eight, he was at his prime, physically and professionally. Lee had a natural aura of confidence and a strong sexuality to which he was oblivious. Perhaps that's why it worked.

The confirmed bachelor still hit the sometimes vibrant, often languid nightclubs. That had never been purely recreational. Club life was an essential part of his criminal practice. Contacts in the drug community used crowded and noisy drinking dens as meeting places where law enforcement couldn't bug them. Quick conversations went unobserved and unrecorded. Just as Lee had once met criminal clients in nightclubs dotting Philadelphia's Society Hill, he crisscrossed the endless variety of Miami night spots.

"You're on my list," Mister Gunther," called the receptionist. "I'll call for a clerk to lead you there."

The woman slid his attorney ID card back with a plastic visitor's badge. He clipped it to his suit jacket lapel, while studying a pair of framed photographs hanging on the wall, decorated with blue ribbons. In one, a bespectacled agent's smile bespoke the self-confidence of youth. The other portrayed an older man, whose GI buzz cut exposed white walls over his ears, lending a look of unflappable determination.

"That's more than a memorial to agents slain in the line of duty last month," a young man called. "It's a reminder for everyone, who works with law enforcement, of how dangerous Miami can be. You're Lee Gunther?"

Lee nodded. The black face that greeted him appeared to be about the age of the younger agent. The office assistant dressed in khaki trousers and a short-sleeve white shirt. His tone was lively, his movements crisp.

"Follow me," the clerk directed.

Lee tried keeping pace as he was shepherded down a long corridor, where video monitors scanned every inch of the way. Finally, Lee stopped and called out.

"Let's take it a little slower," he said, tapping his left leg. "This thing acts up sometimes."

"Sure," his guide replied. "Sorry to make you take this hike. The hallway was designed to avoid house calls from pistol packin' cocaine cowboys."

Lee nodded as they moved more slowly toward an elevator at the end of the hall. An armed guard checked Lee's pass and permitted the twosome to enter an elevator. At the second floor, Lee's guide escorted him to the section of the building used by the organized crime unit. That immediately alerted him. They should've taken him to the white-collar wing. It told him the feds weren't really after tax charges.

*What are they after*? he continued to wonder.

His guide left him in a small room. Austere by design, the walls were white and bare. Fluorescent lights glared overhead. Four empty chairs surrounded a metal table. They made him wait under the focus of another security camera. Lee knew they tailored the treatment to make him feel ill at ease. A few doors away whomever would talk to him was killing time also. Lee never appreciated feigned dramatics yet knowing what the feds were doing didn't help. He was damned uncomfortable by the time three expressionless agents entered.

Special Agent John Ferguson took the lead, carrying a manila file folder under his arm. He was too heavyset and too bald to have served in the FBI during Director Hoover's reign. The guy was lucky to have come around after J. Edgar had left and standards for physical appearance relaxed. Ferguson did the introductions, speaking in a rapid-fire, staccato rhythm. Lee knew he would have to listen intently to keep up: more of the same psychology and gamesmanship.

"Take a seat," Ferguson directed.

Everyone sat at the table except Supervisor Martin, who stood in a corner, remotely as the small quarters allowed. Lee looked the supervisor up and down. Martin was no slouch. He'd spent more than thirty years with the Bureau, and he had seen it all.

*Martin is too high-powered to be on this case,* Lee thought.

He knew Martin had extensive experience in counterintelligence before shifting to criminal work. Lee had come up against the man while defending a client. That experience was the kind he didn't forget. Martin had a cerebral approach to criminal investigation that came from years studying the KGB, the Soviet spy network, and GRU, the Soviet military intelligence. He was a thinking man's thinker, who said nothing until he was ready. Martin looked the part of a former spook, being of average height, medium build, and quiet mannerism. Nothing about the man stood out. If you didn't know him, he was invisible. Lee knew the man by reputation and by the singular experience, which was enough. He wouldn't take the clever man for granted, not for an instant.

The other surprise package in the room was Special Agent Calero. About five feet eight, with raven dark hair and light complexion, the female agent stood out in every way Martin didn't. Calero had striking, yet refined and graceful facial features. A well-toned and physically fit body completed the picture. She didn't hide her good looks. That was rare in the Bureau where petty harassment of attractive women was all too common.

Ferguson fired: "You're looking at serving prison time for federal income tax evasion, Counselor."

"That's bullshit," Lee retorted.

Years of defending career criminals made some responses automatic.

"No. The charges are solid."

Lee looked around. As he suspected, the three agents had their eyes trained on him for his reaction. He fought to deprive them of that satisfaction.

*Screw them*, he thought. *If they want something badly enough from me, they can sweat, too.*

Everything about the setup suggested that the feds wanted something very badly. Lee wouldn't let fear show on his face or in his mannerisms. He still hoped to find a way out with a good bluff. Lee intently listened to Ferguson, who was going strong.

"I can even tell you where you'll do your time."

The agent paused for emphasis.

"Want to know? I've been through this old file of yours, and personally reserved your cell."

Lee realized it was time for him to shoot back.

"Your Philadelphia office looked at that years ago and closed their file. The charges were bogus then and they're bogus now."

"No, our Philly office only started its investigation before you moved down here. We had them complete the job. Want to see what we've got on you?"

Ferguson opened his manila folder and sifted through paperwork.

"Well, lookie here, Counselor. We have a couple sworn affidavits from mob informants, people you represented from the Philadelphia crime family, who've changed sides. Now, they're working for us. They're cutting deals for lighter prison sentences by turning in their mob buddies. They're turning in the goods on you, too."

Lee knew the FBI had cracked the code of *Omerta*—the mob vow of silence sworn by all members in the Philadelphia crime family. Rats, as their brethren called them, had turned as government witnesses. They would say anything to cut a deal for themselves.

"Yep. Just lookie. Proofs of pricy cash fees to paid to you personally for mob related legal work. That cash never made it to your law firm business accounts, and it was never declared as income. Makes us a prima facie case of income tax evasion for each tax year affected. That's a lot of tax years, Counselor."

Ferguson held up his left hand and counted fingers with his right. "Yep, five, I count. And that means you'll serve a lot of time behind bars. I count twenty-five years in federal prison on five mandatory five-year sentences. Aren't mandos a nut buster?"

"You know that evidence was manufactured," Lee said.

"We know a few things," Supervisor Martin interjected. "They're the same things you know. We can prove our case and you can't prove your defense. If we present the charges for indictment, we'll convict you."

Lee knew Martin was right.

"We'll talk to you just once," Martin continued. "You can cut a deal, right now, or you'll go down starting tomorrow. We'll never offer another opportunity for a plea bargain. The U.S. Attorney's Office will act under orders to push this case as a priority, to the limit, and past the limit. An Assistant U.S. Attorney has already drafted the indictment for presentation to the grand jury in the morning. Here's your courtesy copy."

Lee looked at the papers Martin handed him. His shoulders slumped as he read the first two pages. No reason to read more. Lee would have to give the feds whatever they wanted. True or false, the charges against him would stick in a court of law. Someone had planted evidencc too deep.

"What do you want?" he said.

Martin looked at his agents individually. First, he glanced to Ferguson in a way that let Lee know it was Martin's turn to take over. Evidently, the plan was Martin's baby. Then, Martin turned to Calero. Lee saw her eyes were cold, as if her beauty were a mask concealing some ugly secret. He could tell she was all business and felt her icy gaze as she stared back at him.

Jaime Calero studied the lawyer. She wondered if he was up to what they had in mind. She had read the file that the Bureau maintained on the mob lawyer. She knew his connections. He had spent enough years with vermin to become infected by the virus they carried. It didn't astonish her that the Bureau had caught him in a web of tax evasion charges. It only surprised her that they hadn't nailed him sooner. She didn't feel sympathy. The guy had earned what they were about to do to him.

The lawyer had a reputation as a solid courtroom combatant, but she questioned how tough he really was. They were going to make him fight a different kind of battle. His good looks and confident demeanor could be a thin veneer that easily folded.

*How smart is he?* Jaime thought. *Untrained, can he really play the role?*

Jaime was uncertain he or she would survive what was in the works.

*I'm ready, though*, she swore to herself. *God knows I'm ready.*

The special agent had come up the hard way. She had joined the FBI in a clerical position, then gained special training offered by every government agency connected to law enforcement. Her superiors noticed her work ethic and natural abilities. She excelled at each opportunity that came her way, regularly completing training courses at the top of her class. Finally, Jaime entered the FBI Academy to become a special agent. After graduation, she continued the hard work.

As a former Bureau office clerk, they had derisively called her a "clagent" behind her back. That term didn't bother her, but another did. In the California office, where she'd started as an agent, her male counterparts called her, like all female agents, a "breast-fed." No man called her that twice. Jaime knew how to take care of herself. She also had a record of arrests and convictions that few agents could match.

The agent was good at the job she loved—and the job was giving her the opportunity she never thought she'd fetch. Jaime had accepted a mission she may have been born to undertake, one that could also bring her death. She knew the slim odds and accepted them. The plan would bring closure, one way or the other, to a haunting chapter of her life.

Jaime's attention riveted on the lawyer. She stared intensely enough to make him look away.

Lee's eyes darted down. Calero's gaze shot through him; it could have penetrated steel. For an instant, he wondered what had hardened her. Then, Martin grabbed him with words that seemed carefully chosen. The senior agent uttered them almost lyrically, like a baritone delivering an aria.

"You have one way out," he intoned. "Bring us a dictator. You'll convince him to leave his palace voluntarily and walk into the Miami Federal Courthouse where he'll enter a plea to drug trafficking charges and face trial."

Lee was speechless. He realized that was just the way they wanted him.

"You're going to bring us General Manuel Antonio Noriega, Commander in Chief of the Panama Defense Forces, the most repressive dictator in this hemisphere. And you're going to bring him to us so we can lock him in an eight by ten-foot prison cell where he'll spend the rest of his miserable life."

Lee felt his jaw drop.

"You're going to bring us that son of a bitch or you'll take his place in that cell for the next twenty-five years."

Lee couldn't keep a shocked expression from covering his face. He looked up to the security camera, knowing they were recording him. After hearing Martin, he also knew who else was watching: a broad audience of agents engaged in counterintelligence and criminal work. Lee knew they wanted Noriega badly for political reasons as well as for trafficking overwhelming quantities of Colombian cocaine through Panama into the United States.

*How can I be of any assistance?* Lee wondered.

Noriega's own American attorneys had already publicly denounced United States efforts to have him surrender at Miami's federal courthouse. Those attorneys were among the best criminal lawyers in the country.

*The plan's too big for me*, Lee thought. *Maybe I'm better off just serving time on tax charges.*

Noriega was a ruthless killer. News accounts, rumors, and innuendo circulating among knowing members of the criminal Bar and the underworld creatures he represented left no doubt. Whatever the feds were planning, his life would be endangered. Lee had already dealt with one deadly force when the mob had literally kicked him out of Philadelphia. Only his connections in the crime family, through some devoted former clients, had spared his life—at least for the time being. He was still a marked man on some Philadelphia street corners and they could pull the plug on his life, anytime.

He sensed Martin was anxious to recite his plan, but Lee wasn't ready to hear it.

"Hold it," he said. "Don't go any further."

Martin glanced at the camera.

*Someone higher up is watching*, Lee surmised, *someone other than a Bureau chief.*

The deal smacked of covert intelligence work outside FBI jurisdiction. Someone from the Central Intelligence Agency was probably observing. He wondered whether the White House was involved. The Administration was likely staying clear of the operation to avoid political embarrassment if the plan fell apart and became publicly exposed.

*How high does this go?*

He pondered, then mused, "I need time to consider."

"You've got five minutes," Martin said flatly. "And, Mister Gunther, once you're part of the plan, there's no backing out."

"What in God's name *is* the plan?"

"Deal or do time," Martin shot back. "Think of where you'd like to spend the next quarter century. You may also wish to think about what brought you here."

Lee watched the three agents rise, then disappear as somberly as they had entered the room. Martin took the lead and Calero followed. On her way out, she stopped and turned. Calero looked at Lee again, as if studying him for some special purpose of her own. Trailing them, Ferguson carefully locked Lee in the room as he departed.

Eying the camera, Lee intuitively knew that whoever had been watching was still there. He wouldn't put on a show. Instead, he sat motionless considering what the feds wanted him to do.

Then, he reflected on the trouble that had sent him to Miami in the first place, the trouble with the Kelly deaths and the Philadelphia crime family. He was caught between forces that were consuming him like demons riding on his back with insatiable appetites for lifeblood. They could even send him on a deadly mission to Panama.

Lee scanned the room as he vowed so softly his words nearly didn't rise to a whisper.

"I'll never take another shit-kicking like the one I took in that South Philadelphia alley."

He knew what he had to do. To survive, he had to cast the ogres off his back forever. He swore to do it. Lee Gunther longed to get on with his life and to find peace of mind.

His eyes closed. Then, Martin's words gnawed at him as he reflected on a dash down the street he had taken years earlier—a dash that was now sending him on a run to Hell.

# Chapter Four

# Drinking from A Dirty Well

*M*Y *GOD*, LEE THOUGHT, *was it really seven years ago—back in 1982—when this all started?*

It's said that time flies over us but leaves its shadow behind. For Lee, time had cast no darkness to cloak the memory of that Philly night in Harlow's nightclub.

Coasting on a decline, the drink and dance spot wasn't so trendy anymore, but hung onto a certain stature by way of reputation. After all, nightclub glitter tarnishes before it dies. Once their favorite haunt, his old friend Kell didn't join him there so often, these days. That night they were meeting to discuss something troubling Kell, something causing Lee to wonder why his friend had been reluctant to discuss it on the telephone.

Lee rushed inside the club doorway and smacked into assailing breasts and assaulting lips on a faltering form. Her kiss came more as a slurp to his cheek. Through breathy rasps, the tawny blond of colossal proportion slurred.

"Did I ever thank my lawyer for gettin' me outta trouble?"

"Tanya, My Love, only after every time you've gotten into it."

Lee wiped his face with a handkerchief and watched her teeter atop platform shoes. He marveled at mountainous heels that elevated like Himalayan peaks.

"I know *whatcha* thinkin'," she said. "The higher the platforms, the lower the IQ."

Tanya always brought his smile. She pinched his dimples in a vise-lock.

"I ain't drunk," she lamely tried persuading, "just a little fucked up. It's the pills. They make me wacky and get me in trouble. Twenty-five thousand dollars for killer boobs, nose trim, cheek implants, electrolysis, and female plumbing—but to keep a feminine luster you gotta pop so much estrogen that you're cranked up like a premenstrual bitch goddess. So, they pump you full of antidepressants that can kick too hard. Even a teensy drink can put me over the edge sometimes."

Tanya stumbled and wrapped her arms around Lee to keep upright.

"Does that make me a bad girl?"

Her eyes peered longingly. Lee realized they were looking downward into his despite his height.

"Time to sleep it off, Darling," he said.

"Am I having another chemical reaction to my pussy pills—or are you really Mister Right?"

"Mister Right?"

Lee chuckled. He whiffed to inhale her intoxicating mélange of Chanel, gin, and some curious essence he could only attribute to overt sexuality.

Ooh, honey," came her coo, "this little tranny would do anything for her lawyer."

Lee had studied Tanya's medical history after she had first come to him with a motor vehicle accident case. They revealed more than he'd anticipated, fast immersing him in the intricacies and medical complications arising from gender transition.

Procedures were advancing. Transsexuals ingested female hormones to conquer unladylike characteristics like a deep voice and five o'clock shadow. Some male attributes remained pervasive problems after surgeons worked their miracles. So, Tanya popped Premarin, a natural form of estrogen extracted from the urine of pregnant mares. Heavy dosages produced inevitable side effects. As if perennially premenstrual, her estrogen rush induced depression and behavioral swings to such extremes that she had occasional minor scrapes with the law. Her physicians countered the conditions by prescribing antidepressant drugs, which Tanya ingested in varying dosages, as need dictated. The greater her depression, the more happy pills she popped. And, while popped up, antidepressants could set off wildly adverse reactions when combined with modest quantities of alcohol and even certain foods.

Lee waltzed her to a backroom couch, where Tanya curled up, and snored peacefully as any six-foot two-inch baby. Then, he searched for his friend.

Crossing a smoke-filled dance floor, Lee spotted the club namesake, who shared in-common Tanya's identity secret, though Rachel Harlow was confident enough to overtly reveal her own. She was proudly out. With a mane piled like Nefertiti's and a svelte form that was half mannequin, half deer, Harlow swayed. The beauty moved in perfect step with every dancer, while dancing by herself.

A disco ball lighted a thousand twirling stars. Under them one set of eyes burned brighter than the rest. Lee's friend waited at the bar catching Harlow's every move. Lee smiled, knowing Kell's determined look. The exotic creature, who danced alone, would have a partner before the call of dawn.

Kell perched on his favorite bar stool. He balanced a martini glass in a grip that was form fit for stemware. Brown hair, perfectly in place, was whisked back from a high-rising forehead. Unmistakably patrician, the dashing forty-eight-year-old was physically fit. While his father had won Olympic gold for the United States as a sculler, Kell had earned bronze. He still rowed on the nearby Schuylkill River. His physique filled out a Brooks

Brother suit that was more conservative than his political agenda as a wealthy and liberal city councilman. Kell was the spitting image of his father, who had been every bit as suave and just as much a ladies' man.

Kell's father had risen as a brick layer to found the largest construction firm in town. Single-handedly, the senior Kelly had brought his poor Irish-American clan from corn beef and cabbage to caviar. The elder Kelly had raised four children, the most famous being his daughter Grace. She'd starred in a string of major motion pictures before winning the 1954 Academy Award for best actress in *A Country Girl.* The seemingly demur woman from Philadelphia's East Falls had sexual allure behind a girl-next-door image that skyrocketed an acting carrier she had abandoned to marry royalty. Grace Kelly became Princess Grace of Monaco and something happening in her magic kingdom brought her brother to Lee.

Lee studied his friend. Kell's Irish eyes weren't smiling; they were downcast atop a rigid frown.

"My sister's come to me," Kell began, "with a problem in Monaco that's coming to a head. It's more than she can handle alone."

Lee squinted, as if straining for a better look would make sense of what his friend was saying.

"She's Monaco's princess. What problem could she have that she can't handle?"

Kell set his hand on his friend's shoulder and peered around the room. Lee sensed he was about to be pressed for a favor that would test their friendship, a test he might not pass.

"I think her life is in danger. I can't be certain, but you know people who may be able to find out. They may even be able to help . . .."

A slight but perceptible twitch in Kell's hand made his glass stem gyrate. He tipped it high and swallowed.

". . . your mob clients."

Lee observed Kell set his glass down on the bar too quickly, then use a napkin to sponge a spill. When Kell reached for the glass again, Lee grabbed his hand.

"Kell, I've represented people reputedly tied to the South Philly crime family. They're just 'the boys from downtown, as far as I'm concerned. Best we don't discuss them."

Kell persisted.

"Your boys from downtown may be able to tell me how serious Grace's trouble is. I understand there's no real connection between the crime family here and the family in Europe she's confronting, but maybe your clients could make inquiries."

"What are you talking about?"

"People connected to the mob family in Nice are moving on Monaco's casino. They want a piece of the action and my sister has always been headstrong. Grace talks to me about it . . . but I don't know what to do."

"Doesn't she have anyone to handle her problems over there?"

"Grace married into a postage stamp principality. Monaco is the size of New York's Central Park, making it the second smallest nation in the world after the Vatican. There's no army. Even the police are on loan from France—and they can be bribed. Monaco's a beautiful gem on the Riviera. Lots of glitter. No muscle. And, God bless her, Grace doesn't care."

"Better that God protect her than bless her," Lee mused, "with that kind of trouble."

"She's still the little girl from Philly that once kicked a bigger kid out of our backyard. And mind you, the bigger kid was carrying a stick for protection," Kell marveled with big brother pride.

Lee had heard Kell's tomboy tales of Grace's youth, and realized the cocky youngster, who had transformed into a confident and determined woman, might do something rash. She didn't realize what she faced: these interlopers racing through her fairyland carried bigger sticks.

As Lee searched for a way to escape an imposition that could bear nasty repercussions, one thought raced to mind.

"What's her husband doing about this?"

"Prince Rainier? Biding time. Grace figures, if she pushes hard enough, she'll either chase these people out of Monaco or force Rainier to do it himself. I'm not really certain who's she's talking to or what she's doing. I'm worried for her—worried in a big way."

Kell's hand reached for Lee's shoulder. His grip hardened as Kell implored.

"Talk to your boys from downtown."

Lee's elbows thumped on the bar top. His fingertips massaged throbbing temples as he thought. He understood his friend's concern but didn't know what he could do.

"Do you know what it means to ask those people a favor?"

"Find out whatever you can."

Lee looked around the room with a vacant stare until his friend pulled him around, so they met, inches apart, face to face. Kell's eyes implored, his gaze meeting Lee's eyes that responded firmly.

"Asking those people for a favor," Lee warned, "is like drinking from a dirty well. You quench your thirst, but you always pay a price for letting filth pass your lips."

"Lee, I followed one of your cases in the newspapers. You beat a tough rap for a guy named Frankie Cinelli."

"Frankie 'No Throat' Cinelli—that's who you want me to approach?"

"Please."

"Kell, I've handled cases for Frankie. He can be affable, even loyal on his own terms. But they say murder is as familiar to that Italian-American as a plate of pasta. I can't take your problem there."

"Talk to him, Lee. I'm begging for my sister's sake. Talk to him or I'll find the guy myself."

Lee knew he had no choice. He also realized something else. "Fate," he thought aloud, "serves peril when recklessly tempted."

Kell bottomed up and swallowed too fast. Gin and dry vermouth gagged him. He hacked loud and long, each cough expelled by faster and shorter breaths.

*Princess Grace*

## Chapter Five

# A Simple One Man Invasion of Panama

SUPERVISOR MARTIN HAD PROMISED Lee five minutes to consider the FBI deal when the agents left him alone in the interrogation room. They returned sooner. Agent Ferguson unlocked the door and twirled the key like he owned the only pass card to Lee's freedom. His bottom spread wide across the same seat. Agent Calero took her chair, focusing on Lee with her steely gaze. Martin returned to his corner of the room. When they were all in place, Ferguson turned to Lee, who hadn't moved, and began.

"Deal or do time," the heavy setter stated flatly.

Lee didn't look at Ferguson. The man was a stooge. Instead, Lee's eyes fixed on Martin. He sensed that was as visible as the invisible man ever became. Men like Martin preferred to labor behind closed doors.

"Deal or do time," Ferguson repeated.

Lee never really had a decision to make.

"I volunteer," he said, "but the criminal charges have to disappear."

Ferguson exploded.

"When you bring us Noriega, they'll go. You know how this works. We're extending this deal the same way we would offer a plea agreement based on a controlled drug buy. You've been down that road for your clients enough times to know the drill."

Lee understood. When a client was prepared to cut a deal in a drug case by turning in another drug player, the rules were simple. To receive a lighter sentence the client had to see the other player was involved in a drug transaction controlled by the government, arrested, and convicted. Only upon that conviction, did the client satisfy the terms of a government deal. This wasn't like tossing hand grenades: close calls didn't count. He realized he would have to do more than just participate in the Fed's plan, whatever it was, for the criminal charges against him to disappear. He actually had to get the Panamanian dictator into the United States. Anything short of that meant they would still prosecute him.

Lee made a simple inquiry.

"How do you propose I bring in Noriega, beguiling charm or a simple one-man invasion of Panama?"

He directed the question to Martin: he was the man with the plan.

Martin took a seat at the table for the first time. He cleared his throat, then laid it out.

"It has been said," Martin began, "that Manuel Noriega is like an unwanted mistress. He served his purpose for a while but doesn't have the decency to go away quietly now that the affair is over."

Lee looked uncertain.

"Well, you see," Martin said, backing up a bit, "years ago the CIA trained the son of a bitch as an informant for us. Noriega was a young military academy cadet. His handlers found him to be a perfect recruit. He was resourceful, amoral, and willing to work cheap. The guy grew up so poor, he worked for beer money in those days. They helped him advance through the military ranks and even gave him special training in counterintelligence, political science, and military tactics. He was a star pupil at our army jungle training center at Fort Gulick in Panama.

"When Castro seized Cuba in 1959, stabilizing Central America became increasingly important to United States foreign policy. This was especially true in Panama where the canal has always been a vital economic and military interest. Noriega was one of the people we depended upon. Ultimately, he became our 'go to' in Panama. Being our 'go to' anywhere gives you latitude. This guy stretched it to the limits, then further.

"We overlooked his repressive political ambitions. The United States has an unwritten policy that an anticommunist regime is preferable to a left-wing ruling party, even one that's democratically elected. Sometimes, our agenda requires a degree of selective blindness. After all, when he had members of his political opposition beaten, raped, and murdered, he wasn't adversely affecting American concerns. He was preserving our interests."

Martin paused to clear his throat again. A raspy smoker's cough echoed through the room. Evidence of years chain-smoking, while plotting and scheming in some dank sepulcher, filled their ears. Then, he loosened his necktie and continued.

"We would still be closing our eyes to what he's doing down there, but he became problematic. He was too greedy. Panama borders on Colombia. The Medellin drug cartel was the first to approach Noriega with a deal. They wanted an easy port of debarkation for Colombian cocaine shipments to the United States. Next door, the Panama Canal gave them unlimited shipping access to ports of entry all over the world. Naturally, we never much cared about the whole world, just our piece of it.

"The drug cartels began pumping cocaine into the United States, mostly through Miami, long before Noriega came along, but Manuel increased the pace. He became rich from trafficking drugs and laundering drug money. The man wasn't just an out of control despot. He was a drug kingpin with an army at his disposal, pumping

Colombian cocaine—billions of dollars of it—into the United States.

"We asked him to stop. He gave us the finger. Last year, we finally indicted him in our Federal Courts. He retained lawyers and we offered him a deal. We told one of the richest criminals in the world to keep all his money. We would give him a 'get out of jail free' card. All he had to do was turn over power gradually to a democratically elected leadership. We would even assure his safety in Panama or find him a safe haven somewhere else in the world. We thought he'd go for the deal. A man who grew up poorer than either of us can imagine could retire wealthier than we can even dream.

"His lawyers said it was a done deal. We told the President it was a done deal. Afterward, the son of a bitch changed his mind, so we supported a military coup d'etat to overthrow him. When that failed, the little bastard murdered the coup supporters and destroyed their families.

"His Battalions of Dignity went on a rampage of terror that hasn't slowed. Cocaine flows more heavily now than ever. He's made vague threats to close the canal to American interests and we can only expect those threats to escalate if we push him harder. Right now, he refuses even to talk to us through his lawyers.

"The Administration tried imposing economic sanctions, but the guy doesn't care. He lives above his national economy and his Battalions of Dignity protect him from any civil disturbance. Panama's a scary place.

It's a country where the police are the bad guys, supported by the army, and no one dares stand up to them."

"He's an indicted drug lord," Lee interjected. "Why don't you just send in the Marines to pick him up? Say he's a threat to American civilians in the canal zone."

Martin flashed a quick glance to Ferguson, the only trace of emotion Lee had ever seen from him.

"More aggressive measures have been considered," Martin offered cautiously, "but the Administration is committed to a conservative remedy. Diplomatically, there's a fear of upsetting Latin America. Politically, no one wants to risk our men and women in uniform."

"So, I'm your remedy of last resort," Lee said. "That's what this is all about, isn't it?"

The agents didn't answer; they didn't have to explain. Lee understood. If the plan didn't work, the United States might invade Panama to get Noriega. Yet, something remained a mystery.

*How*, he wondered, *can they use me?*

Martin answered the question without being asked.

"We'll prepare you for an introduction to Noriega."

"How?"

"He's always interested in an opinion from a hotshot mouthpiece. You have the credentials. You'll become his next legal wizard. You'll meet and persuade him to surrender in the United States. Tell Noriega anything it takes. There's no script. Play it as you find it. Tell him the case can be fixed, if you want, but get him here."

"The guy's represented by Frank Rubino, Neil Sonnett, and Ray Takiff," Lee noted. "He already has top criminal attorneys working for him. Why would he listen to another lawyer?"

"He doesn't like what they've been telling him. Noriega's been asking around for other options. There's already been talk of finding new counsel and you've successfully defended major and minor drug players."

"I've never represented his people."

"We know the nature of your mob connections, Mister Gunther."

"Reputed connections," Lee corrected.

"Yes, reputed," Martin conceded with a thin smile both saw through. "But Noriega's people are always on the prowl for sharp legal talent. Your name's already been raised in their circles."

Lee realized they had someone inside Noriega's operation to know that.

"We'll see that some of his people come to you for representation, immediately. The cases will be assigned to a federal judge who knows the plan. Counselor," Martin spit almost derisively, "you'll obtain fast and impressive results."

"The government will fix cases for the defense?"

"You'll obtain fast and impressive results," repeated Martin. "The Assistant U.S. Attorney assigned to prosecute the cases will work out details with you. You'll put your heads together, on a case by case basis, to dispose of charges on pretrial motions and other summary procedures."

"You're about to become the hottest thing to hit this judicial district," Ferguson chirped. "Noriega's people like a lawyer who's hot. We expect some to drop their current lawyers and show up in your office once word spreads. When they do, you'll find swift justice for them, too. Tough cases that languished will suddenly resolve in their favor."

Lee pressed for details.

"When will I meet Noriega?"

"Whenever he invites you to Panama," Ferguson said. "It'll happen fast. When it does, you'll go in a hurry."

"I travel there alone?"

Martin took over again.

"We learned about you. You don't know Spanish and we can't rely on Noriega's interpreters. You'll go with Agent Calero. She'll work undercover. The two of you will meet, *conspicuously*, in one of Miami's nightspots. Over the next few weeks, you'll be seen around town together at the clubs, the restaurants, the usual places drug players hang. You two are going to be a hot item."

Lee looked at Calero. She, at least, was a hot item but how well could she play the part? Lee's life would depend on it. He wasn't trained in covert operations and would have to depend on her.

Jaime returned the lawyer's stare.

She would go with him, but she would take her own agenda. For Jaime, the mission was more than a matter of bringing Noriega to justice. Venom boiled in her blood. Vengeance stirred in her heart. Until she released it, she would find neither peace of mind nor heart.

Had the operation come to ease her pain, or had she been born to fulfill it? Did it arrive mercifully, or would it tear her apart like all the others that had already been shredded? Every piece of her life fit snug into a shell casing that was ready for firing. Even the man they had found to make her cover work was perfectly suited for the role he would play. She studied him approvingly.

*Yes*, she thought, *this guy has the demeanor*.

He was more than just a pretty face on a well-honed mob mouthpiece. He was ballsy but where fate was sending them, tougher men had theirs cut off. She knew firsthand how cruel destiny could be and realized the lawyer didn't know how slim his fortunes had become. Jaime let out a long breath for a sorry stooge.

"We'll meet at The Forge," she told him.

Calero's words startled Lee. They were the first she had spoken, and he immediately detected her thick Spanish accent.

"Their Wednesday night party is the liveliest ticket in town," she said.

Lee knew. He often met his people there.

"Agent Calero will be your only contact with us," Martin interjected. "She's your lifeline."

"Can I count on her to pull me through this?"

"Don't screw up," Ferguson answered fast as a pig being poked. "Noriega's people can take you out anytime they want on Miami streets. And, once you're in Panama, you're in no man's land. Outside our military bases in the canal zone, there's no help for you. Blink wrong and you're both dead."

Lee knew the fat man was right. He also knew they weren't telling him everything. They were holding back, especially Martin, who probably was keeping his agents partly in the dark as well. Still, Lee knew how to play the game. He could hold back, too. He would use his own resources independent of the FBI and other agencies behind the operation. Maybe Martin was even counting on him to use them.

Lee sized up Calero again. The Latina agent seemed to be doing the same of him. For an instant, he contemplated the alternative to cooperating, the certainty of prison, and realized he had no other hope. He would have to bring in the ruthless and sadistic Panamanian dictator. To do it, he would have to reach old friends fast.

# Chapter Six

# Journey to the Devil

THE IDES OF MARCH, the fifteenth day of March in 44 B.C., was a day known to Lee from so often rereading his favorite of Shakespeare's plays. In it Julius Caesar was assassinated that day by his friend Brutus, who betrayed him with a cast of murderous Roman senators. The thought came to Lee on the Ides of March, when he called his pal Frankie, who also had murderous associates, and arranged for the twosome to rendezvous in a renown Miami locale.

Days later, Frankie No Throat squeezed into the crowded Forge lounge. Amid South Florida blue bloods and blood spillers—those who accrued wealth legally and those who amassed it illicitly . . . packed among brats, who had too much, and pretenders, who had spent their last dimes on designer fashions for just the night, everyone elbowing the beautiful people, who clamored for attention . . . Frankie spotted the show that caught every eye.

His lawyer and a Latina dame stopped exchanging furtive glances. They passionately embraced at the far end of the bar. Frankie watched Lee lip wrestle her, then looked around the room for a broad to stir his groin. He was always on the prowl, although he had a woman at home, one he had inherited.

Frankie was a "made guy," a man formally accepted into his crime family as a member. As part of his initiation into the family, he'd whacked a few guys . . . simply as a matter of making his bones. Since then, he had killed often. Bringing death was never a problem, though once he had run into trouble accepting blame.

His sister's husband wasn't part of the mob. The younger man was a tough guy from South Philly, who ran his own legit hardware and building supply business. He had a long-standing dispute with a made guy in Frankie's family. One late night, the two men walked behind a garage, and resolved their grievance the only way it could be settled: one walked out alive. Desperately, the survivor besought help.

"Jesus Christ!" Frankie shouted at his brother-in-law. "When did I become the patron saint to lost fuckin' causes? You took out Louie Grapes. He's a made guy!

I can't even do that without getting approval from my family."

"I know," the terrified, younger man said, acutely aware that what he had done in a heated moment probably meant he would receive a mob death sentence. He lifted the bottom of his oversized sweatshirt to his face, wiped his eyes, and wailed.

"You *gotta* help me, Frankie. You're the only hope I got."

Frankie's head spun. It spiraled faster when the arrogant prick leveled a reminder.

"You're godfather to my oldest kid, Frankie, the cute one with braces."

Frankie No Throat felt deep loyalties to those he loved. So, he did what he had to do to keep his sister from becoming a widow: he accepted blame for the death. When he was brought before a mob council, he parted words slowly, deliberately, but most of all hopefully to unbelieving jurors about to cast their life or death ballot.

"I was trying to settle bad blood," Frankie told the family members, who listened intently. They sat around a small table in an uncomfortably cramped room.

"And while I was talkin' to him—

Frankie paused, uncertain how best to frame his story for men who long shared an affinity for the decedent. Unlike making the classic old movies he so loved to watch on television, there would be no rewrites if this scene didn't pan out. There would only be one take.

*Damn*, he told himself, *just say it and hope to live.*

"You know," Frankie continued. "Well, we all know, don't we? We all know how hot Louie gets when he's drinking."

Frankie paused for emphasis, just as he had seen Lee do in courtrooms, when driving home an important point.

The guy came at me and I couldn't do nothin' else. In self-defense I took a knife to him."

"In self-defense you stabbed Grapes twelve times in an alleyway," his boss said suspiciously.

Frankie didn't like the tenor of the comment. His story was shaky, but it was the best he had.

Rocco Baratta was the Philadelphia crime family Don. Age spots freckled his forehead and bald scalp. Silver hair, full along the sides and hanging over his ears, lent a compassionate, almost grandfatherly appearance, which concealed the man's true nature. The older man was a killer, who had a fondness for Frankie.

*But, even if I get his vote*, Frankie wondered, *will it carry enough weight to save a longtime pal*?

Seated next to Rocco was one of the family rising stars. Little Vinny Talarico had a thirst for blood. The man of violence was well acquainted with the decedent, whose fondness for homemade vino had earned him the name, Grapes. Frankie surmised that the smaller man, who had an equal vote, wasn't buying Frankie's story. The dapperly dressed hood with perfectly coifed, slicked-back hair shot a fractured, psychopathic glance that made Frankie doubt he'd see tomorrow.

"Frankie, wait outside for us to consider this business," Rocco told him. "Taking the life of a made man is a serious matter, even if you were acting in self-defense."

When they invited Frankie back into the room, his knees locked. He stood at rigid attention as his verdict was delivered.

"Frankie No Throat," the Boss began, "what you've done troubles us. You've always been loyal. Your knowledge of banking laws is valuable. But you whacked one of our boys without permission."

Frankie saw Little Vinny fidget with something inside the jacket of his sharkskin suit. From where he was standing, Frankie couldn't tell if the small, yet perfectly proportioned, man carried a gun.

"You must pay the price," Rocco said.

He paused to let loose a raspy cough before continuing. "You'll pay the family by taking care of Jimmy Picardo's wife while he's in the can. You'll move in with the woman and treat her with respect. And you'll care for her children until Jimmy's out of prison and back on the streets."

"Jimmy's serving a life term!" Frankie cried.

"He's appealing his conviction and we can't let his wife become unhappy. If she divorces the guy, the District Attorney can compel her to testify against Jimmy at a retrial. If she stays married to him, the D.A. can't force her to take the witness stand against her husband.

You'll keep her happy, so she'll stay married to Jimmy during the appeal and his retrial if he wins the appeal."

"Boss, the appeal could take five to ten years."

"I suspect it will."

"The woman's a fat cow!" Frankie was almost beside himself.

"She's a cow but she's got a nice pair of udders. Frankie, I suggest you enjoy them and be glad you're allowed to live. That's your punishment, Frankie No Throat."

Head-down dejected, Frankie slunk from the room. As he wondered if he would have been better off carried out dead, another man called to him.

"Hey, Frankie," he said. "Mooooooooooo!"

As if a goddamned barn door had opened, Frankie heard cow calls from all his cronies for the next few weeks. He moved in with Jimmy's wife and cared for her. When he went to Miami, though, he prowled for female companionship, preferably on the skinny side.

He settled onto a barstool and eyeballed the room. Nothing grabbed his attention like the Latina number in the red dress whose lips were still locked on his lawyer.

Now that's a woman, he thought.

Ninety miles south of Florida lies Cuba. Seven-hundred miles farther is Panama. At the same moment Frankie watched Lee lip lock Jaime, another man in a Panama City nightclub eyeballed an attractive couple at the bar. From his Naugahyde booth, he saw them snuggle and laugh.

*The woman*, he thought, *ah, she's a beauty*.

With long, flowing dark hair and dark skin, wearing a brightly colored floral print dress, cut low to display her cleavage, she was indeed a vision to behold.

Rodolfo Angel was on an assignment. He had found a man whose loose talk had subjected him to scrutiny of the Battalions of Dignity. The man was a middleclass executive, a Panamanian citizen working for an American company in the canal zone. While he worked in the American controlled zone, he was safe. When he came home to his family each night, he returned to the Dark Angel's world. The man, who had spoken openly opposing President Noriega, was about to learn a lesson.

What was the man's name? Angel neither knew, nor cared as he watched them leave that nightclub. He was merely satisfied that his men had done their homework, filling a dossier with ample background information: the couple had three youngsters at home, the wife's mother—herself a widow—lived with them, babysitting when they occasionally spent an evening on the town.

*Such obvious affection*, Angel reflected.

He seized upon adoration evident in eyes that still lingered, long after devoted vows had been cast.

*Love comes easier*, he understood, *to their kind*.

Angel recognized the man and his wife for all they were, and for all he was not. Too poor to obtain a formal education, he had risen—slowly and hard—through the military ranks to attain his station in life. Unlike the blessed twosome, Angel knew he lacked sophistication that bred its own rewards. Instead, he was framed inside a small shell of diminutive features, unattractively cast: eyes too close, nose flat, forehead back sloped, and skin seemingly ingrained with uneven grime, rather than dark pigmentation. A mestizo, like his boss, Noriega, Angel had grown up with—and accepted as natural—a resentment of those better advantaged.

Yet, bitter feelings turned sweet with realization that his plan was unfolding. Angel rose, walked outside, and approached his troops who were detaining the couple. He studied the couple's fancy attire.

"White handkerchief," he pronounced as he lifted a silken square from the man's pocket. "The symbol of political opposition to President Noriega. Worn . . . so defiantly."

Angel grinned at the sight of fresh sweat beading on the man's brow, then calmly continued.

"*Senor*, we've heard about you. Your tongue wags too loosely about our President. Just because you work in the American canal zone all day, you think you're free to say whatever you choose."

*Terror dances to its own rhythm*, Angel reflected.

He appreciated just how fast it swept the man's face, steeling every trace of confidence, stripping dignity.

"You still sleep in our world."

The man's eyes could not meet his own, lifting Angel to grandeur heightened by the docility of his prey.

"Tonight, Amigo, you'll learn about patriotism."

The woman threw herself between Angel and her husband.

"No," she cried, "it's our wedding anniversary. Don't take him away."

"Ah," Angel sighed, not missing a beat of her rapidly pounding heart. "Of course not, My Dear," he assured, catching a flash of relief that instantly stroked her husband's brow like a cool, damp cloth. "We're taking you."

Angel turned to his troops and issued a simple order, "Release him."

Stone-faced soldiers freed the man and escorted his woman to a waiting troop truck.

"No," the man cried. "Take me," his cracking voice pleaded. "Please. My Rachelle has done nothing."

A soldier bashed him in the skull with a rifle butt, then watched the man slump to the ground, bleeding and unconscious.

*A piss ant is all he is*, the Dark Angel thought, *married to a beautiful lamb*.

He would give the piss ant something to remember. When they were through with his wife, he wouldn't be so loose with his talk.

They took her to the Battalion Headquarters, where Angel engaged in special work that was his pleasure. Inside a dank and nearly empty room it began.

"Rachelle," the Dark Angel cooed to her. "Your husband has been saying bad things."

Her eyes widened; her lower lip quivered.

Two soldiers held Rachelle on her knees before him. Three more stood behind her. They leered at her in the special dress her husband had bought to celebrate their anniversary. No one could help her. Her husband couldn't even go to the police. In Noriega's Panama, they were the police.

"You are a beautiful woman, my Dear," Angel said. "You're the kind of woman who makes a man hard."

He approached, reached inside her dress, and fondled her breasts as he spoke.

"You've made me hard, and I can see what you've done to my men. It's only fair that the wife of a man who talks so freely, a woman who makes men so hard, be taught a lesson in respect. After you've learned, your husband will be more mindful of what he says."

Angel laughed and turned away.

"Strip her," he said as he left, "and send her back to her husband in a way he'll never forget."

Lee looked up from Jaime and saw Frankie No Throat at the bar. He signaled to Frankie. Separately, they headed to the men's room to talk. Lee entered first, and strode to a brown marble sink, noting that even bathrooms in the place were splendidly plush. As Lee removed lipstick smears from his face, Frankie walked to the sink next to his. Frankie turned on the faucet and spoke softly above the noise of running water so the attendant by the doorway wouldn't overhear.

"You gettin' ready to do that babe on top of the bar, Counselor?" he said.

Lee smiled. Frankie could be crude, but he was good natured in his own way. Just as Frankie was grateful to Lee for keeping him out of jail, Lee was indebted to Frankie for keeping him alive after the fiasco in Philadelphia had blown up in his face. Lee looked down at the man's right hand. It bore a jagged scar from the laceration he had sustained reaching through Lee's car window in that Philadelphia alleyway. Lee thought of the limp that had plagued him since that night. The aggravation of his football injury was his memento. Lee and the hood had become a matched pair.

"Word's out that you're handling some new clientele," Frankie said.

*How did Frankie know so quickly?* Lee wondered.

"There's been some Panamanian traffic through my office in the past few days."

Noriega's people," Frankie said matter-of-fact.

"Yes, Noriega's people."

"You know, I used to take shipments of cash to deposit down in Panama. I always enjoyed myself on those jaunts. We had a deal with Noriega. He was supposed to protect us. The guy works primarily with Colombians, but for a price, we were doing some banking there. Well, it made sense to spread our deposits around rather than keep them all in the same country. So, from time to time, I went to Panama and stayed at the Caesar Park Hotel. The place had a suite with a walk-in steel bank vault nearly the size of this bathroom."

Frankie paused while another man walked up to a third sink beside them, washed his hands, then quickly departed when Frankie gave him a sneer. Frankie could even flinch in a way that gave the sinister message he intended.

"Anyway," he continued, "I'm down there with another guy from Philly. We stashed six million in bills into the vault from floor to ceiling. We've got a bank truck scheduled to pick it up—and remember, a deal with Noriega's people protects us there. We paid the son of a bitch handsomely, 'cause you can't keep that kind of money in Panama without his blessing.

"So, we're waiting for the bank truck to arrive when, instead, a little weasel knocks on the door. It's one of Noriega's guys. He's got ten soldiers with him in full battle gear, tiny little soldiers. They looked like the midget marines. Angel—somethin' or other—was the guy's name. He makes us lie on the floor while they open the vault and take out every bill. Then, they empty our wallets and snatch all our cash and credit cards. After they take off, the hotel manager knocks on our door and tells us to leave because he understands we can't afford to pay the room bill. We can't report the robbery because the guys who robbed us are the police in Panama. That slimy little bastard, Noriega, took us for six-million bucks and didn't even leave us with cab fare to reach the airport.

When we got out of the country, we were glad to be alive to tell the story."

"Do you still deal with Noriega?" Lee said.

"Nah. Organized crime relies on stability in government. His people made overtures for us to return, but I doubt we'll go back. There was even talk of whacking the bastard because he still has our Panamanian deposits tied-up."

"I may travel there to meet Noriega. Not right away, but soon. I'll need your help, Frankie No Throat."

Frankie spoke carefully and with conviction.

"Your new clients from Panama are more dangerous than you know. Stick to your old friends, Lee. Avoid these new people. And, whatever you do, stay out of Panama. Traveling to meet Noriega is like taking a journey to the devil."

"I need you to take that journey with me."

Frankie's head jolted backward.

"Maybe you didn't hear me. I'm never returning to Panama."

Lee knew he would have to cash in everything he had to land Frankie's help, and someone was bringing what he'd need to change the mobster's mind.

"Frankie, I'd like to see you in my office later this week."

"No can do. I'm on my way back to Philly."

Lee stared hard into Frankie's eyes. Like his friend, he could silently convey his meaning. Without a word spoken, Lee knew Frankie would delay his return trip.

Somehow, he would have to persuade the man, even though he knew Frankie was right. He would be taking a journey to the devil.

Rachelle woke feeling dirtier than she'd ever been in her life. She bled vaginally and rectally.

"No," she cried out. "I don't even know how many of them took me."

She cried fruitless tears. As a Roman Catholic, the Church mandate against birth control assured she was fertile at that time of month. Surely, she was impregnated by one of the many men who had raped her.

She continued to wonder: *How many was it?*

Rachelle had passed out and lost count.

They had left her alone, naked in a room that was empty, except for a full-length mirror. Unsteady on wobbling legs, she rose to see her reflection in horror. They had shaved her beautiful, long hair, leaving her totally bald. Dried blood caked the side of her head, where the straight razor they'd taken to her scalp had dug too deeply and opened a wide gash. She looked more closely and saw they had shaved every hair from her body. She no longer even had eyebrows.

"No!" she cried out again.

Her cries brought two of Angel's men.

"Your husband is here for you," one of them said. "Time to go, now."

Rachelle staggered in shock.

"Where are my clothes?" she asked with tears streaming down her face.

The men said nothing. They just grabbed her arms. That was how they would take her to her husband.

"No," she cried. "You won't return me to my family this way. And I won't bear the child of a monster."

Rachelle shook herself free and grabbed for the pistol of one of her captors. She jerked it from his holster. Before they could stop her, she jammed the pistol barrel between her lips and pulled the trigger.

Smoke rose from Frankie's mouth. Perched on his same bar stool, he clutched a Cubano cigar and watched his smoke ring drift. As the wispy spiral snaked toward the ceiling, he considered the lawyer's words.

*So, he wants me to travel to Panama,* Frankie mused.

He would never go. The younger man had already sent him on one trip, without even being aware, and once for Frankie had been too often.

# Chapter Seven

# Boys with Bigger Sticks

"WHAT A DAY," marveled Frankie No Throat, "*fuckin' glorious*."

April of 1982 came sweet as the espresso he laced with extra sugar, then long savored under his palate before swallowing. Frankie sipped at a linoleum-topped table in a storefront parlor. Outside, a crooked sign hung above the door identifying the joint as the "Amici Social Club." Situated in a South Philly mostly residential neighborhood, the club was a meeting spot for the boys from downtown. There, Frankie's boss met his *capos*, lieutenants, and wise guys.

Law enforcement knew what transpired there. The FBI planted listening devices in known mob hangouts. Recorded conversations were ripping apart the Gambino crime family in New York criminal trials, so the

Philadelphia family constantly swept their club for bugs. Periodically, special agents on the FBI organized crime squad wrote down license plate numbers of cars that pulled up and took pictures of people as they entered and left, employing open surveillance tactics calculated to harass the mob as much as to gain information.

Little Vinny Talarico had recently assumed control of the family in the usual way. He had the old boss whacked, led a bloody gang war, and came out on top. The brutal killer trusted no one and ran the family with iron knuckles around a freewheeling fist. As a measure of self-protection, he rarely spoke inside the club. When his men sought permission to partake in a venture, he simply nodded. If Little Vinny needed to talk, they took a walk or car ride.

Frankie accepted losing former boss and friend, Rocco Baratta, the same way you say goodbye to a retiring United States President.

*Sometimes*, Frankie realized, *your time is up*.

The trick to surviving transition in mob leadership is staying on the sidelines until a winner is declared, quickly vowing allegiance to the victor, and remaining indispensable to family business. Frankie had that kind of business, so he waited for the little man to arrive in his big ass Cadillac. Their under boss would drive as Frankie and Vinnie talked.

In Monaco, her Serene Highness, Princess Grace was propelled by her own purpose. Before she had met Prince Rainier Grimaldi, III, the Monte Carlo Casino drop—meaning the money or credit gamblers paid for wagering chips—was hitting all-time lows. Monaco revenue was dwindling. Rainier had tried glamorizing the casino to attract wealthy gamblers, but nothing worked until he married his alluring charm. When stars attended the Cannes Film Festival on the Riviera, Grace whisked her Hollywood pals to Monaco and showed them off in the casino. Soon the rich and beautiful, as so often fickle attributes mix, scurried in the doors. Having seen her fairy tale wedding on television and in magazines, they came to taste the magic. Overnight, Monaco thrived. The principality subjects, who thereby retained their status as the only tax-free citizenry in the world, naturally rejoiced. Everyone loved the beguiling princess. Well, almost.

People, who weren't so beautiful, cast covetous eyes at Monacan prosperity. The crime family from nearby Nice, France, reared its ugly head to filch action and Grace prepared to stop them. She summoned a trusted attendant when her husband failed to combat the incursion.

Jean Claude Methot was a lean, physically fit, and square-jawed specimen, who had faithfully served the royal family for years. The prince had assigned him to protect his princess and their three children. The former Parisian police officer, who was slow to speak but quick to serve, heeded the Princess' call to meet in her private office.

In a room appointed with dainty antiques, the place where she planned festive soirees, Grace play-acted the role of commander-in-chief about to unleash her army of one. She tilted her head, tossing golden locks that framed a porcelain doll face, albeit rounder since lighting movie screens.

"Jean Claude," Grace directed, "learn what these people are doing in the casino. Collect their names and see which of our people have ties to them. Can I count on you?"

She expected a crisp response, perhaps even a loose salute before her man embarked on the reconnaissance mission. Instead, John Claude paced to the other side of the room, where he stared out a window with panes stretching from floor to high ceiling. Uncharacteristically, he fidgeted with a button on his jacket, as if that would spark a better idea.

"These are dangerous men," he said, "with serious intentions."

"Who?"

Grace demanded to know with American directness. She needed definitive information for the *Gendarmerie*, if she were to gain assistance from the amply better equipped French national police force.

"If the royal family pays people threatening violence," Grace persisted, "we lose control of the Monte

Carlo casino and the country falls into the hands of mobsters."

"Yet, it seems the Prince is not so compelled."

"My husband and his advisors fear any scandal will chase away gamblers or give France cause to meddle in principality affairs. They dread losing autonomy to the French as much as to these hoodlums.

"So," Grace continued in a drawl, "they're inclined to pay just to rule, at least for now. They're blind to where that will take us."

Jean Claude nodded understandingly.

"Help me lay groundwork," Grace implored. "My husband can't keep his head buried forever. An official call to the *Gendarmerie* must come, if we are to survive."

In South Philly, a black Caddy sailed like an ocean liner down narrow streets, docking curbside at the Amici Social Club. Frankie No Throat ambled outdoors under bright afternoon sun, while high above on a rooftop a pair of birds sang as if paired in a love ritual.

"Even birds do it," he observed, drawling the line from song master Cole Porter, who had penned the lyrics for "Let's Fall in Love," another great favorite Frankie couldn't hum.

He jumped into the rear seat with his boss. Little Vinnie's small stature and often charming demeanor concealed his true nature. His peepers gave him away.

Those with enough courage to glimpse into them could see the paranoia and blood lust that earmarked his regime.

Their car ambled up West River Drive beside gentle waters of the Schuylkill, where trees with fresh buds lined the river edge and joggers traversed running paths. In that bucolic setting, fresh with springtime promise of new life, Frankie outlined a lethal venture. He had figured angles to reap a piece of the action from the crime family in Nice. Frankie paid a percentage of anything his crew earned to the Boss, but before they could undertake an enterprise, they needed his blessing.

Rolling tires hummed as Little Vinnie conjured, then decided.

“Frankie, look into this business. Let the lawyer think you’re making inquiries for Councilman Kelly, then see if you can help our friends in France . . . in a way that benefits our family.”

Frankie was emphatic.

“The boys in Nice will make a fortune if we help keep Monaco’s royal family in line. We can furnish a valuable service by handling the councilman. That’ll muffle his sister.”

“Perhaps,” Little Vinnie mused. “Our associates in Atlantic City know all the casino rackets. Meet with Tony Quick Fish and learn what you can. Grab him in a neutral site, say Jerry Blavat’s Margate club. You know the place: “Memories.”

Frankie knew Antonio DeBona, the tough old geezer who headed the Atlantic City crime family. The guy was an old school hood, who'd earned his moniker, Quick Fish, by planting victims in cement and feeding them to the fishes. He had risen through the ranks of the smaller Mafia family that took control of the seashore town's nefarious dealings following the untimely death of Irish mobster and elected politician Enoch Lewis Carlson, better known as "Nucky." DeBona had become "Boss of the Boardwalk," the boardwalker running all the rackets in the seashore gambling resort.

"Frankie, you've always been valued as a money earner for the family. But remember something. You may be called upon to assist our friends in Nice by taking out the councilman and the lawyer who brought this business to your attention."

The boss paused, as if reflecting.

"I know you have a relationship with the mouth-maggot," he continued. "Don't forget your fucking priorities. Remember the meaning of *La Cosa Nostra*: this thing always comes first."

Frankie knew Little Vinnie would hand a contract on the lawyer to someone else if he felt Frankie wasn't up it. Ralph the Bull's crew usually flexed family muscle, enforcing debt collections from book making and loan sharking operations, as well as contract killings. They transported corpses to Ottaviano's Butcher Shop where they'd hang 'em upside down. After blood drained, they'd chop the carcasses to toss out with garbage.

Frankie was a unique man in their organization. He specialized in white collar crime but had a blue-collar work ethic. Generally, blue-collar crews handled dirty jobs like street crimes and heavy-handed enforcement while white-collar boys operated more sophisticated rackets. Frankie's savvy made him invaluable as the family money launderer, yet he had nerve to whack a man.

As they returned to South Philly, Little Vinny's eyes trained on Frankie.

"Does the lawyer know of your connection to his father?"

"No reason for him to know."

"Someday you may have to clip your wings as the kid's guardian angel. That a problem?"

Frankie No Throat saw madness inside the smaller man's soul and knew only one answer.

"*Bonjour*," called Pierre, who was a dear friend of John Claude. They had long worked together in the French national police force before John Claude moved to serve in Monaco. At John Claude's request, he had agreed to act as intermediary between Monaco and Paris. Dressed in plain clothes, Pierre called with greater voice to the twosome he was slated to meet.

"*Bonjour!*"

The older man he spied was a picture of élan, elegantly attired, grey trim on dainty sideburns lending a trace of distinction to dark hair so delicately scented with musk.

"In English please," the elder Frenchman said, "for the benefit of our American friend."

"*Oui,* but of course," the officer replied, lowering his head in deference to the foreigner.

Frankie No Throat didn't respond, nor would he. Frankie never showed respect to a cop on the take. Instead, he surveyed their surroundings in the near empty bistro.

"Quickly, your recommendation," the senor gentleman prompted.

"The Prince is no problem."

"And the Princess?"

"Her Highness is the royal rose that sticks a thorn in your side. She is the one attempting to enlist French Police assistance. Her convictions require, shall we say, immutable modification."

"And, your friend, who came to you, what is his name?"

"Jean Claude, *Monsieur*. Jean Claud Methot."

The elder man nodded, dismissing the officer before assuring Frankie.

"If this 'immutable modification' can be accomplished in a way that can't be traced to my family, we shall be . . . grateful."

"You have loose ends in Philadelphia as well," Frankie sparred.

"*Oui*, and with this Jean Claude."

"Then, let us agree upon appropriate consideration."

"Yes, it is time, *cher ami*, and our gratitude is assured. After all, we are roasting a bejeweled pheasant that is large enough for all to feast upon.

Grace was adorned in fine jewels and a feathered mask for the masquerade ball. She had come to take Monacan pageantry for granted. The little girl from Philadelphia's East Falls had even grown accustomed to people bowing and addressing her as "Your Serene Highness." What she did not expect was commotion stirring in the corner of the ballroom.

Grace peered through the crowd and grabbed her husband's arm. Rainier wasn't classically handsome, though possessing panache inherent in royal breeding, which is another way of saying: money always looks good on you. He flicked his mustache as a servant whispered in his ear, then conveyed the information to Grace.

"A guest has taken ill and passed out in the back of the room. Too much champagne."

Furrows etched in Grace's forehead relaxed until the servant hastened back, this time whispering in the Prince's ear. Rainier turned ashen.

"What's the matter, Dear?"

Rainier's words came slowly.

"That was no guest. Jean Claude is dead. Stabbed through the heart."

"What?"

Grace felt her knees weaken and held her husband until faintness passed.

"Who did this?"

Rainier peered around the room.

"Anyone. Every guest is masked."

"Have the palace guards . . . have them interrogate everyone."

The prince shook his head.

"We can't tell guests," he said. No one can fear danger lurking in Monaco. Pretend nothing happened."

Grace's lower lip twitched. She bit it hard, maintaining composure with her best stage face, all the while realizing that the people forcing their way into the casino had just announced their presence.

Days later, on a busy street corner, Frankie caught Lee returning to his office from a courtroom. Under the gaze of William Penn, Philadelphia's iconic statue atop City Hall, the mob capo delivered a simple message.

"If Councilman Kelly wants to help his sister, they must find blind eyes. You, too, Counselor."

A street sweeping truck approached, brushes collecting gutter trash with a clatter. Rather than shout, Lee nodded, knowing what he had to do.

He'd warn Kell without knowing the Princess was already among the walking dead.

# Chapter Eight

# Over Rover

"WHAT A DAY," marveled Grace. "*divinely glorious.*"

Monday, September 13, 1982, Grace woke at the Grimaldi home known as Roc Angel. Though the night before she and teen daughter Stephanie had engaged in another raucous argument, which had compelled Grace to call her chambermaid for a handful of phenelzine pills to down with gin, the new day brought promise. Swiftly, she rose to get underway.

She and Stephanie were patching up by spending the day together. First, they'd see her couturier in Monaco to have dresses altered. Afterward, they would travel to Paris, where she at long last would meet a Captain of the French National Gendarmerie. Arrangements had been fashioned by John Claude before he had died, leaving

Grace without his loyal voice and with profound sorrow in her heart.

The clandestine rendezvous would take place in a favorite boutique as the initial step toward engaging French law enforcement assistance. Grace felt the thrill: playing a role in a plot worthy of a Hollywood screenplay.

Racing through the foyer, she almost didn't hear her chambermaid.

"Madame!" she called.

Grace turned to the thin woman, who looked winded from trying to catch up. A tray in her hand shook, almost spilling a glass of orange juice.

"Your Highness," she puffed, "your morning medications."

"What?"

Anymore, pill popping to ease anxiety seemed a ritual. Grace gulped them down before rushing outside where Stephanie waited beside the family Rover 3500.

"Are my dresses in the car?" Grace called.

"Everything you want altered," the willowy, brunette beauty said. "On the back seat."

"Oh, damn. We don't have room for a driver."

"Your maid didn't want to wrinkle them in the trunk."

Grace decided whether to rearrange. If servants placed her dresses in the trunk, she could relax on the ride. On the other hand, she and Stephanie needed to talk privately. Hankering to get underway, Grace simply decided.

"Oh, I'll drive. Climb in!"

At nine-thirty, they headed onto the Moyenne Corniche, where long-past images came to mind. Thirty years earlier, before even dreaming she'd become the country's princess, Grace had filmed scenes on the famed highway, making *To Catch a Thief* with Cary Grant. The panoramic backdrop always enthralled with a twisting road edging sharp drop-offs and ravines.

She turned to her daughter, who rested her eyes. Grace had things to say to the young woman, who was every bit as headstrong as she had been at that age, but they would have time. Grace relaxed, too. Effortlessly they glided down the familiar roadway. Without realizing, Grace took curves a tad faster, rounding a bit closer to the highway edge. Tires began to cry but so faint was their lament that muffled ears ignored them.

Her thoughts turned to Rainier, heart pounding in a vivid daydream as she rushed to him. Flickering candles lighted the boudoir where he waited, welcoming her bed-ready body. Every contour of her physique merged into familiar folds of the man who was her prince, the father of her children, her husband, her lover. As if cascading from heaven to a meadow of delicate blossoms, they collapsed on a downy mattress, blood racing through her veins. Slightly parted lips sped to hers and his kiss ignited her nerve centers!

Pounding pressure in Grace's brain exploded, pain riddled, paralysis gripped. Everything moved in slow motion, sounds echoing as if from afar. Screeching tires orchestrated a sonata, Stephanie's barely audible wails a soprano's refrain. The Rover approached a curve Grace was powerless to negotiate. Transfixed by scenic farmland far below—virtually straight down a rugged ravine—she couldn't turn the steering wheel or lift her foot to the brake pedal.

"Are you all right?" Stephanie shouted.

Grace didn't comprehend.

The nose of their car pointed toward a wondrous Neverland approaching a 110-foot drop.

"Mommy, wake up!"

As the front wheels left solid ground, the bottom of the Rover scraped. For an instant, the Rover teetered, then tipped down, giving a clear view of the rocky hillside and green pastures below. Nose front, it plunged.

Stephanie squealed as earth seemed to rush up at them.

Thudding into the steep slope, their car somersaulted over and over.

Grace didn't feel the blow to the front of her skull. Instead, as the Rover flipped again and rested on its roof, the gentle hand of sleep closed her eyes.

Steam discharging from the radiator rose in vaporous clouds. Stephanie watched it spew as she pulled herself from the wreckage. Wobbling in shock from a concussion and fractured vertebrae, the ground called her name. She dropped to her knees and fell forward, lamely praying, imploring, begging.

"Please, God, let my mother be alive."

"It's just media exaggeration," Prince Rainier declared publicly. "You have a bump with your car. Five minutes later, it's become a bad accident. Next it is really dramatic; the car is wrecked, and you're injured. It ends up with you being thrown out into the road and you're killed."

An aid watched the prince leave the press podium. As reporters raced toward telephones to call in their stories, he turned to a fellow advisor.

"What's he talking about? They can barely sustain the Princess on life support."

Grace lay unconscious in a hospital bearing her name. Rainier anxiously waited in the intensive care ward lobby, surrounded by their children, realizing each was silently praying for hope that further withered with each passing moment. Head low, Rainier cried for the first time since it happened.

"You may see her, now, Your Highness," a physician whispered in his ear. "Your children may accompany you, as well, but I must warn each of you that. . .."

He heard nothing else as the family entered the hospital room. An oscilloscope showed faint life signs.

One at a time the children kissed their mother, then left Rainier. Where only the twosome would ever know, he swore a sacred vow to the only woman for whom he'd ever bestow more than a dalliance. Raising her hand to his lips, he pecked sweet fingertips, then turned her palm to stoke his cheek. Through lips that never moved, he heard her voice, letting him know to return home where he came to stand in solitude beneath her portrait.

As he studied her face, memories raced. Rainier almost laughed at himself, recalling his startled reaction at their engagement reception when a Philadelphia newspaperman commented upon the couple's relative heights by declaring too loudly: "Say, he's titty high!"

Comforting remembrances of times together flashed yet he chided himself for too many moments wasted, never thinking their days together would end, now realizing: If only I—

A soft whisper kissed his ear, unmistakably hers.

"It's time for me to go, My Love."

Reluctantly, Rainier picked up the telephone and gave the direction.

"Remove my wife from life support."

Tragedy gripped the small nation's populace as a palace spokesman solemnly made the official pronouncement.

"Her Serene Highness, Grace Kelly Grimaldi has died."

Mob members from Nice joined in the outpouring of grief. At her wake, a sea of flowers surrounded the former starlet, many contributed by those now preparing to move in unopposed. Natural causes had snuffed life from the Princess of Monaco. No one would challenge so obvious an assessment following the accident—nobody save one man who couldn't release his sister's memory.

Two years later, maybe just a tad more, Kell met Lee at their Society Hill watering haunt, his Irish smile conveying hope. Lee opened a file folder atop a table for two and explained why he didn't share it.

"I read these hospital and medical records you collected, Kell. I just don't see how foul play factors in. Royal physicians say CAT scans revealed two cerebral-vascular concussions."

Lee pointed to record entries, then eyed Kell to assure he saw them, too, before continuing.

"One concussion deep in the brain and the other in the frontal lobe. They say she suffered two strokes. The first caused her to lose consciousness behind the wheel. That's what caused the accident where she suffered the second brain injury that killed her."

"I've hired investigators," Kell interjected, "who are digging further. The key is determining what induced the initial concussion. Physicians and forensic experts are helping me weed through this. My sister Peggy's ex-husband is helping, too. We have a theory and I need your friend's help, again. Call—"

Lee jolted and interrupted.

"Frankie issued a warning for you, me, Grace, all of us for God's sake . . . to back off."

"Will you call him for me, again?"

Lee knew he couldn't dissuade his headstrong friend.

"I already left a message for Frankie to contact you. He may or may not. He's unpredictable with this."

Lee shook his head and peered around the room.

"I'm giving you advice," he continued, "not as a lawyer but as your friend, forget the whole damned thing."

Kell didn't hear from anyone until he vacationed in South Florida. A phone ring broke silence of night, relentlessly beckoning. Groggy but waking fast, he was given explicit directions to meet on a Fort Lauderdale street corner for dope on Grace.

"Be there in thirty minutes," he was told.

"That's a forty-minute drive," Kell blurted.

"Come alone and park two blocks south of the corner."

Kell realized he'd be watched to make certain no one accompanied him.

"Say," he pressed, "how did you get this telephone number?"

The phone clicked dead in his hands. A dial tone burning in his ear told him he didn't have time to waste. Somehow, he arrived in time but that hadn't allowed him to consider what he was doing. On the dark and lonely corner, Kell wondered if he should have come at all. As he readied to leave, something moved.

*Is it a person or an animal?* he thought.

He detected something. Then, the form of a man emerged from the dim but Kell couldn't make out the face.

"Turn around, councilman," the shadowy figure called.

Kell turned. Footsteps grew louder as the man approached, then treading stopped. Hot breath on the back of Kell's neck told him how close they were.

"Talk, Councilman."

Anger surged through Kell's veins as he contemplated what had happened to his sister, overcoming trepidation.

"I need information about my sister's death," he said.

The man didn't reply.

"Name your price."

Still, no answer came forth.

"I have a theory and want to see the people responsible for her murder brought to justice."

"Lee Gunther told me your theory. You think someone slipped your sister a Borgia cocktail."

"A Borgia cocktail?"

"In the old days, that's what they called a drink laced with arsenic. Today things are more sophisticated but the result's the same: no signs of foul play and no questions asked."

Kell suspected but remained uncertain of who spoke so near his back that he could feel the breath that carried those words.

"But, Councilman, you're just speculating, and Lee tells me there's nothing in your sister's medical history to suggest you're guessing correctly."

"Evidence is emerging," Kell said. "It's no secret that Grace was under stress and using antidepressants. Her physicians placed her on an MAO inhibitor called phenelzine. They warned her not to mix it with certain foods and drinks. Know what they have in common?"

Though Kell received no answer, he knew he piqued the man's interest.

"They all have high tyramine content," he continued. "It's a tasteless enzyme. Tyramine can easily lace a drink, then mix with the antidepressant to induce disorientation or a stroke, like the one my sister suffered. Someone could have slipped it into my sister's morning coffee or into a—"

"Councilman, turn slowly with your eyes closed."

Kell rotated.

The man spoke slowly and emotionlessly.

"Now, open your eyes."

Kell obeyed and saw a pistol pointed at his groin. Simultaneously, a flash blazed from the gun barrel, a blast rang in his ears, and lead kissed his testicles. His cheek rested on concrete, though he didn't recall falling. As he moaned on the ground, the man standing above him spoke calmly, as if nothing had happened.

"That's your warning shot. Keep your nose clean of this business."

Kell grabbed the wound with both hands and rocked back and forth. Blood seeping through his pants covered his fingers.

"Enjoy your crotch cramps, Councilman."

They had placed the bullet where the ladies' man would remember.

Kell heard footsteps departing. Frankie No Throat swiftly disappeared as Kell vowed through agonizing groans.

"Those bastards won't stop me."

The former Olympic sculler had been in excellent physical condition. He worked out in a gym and ran five miles every day along the East River Drive, so he quickly recovered. Kell realized the mob would be hard pressed to kill him.

On March 2, 1985, John B. Kelly, Junior—always a popular Jack called Kell—was a high-profile Philadelphia politician, businessperson, and socialite. The United States Olympic Committee had just named him their President. Lee's "boys from downtown" could never shoot him dead on the street. So, he continued his investigation, and gave Lee a copy of the file to hold in safe keeping.

Time does as it does, always moving, while routines we favor remain predictably stagnate. Kell took his customary morning jog to boat house row on the Schuylkill River, as his warmup for a chilly jaunt in a four-man boat. The water was calm, smooth as glass. Kell hardly worked up a sweat by the time they put the boat away.

He began his easy jog home. Along the way, he spotted another runner on the ground, gripping an ankle that appeared swollen. Instinctively, he went to the aid of a fellow sportsman without mustering a second thought.

"Need a hand?"

The jogger looked up and shook her auburn mane free from a woolen winter cap.

"I think it's a sprain," the attractive young woman offered uncertainly.

Kell had seen many sport injuries and her sprain looked genuine.

"Can you help me to my car? I don't think I can stand without help."

She took his hand and lit a smile. Fortunately, she didn't have far to go. They chatted amiably until reaching her beat-up Volkswagen.

"Could you stay just a minute." she implored, "while I try getting comfortable behind the steering wheel? I've got a couple of juice bottles on the back seat. Would you get me one? Take one for yourself, if you want. You look like you could use something to drink after your workout."

Kell grabbed two eight-ounce bottles and handed her one. He opened the other for himself and chugged hard. It went down sweet. He wiped his mouth with his sleeve without noticing the young woman had simply placed her drink under the car seat.

A jogger heading in the opposite direction turned to her running partner.

"Wasn't that Councilman Kelly?"

The man turned his head.

"Looks like him," he said, "but who's the woman in the VW?"

Both grinned understandingly. Although Kell had married a lovely woman much his junior and dedicated himself to the marriage, his enduring reputation as a ladies' man proved legends have a life of their own.

The fetching smile on the auburn-hair beauty would have sent any man's heart racing, but not as fast as what laced his juice. Kell reached Callowhill Street near 18th Street in center city. At 10:05 a.m., he felt sudden and severe chest pains. A sharp ache in his left arm radiated into his neck. Nausea overpowered.

"What the—"

An explosion in his heart wrestled him down and the fifty-seven-year old died.

Kell was right: the mob couldn't shoot him dead on the street. He died of a heart attack attributed to an enlarged heart, a natural condition for a man so physically active. Who would ever question the diagnosis? Lee wouldn't have looked more closely, if it hadn't been for another tragedy the Kelly family suffered hours later.

Eugene Conlan had divorced Kell's sister Peggy but remained close to the Kelly clan. Down on his luck, he'd taken a room in the YMCA. According to one news report, a desk clerk at the "Y" had often seen Kell call on his former brother-in-law. Apparently, they had been working on something.

Hours later, blocks from where Kell fell, Gene Conlan dropped. Taken to the same hospital as Kell, he was also pronounced dead on arrival, having succumbed to natural causes.

Philadelphia media accounts noted the coincidence of two evidently healthy, middle-aged men meeting such untimely deaths. Two days later, on Monday, March 4, 1985, the Philadelphia Inquirer bugled taps in three front-page news stories. The lead story headlined "A Rower and a Gentleman," followed by the headline "Kelly had Mild Ailment Officials Say," and yet lower laid the headline: "Former Brother-in-Law in Kelly's Shadow to End." The latter article bore deck copy reading:

> Conlan was felled by a heart attack outside Suburban Station about 4:15 p.m. only blocks from the spot where Kelly died earlier in the day while jogging.

Lee placed their hospital records and related police reports into the file linking the mob to Grace's death. He wondered what to do with the binder, until Frankie No Throat solved that mystery in Lee's office.

"Counselor, you have until the day they bury the councilman to deliver his entire file. You know the one. Don't let any copies survive. Spare his family more . . . anguish.

Lee simply stared at the man.

"Deliver it to me the evening they bury him. And don't fuck up. Heart attacks are becoming epidemic."

Raw edge in Frankie's voice revealed how badly the hood wanted the file. Lee fully understood what he must do.

The following Friday, Lee attended Kell's funeral service at Holy Sepulcher Cemetery, where the widow wept and children by prior marriage grieved stoically. Not to be overlooked appeared Philly Mayor Goode and former mayors Green and Rizzo. Paparazzi clamored for better camera views of Monaco royals: Prince Ranier, Kell's nephew Albert with nieces Caroline and Stephanie, the latter princess raising reporters' ire for "standing out defiantly" from conservatively attired mourners.

Well, Philly is a big city with a tiny town temperament. Stephanie displayed her lithe form in a black minidress, under a black leather jacket, with black stockings and little black boots. To Lee, it seemed befitting homage to the deceased ladies' man, who would've been appreciative.

Lee studied the casket and considered his promise to hand the file to the mob capo. Rage stirred then brewed, heated by nascent realization.

*A man, who can't be angry at evil*, he thought, *lacks the genesis for good.*

His acrimony wasn't directed at murderers, but at himself as he whispered the one way to stay alive.

"Turn the file over to the boys from downtown."

So, Lee waited at Harlow's nightclub for Frankie that night, where the binder grew heavy under an arm that couldn't set it down. Near closing time, he observed the shiny dome on a head shaver from Frankie's crew. The wise guy twitched the tip of his nose with a finger, then pointed nose and finger at Lee, and strode toward him.

*It's not like Frankie to send someone in his place*, Lee thought.

The hood came close and huffed, catching his breath before speaking.

"Frankie got tied up," he muttered in a raspy voice.

"I'll hand this file to Frankie," Lee said. "Nobody else."

"He wants to meet you tonight behind the butcher's shop: Ottaviano's. Know where?"

Lee nodded. He knew. He also knew better than to go alone so late.

"No Throat wants you there in thirty minutes."

Lee paused to reflect.

*Go or refuse*, he pondered, before casting his own fate.

"It'll be forty minutes to reach my car and zip there, he said, "maybe longer."

"Thirty minutes, Counselor."

Lee's nod sent Frankie's man on his way.

As lights in the club brightened, bartenders shouted: "Last call!"

Lee considered bracing for the late wintery chills and winds.

*Maybe*, he thought, *I should order a fast double.*

But time was running short. Lee grabbed his coat and hustled into the night. His engine churned slowly in the icy cold before the 'Vette found its form and revved downtown. As each block passed, rancor he had never known filled his soul . . . animus that could only be soothed one way.

“In time,” Lee vowed, “I’ll take my own revenge, drawing blood with a gavel of justice that swings like a sledgehammer.

**Sports Extra: 56 points**

# The Philadel

Vol. 312, No. 63 ©1985, Philadelphia Newspapers Inc. Monday,

# A rower and a 'gentlem

John B. 'Jack' Kelly Jr.
*Cause of death undetermined*

## Kelly had mild heart ailment, officials say

By Paul Nussbaum
and Robert J. Terry

John B. "Jack" Kelly Jr. suffered from a mild heart ailment and had an enlarged heart when he died Saturday, police said yesterday

Sandra Kelly (left) and John B. Kelly 3d (in dark suit

Philly Inquirer front page on March 4, 1985

Sandra Kelly (left) and John B. Kelly 3d (in dark suit) ... Palace Hotel yes

# Former brother-in... in Kelly's shadow

**Eugene M. Conlan**
*Died of heart attack Saturday*

By Robin Clark

Eugene M. Conlan merited only one mention in *Those Philadelphia Kellys*, Arthur H. Lewis' 1977 biography of the famous Kelly clan.

It was in the chapter titled "There's Never Been a Good Kelly Marriage," and the brief passage did little to illuminate the character of the Ohio salesman and sports enthusiast who was **married briefly to Jack Kelly's sister Margaret in the mid-1960s.**

**On Saturday, Eugene Conlan died much as he had lived — in the shadow of the man who had been his longtime friend and mentor.**

**Conlan was felled by a heart attack outside Suburban Station about 4:15 p.m., only blocks from the spot where Kelly died earlier in the day**

while jogging to ... from a morning ...

Both men were ... friends say, is w...

**While Kelly was** president of the U... had spent his last ... room at the Arch ... a bathroom with ...

In many ways ... story of the prin...

"There's ... Gene," said ... both Kelly and ... downhill ...

Lower on the same front page

# Part II

# Chapter Nine

# Ain't Nobody Guilty Round Here

THE WHACK OF A GAVEL REVERBERATED through the Miami courtroom.

"Case dismissed," the federal judge declared. "You're free to go, Mr. Batista."

"I'm . . . I'm free to go?"

Elderly and patient Judge Ramis never looked up. She tweaked the tip of her pronounced nose, then looked down at the briefs and exhibits that had been submitted for her consideration.

"Yes, Sir," the jurist said. "Your counsel aptly demonstrated how your civil rights were violated when the DEA searched and seized your yacht."

Thanks to *Senor* Lee Gunther, Jose Batista suddenly realized, he was a free man. His new abogado had declared illegal actions taken by DEA agents, as they had seized his cocaine and cash, tainted government evidence. Their conduct rendered the evidence inadmissible at trial. Without that evidence, *Senor* Gunther had explained, the law obligated the Court to dismiss the case.

The government *abogado* leaped to his feet. The big black man was beside himself with rage, his bellowing voice filling the courtroom.

"Your Honor, this means thousands of hours expended by law enforcement officers on this investigation are wasted. The evidence includes cocaine with a street value of three-million dollars on the defendant's yacht, cash—"

"You heard my ruling on the search and seizure motion," the judge interrupted. "Defense counsel's arguments are compelling. The evidence is excluded, and the charges are dismissed as a matter of law."

She rose, straightened her black robe, and turned to *Senor* Gunther, to conclude.

"Good job, Sir."

As Judge Ramis left the bench, Batista marveled at his good fortune. He would be processed, given his street clothes, and released. By the end of the day, he would be on his way home to Panama, where he would immediately report to his boss, President Noriega. His arms wrapped around his savior.

"*Gracias, Senor* Gunther. Will I get my boat back?"

"I'll see to it."

Jose had been in many courtrooms. The burly, middle-aged drug runner for Noriega's crew had seen his share of *abogados*. Yet, he looked at the one beside him in awe—a genius. Jose's speedy yacht would have been forfeited under United States drug laws upon conviction. Yet, not only was he a free man, his boat was a free boat, leaving him to think the inevitable truth.

*Life is great, when you have great representation.*

"What about the cash they confiscated when I was arrested?"

"You assigned one-hundred-fifty thousand of it to me for legal fees," Lee reminded him. "Is that still a satisfactory arrangement?"

"*Si.*"

Of course, it was all right. No price is too high for freedom. Besides, Batista was reclaiming a boat worth ten times the cash.

"Does this mean you'll get my friends, who were arrested with me, released as well?"

"Out before the end of the day. I'm meeting the Assistant U.S. Attorney in his office this afternoon to discuss your associates. Be sure to tell your friends who's springing everyone."

Jose smiled broadly. He had thought he'd go to a trial where the government would convict and lock him behind bars for years. He still couldn't believe his good fortune.

"I'll let everyone know that with you, *Senor*, ain't nobody guilty round here."

Jose watched his *abogado* leave as a uniformed court officer grabbed his sleeve.

"You'll have to be processed before you're released, Sir," the man said.

Jose jerked his arm away.

"Hands off," he sneered. "I'm a free man."

The softness of his voice barely concealed the violence pent up inside him. Easily triggered, that rage would spew again.

Lee walked into the small office of the man with whom he had so heatedly argued. Robert Sheppard would be his courtroom adversary in the days ahead. The Assistant U.S. Attorney sat behind his desk, shuffling paperwork. Lee sat and studied framed photographs of an attractive black family displayed amid clutter. Files covered every inch of desk space and littered the floor. It looked more like the office of a defense attorney than a prosecutor. Government lawyers typically worked more neatly than their brethren among the defense bar.

*Must be something about their thinking process*, Lee figured.

The same reasoning normally dictated that prosecutors wore unimaginative wardrobes: predictably drab suits, button-down collar shirts with too-staid-to-get-laid neckties. Robert Sheppard was different, dressing with panache. The man was sharp as the creases in his designer suit. Well spoken, about Lee's age, he was on his way up.

Lee continued to scan the photographs. Robert wore a U.S.C. sweatshirt in one. From the way he filled it out, the guy could've played football for the Trojans as a full back. His wife looked like she belonged on a sitcom: the pluperfect TV series wife, attractive without being flashy, exuding warmth clear across the room. Robert's two sons flanked him in another picture. For an instant, Lee wished he had raised a family of his own. His life had just been too unstable after the Philadelphia affair. Momentarily, Lee envied his adversary.

Another picture behind the rest stood out. In it, the government lawyer wore Marine Corps dress blues with captain bars.

Robert caught Lee staring.

"Marine reserves," he said with evident pride. "That's the advantage to working for the government. They give you time off to complete your reserve obligation in the field each year."

Robert continued searching through desk papers until he found a legal pad and pen to take notes. Then, he broke the ice.

"Counselor, I hear you're lucky in the courtroom and lucky in love."

Lee knew he would like the guy. Anyone, who could ham-up the feigned indignation Robert had mustered in the courtroom, was all right. Lee pegged him as a forceful advocate, who didn't take himself too seriously.

"Each time we meet in the courtroom," Robert continued, "I'll put on my act, but I'll be there to help you. You'll get scumbags acquitted in front of our District's senior judge, who's part of the plan, too. It almost doesn't seem fair. I help you win in the courtroom by day so you can date the best-looking FBI agent I've ever seen by night."

"That's the advantage to working for scumbags," Lee said with a wink.

Robert stared at the file he had just closed with the dismissal of Batista's drug charges.

"We put a rabid dog back on the street without a leash or muzzle," he said. "It's frightening. He's not just a dealer. We believe he's killed at least three people on Miami streets for Noriega. Lord knows what he's done in Panama. Still, we had to let him go for sake of the plan. If you don't come through on this, Lee, a lot of people are going to have explaining to do."

"I'll need his buddies sprung today," Lee reminded.

Robert shook his head.

"We'll argue before Judge Ramis in the afternoon. She'll toss out their cases, too. We could do this on paper but it's important that your clients see a show. Tonight, they'll be with Batista on that yacht, cruising toward Panama. You're going to be a hot item in their circles."

"What about the cash that the DEA seized?"

"We'll give you some to use as expense money. The government keeps the rest of your fee. Nobody will be looking for you to put it into your business account."

That stung. Lee knew Robert was referring to tax evasion charges that had led Lee into their plan. The stigma of false charges lingered.

He handed Robert a slip of paper.

"Tomorrow these boys are showing up on my doorstep," he said. "More of Noriega's people. Let's figure out how to keep these sweet things on the street with their buddies."

The prosecutor let out a long breath that seemed to deflate him.

"The Diaz brothers," he sighed. "Man, these are serious bad guys. Blowing out their charges is going to piss off a lot of people. Nobody in this office, besides me, is cleared to know the plan. The DEA popped the Diaz brothers and none of their agents have clearance for this operation. Shit is about to sprout wings and fly at jet speed."

Robert called for his assistant to pull their file. Before returning to court for the afternoon session, he and Lee would review the investigation and evidence sections of the files to find ways to spring them. Lee realized it must feel unnatural to the dedicated prosecutor. They were releasing hardened criminals, who would return to their work—dealing drugs and killing on command.

Jaime Calero prepared for night work; she and Lee were going out on the town again. She had taken a high-rise condominium in Miami Beach as part of her cover. One side of her twenty-first-floor apartment had an expansive ocean view; the other overlooked the intercoastal waterway.

The FBI had picked up the condo years earlier when they arrested and convicted its owner for dealing. All property the government could trace to earnings from illegal drug activities was subject to forfeiture under the law. Law enforcement authorities would sell or use seized property to battle crime. The Bureau kept the condo as a safe house, a place where agents could meet informants without being seen. When Jaime needed a cover, the Bureau assigned her the safe house as her temporary home. That was good living, consistent with the lifestyle of the "party girl" she was supposed to be.

Jaime primped in front of a small makeup mirror and sipped a glass of red wine. She hadn't told Lee something and tried to think of the best way to explain. She had put it off but that night she would let him know.

She finished her hair, took another sip, and peered into a full-length mirror.

"*Shee-it*," she exploded.

Her hair wasn't right. Jaime stuck both her hands in her thick black mane and tossed it like a salad to start all over.

"Do I like this guy too much?" she asked herself.

A long time had passed since she had cared for any man. Her career hadn't given her time. Jaime checked her reflection in the full-length mirror again and posed a question.

"Why should I care so much about how my hair looks tonight? Maybe I do like this guy too much."

She sipped more wine, pondering until she decided upon the truth of the matter.

"Nah," came her realization in a sigh. "This is for the job—*especially for this job*."

Riding the elevator up to Jaime's apartment, Lee contemplated what he had done in the morning and afternoon court sessions. He had often freed clients by using well-honed courtroom skills. Yet, what he had just done seemed different, somehow unsavory. As a law student and young lawyer, he had never thought he would utilize skills acquired from years of education and hard-earned experience that way.

*You're only innocent once*, he thought, then wondered: *Was I better off when I was still naive?*

The elevator stopped at floor twenty-one and Lee walked down a long hallway to Jaime's apartment. It reminded him of the stroll he had taken in the FBI building corridor the day they met.

Jaime quickly answered his door knock and let him enter. She was stunningly beautiful, just the way Supervisor Martin had ordered.

"Breathtaking," he said.

"Are you commenting on me or the water views, Counselor?"

He looked around her apartment for the first time.

"Safe house," Jaime simply offered. There was no need for further explanation.

Lee leaned close for a kiss, but Jaime turned her head so fast his lips found a cheek. She stared at him as he backed off.

"There's a line," she said, "a line we can't cross."

"What line?"

"Never forget we're role playing. The Bureau maintains a 'kiss only' rule for undercover agents. That's the line. I like you, Lee, but I love my work. I've sacrificed for my career and nothing's going to jeopardize it."

Lee scratched his head.

"Tongues from defense lawyers OK?"

"Let's have dinner in South Beach," Jaime answered.

"I can't imagine anyone with whom I'd rather spend a lovely evening."

At last, Jaime's quick smile flashed, though lighting little more than a glimmer. Lee accepted it with satisfaction.

*Perhaps, despite herself,* he thought, *that icy attitude is defrosting.*

"All right, my Charming Prince of Baloney," she laughed, "a little tongue may make the menu."

Her arms wrapped him, and moist lips merged.

Frankie No Throat also had someone with whom he would spend the evening. His invitation had been straightforward.

"Meet me at the pissers."

So, they met in the men's room at the Bermuda Bar, standing at urinals next to each other. Every time someone walked by, they flushed in unison to muffle their voices. When they finished their conversation, Frankie was first to leave. He returned to the bar as his companion walked a different direction.

Without anyone having seen him talk to the Philadelphia mob *capo*, Jose Batista stepped into the night.

That evening, warm and gentle ocean breezes blew pixie dust. Jaime and Lee could think of no other explanation for the magic mood.

They cruised top-down in Lee's Corvette along the South Beach strip. To their left, sand and surf invited promenaders. To their right, strollers and roller bladers jammed the sidewalk. Restaurant diners enjoyed open-air meals. Lusty Latin rhythms filled the air.

They were about to discover how fast night can disappear and how unready two can be to part at dawn. Words between them came so easily. And, though skies turned angry, neither had eyes that noticed.

The man of few words joined his crew at the dock. Batista's men had been waiting, ready to cast off. They examined damage that Drug Enforcement Agency agents had done when they boarded the vessel with Coast Guard assistance. Agents had pulled the boat apart looking for drugs, weapons, and other contraband. No matter, the vessel was seaworthy. They'd cruise home. Jose was anxious to set foot on Panamanian soil. The place was more than a safe haven from American authorities: Panama was his homeland. Infused with nationalistic pride, typical of his countrymen, he longed to reach its shores.

"A storm is brewing over the ocean," his senior man called. "We'll hit bad weather."

"True."

"Can't we wait for calmer seas?"

Batista shook his head.

"I have a message for the ears of President Noriega . . . a message that can't wait."

He started the boat with a roar from its engine. As they cast off, Jose looked to the dark and starless sky, knowing they would face a storm. He considered what Frankie had told him about his new *abogado*, who had obtained such swift justice, then turned to his man.

"I just met with someone who has come to our country for years—the skinny Italian with no throat. He may share some information for a favor."

Batista paused to study the ominous skies.

"Perhaps our *abogado* isn't so brilliant, after all," he mused. "Perhaps he's no more than a fool—the kind who pays for stupidity with his life."

# Chapter Ten

# Curds on Sour Milk

LEE FELT FOOLISH. JAIME'S ADVANCES HAD clouded his thinking. She was doing a job and he had to do the same. On their mission, a lovesick puppy would become a dead dog.

Close faces refocused his thinking. He sat in his spacious office behind an oversized glass-top desk, the clear surface allowing him to eyeball movements across from him. People he met in his law office were sometimes high, usually mad, and always dangerous. In his practice, neither sainted women nor holy men found the door. For fifteen years, he had represented con artists, thieves, drug dealers, and button men.

After leaving Philadelphia, Lee had never really started anew. Miami burned with the same action that quickly filled his file drawers with a heavy case load.

Clients eagerly sought representation from the forceful trial lawyer. Just as fervently, he championed unrighteous causes. Frankie No Throat was the first to throw business his way. The *capo* had called the moment telephone lines were installed.

"Lee," he summoned urgently, "cops picked up two of our guys in Fort Lauderdale. Nailed 'em with a couple keys of coke. The boys, up here, want them sprung. They're held on a half-million dollars bail each."

Without even thinking, Lee scheduled an emergent bail reduction hearing to place Frankie's guys back on the street. Like old times, a messenger delivered the fee to his office in a brown paper bag. He spread cash across the glass desktop to count stacks of thousands. Lee was back in business with scum. They still sought him out when their associates had problems in South Florida. He figured they would always engage his services, though they might never forgive his role in the Kelly affair.

The men in Lee's office that morning weren't connected to the Philly mob but one thing remained constant. He spread stacks of thousands across his desktop, collecting from the Diaz brothers. The two men were carbon copies of one another, identically dressed in white shirts and black trousers. They greased their hair back from low brows. Huge nostrils quivered when their Latin tempers flared. The older spoke no English so the younger translated. Patiently, Lee made certain Noriega's men understood him.

"They arrested you in a sting operation," he explained. "Drug sales you made were part of a setup. A man you once trusted—a man who regularly bought drugs from you—was arrested months ago. To get a lighter jail sentence, he agreed to work for the Drug Enforcement Agency. The DEA kept his arrest quiet so they could use him as an informant. Your friend set you up. Surveillance cameras monitored the last two drug sales you made to him. The associate he brought with him wasn't one of his men; he was an undercover officer. Each word you spoke and every move you made was in the presence of a government informant and a DEA agent . . . and all of it was recorded on video tape.

"In the second transaction, they purchased drugs from you with marked bills: money smeared with a dye that's only visible under ultraviolet light. The DEA recorded the bill serial numbers before the deal took place. When they arrested you, agents identified the cash in your possession as money paid by the government in the sting. They made you . . . and made you good."

Lee waited again, while the younger brother translated. Then, the two men spoke between each other in Spanish. Lee picked up a phrase or two. "*Assinato*," was one word he understood. The two men planned to murder the informant and the DEA agent. They were arranging a dual assassination in his presence, thinking the gringo lawyer didn't understand them. Lee wouldn't let on that he knew *un poco*, a little, of the Spanish language. That might give him an edge, later, but he couldn't let them plot a double homicide.

The Diaz brothers were matched maggots, who came under Batista's rein in Noriega's hierarchy. Robert Sheppard had pulled their rap sheets for Lee. The paperwork traced lengthy histories of arrests without major convictions. So far, they had been lucky in the court system. Their recent arrest should have been different as the government finally had an ironclad case to prosecute. Those two would have been on their way to prison except for one thing: they walked into Lee's office. Although they didn't know, they had a free ride. They didn't have to kill anyone to beat the charges. Lee also knew they might want to kill the informant and DEA agent just for revenge. Either way, Lee had to defuse their *assinato*, somehow, without letting them know he understood anything they said. He leaned back in his chair.

"I can beat this rap," Lee began, "based on errors the informant and DEA officer made in the sting operation. To do that, they must testify against you at a preliminary hearing. When they do, I'll cross-examine them and bring their mistakes to the judge's attention. They'll look like fools and the judge will dismiss the charges against you."

The younger brother translated. Again, the two men discussed their plans, growing louder and animated, their hands swatting and tongues waggling faster. Lee wondered if he should warn the feds. Federal officers are under an obligation, which the law mandates, to alert anyone whose life is endangered when they overhear those kinds of threats. The situation often arises when agents bug mob telephone lines. Yet, Lee wasn't under a reciprocal obligation. Besides, his tactics seemed to appeal to his clients' machismo. Public humiliation of the informant and DEA agent seemed to appease the brothers, apparently as much as murdering them. Lee thought they were saying that, anyway. He couldn't be certain.

As they bade *adios*, both tipped their heads to Lee in deference to his professional standing. Attorneys are revered in their homeland, more so than lawyers in the United States, who so often come across to the public like well-dressed used car salesmen selling clunkers. They appeared comfortable with him handling their case. After years working for those kinds of people, Lee was still at it—making new friends among rawer slices of humanity. Like crusty curds on sour milk, they left a bitter aftertaste in his mouth.

Lee swallowed hard, then scanned a stack of pink telephone message slips his legal assistant handed him. She had placed one on top that immediately caught his attention. Mary knew him well enough to land it there.

The middle-aged woman, who fancied rather than concealed her premature grey streaks, gave a knowing wink. A grin spread across her round face. She knew that message would send Lee from the office early to meet someone for whom his fondness was genuine.

Across town, Jaime and Robert Sheppard sat in his office with the Drug Enforcement Agency special agent who had popped the Diaz brothers. The man screamed, his words reverberating off close walls.

"What do you mean?"

His eyes bugled as his tongue lashed.

Why would my bust be tossed out?"

Neither Jaime, nor Robert, could divulge the plan. The Drug Enforcement Agency was out of the small loop, so Robert did his best to cover.

"Lee Gunther," he calmly repeated, "filed a pretrial motion that may blow the charges out. Defense counsel raised some serious issues."

"My people popped 'em clean!"

"The Bureau's been tailing their organization," Jaime interjected. "That's why I'm here. We'll pick up the case, if they get lucky in court."

Veteran DEA Agent Dave Tillis didn't like it. The pasty-faced and bulky-bodied agent had worked at the agency for ten years. He knew his job. Something smelled. The FBI was in on it. He didn't know what it was, but he'd find out. The DEA had expended too many investigative hours taking down the Diaz brothers to let them fly.

Robert took over again.

"Tillis, your agencies have different methodologies. The FBI is organization oriented. They tackle an entire crime organization, all at once. The Drug Enforcement Agency is transaction oriented: it takes down drug deals as it finds them. The DEA theory has always been, if you take out enough players, you'll make a dent in the war against drugs. I'm not here to resolve philosophic differences. I'm under orders to tell you the FBI will handle the Diaz brothers. Back off their case."

"Perhaps Miz Calero's nighttime antics have clouded her daytime thinking," Tillis suggested.

Jaime's eyes discharged ballistic missiles at the DEA agent.

"What do you mean?" she fired.

"Our people have spotted you around town with the courtroom Galahad who's defending these turds."

"My private life is my business."

"We'll find out," the DEA agent promised. "No one blows out my busts and no one takes away my cases."

Tillis fled the room. Trained to be suspicious, he sensed subterfuge. The agent didn't trust the Assistant U.S. Attorney and he sure didn't care what the bitch-with-a-badge said.

"Somehow, I'll get to the bottom of what they're doing—no matter what they're doing," he puffed, "and explode it in their faces."

Faces lighted, heads spun, and necks craned as Tanya paraded from the baggage claim area. Blond hair teased high, wearing black boots, leopard print stockings, and a tiger top, she looked ready to revolt against any sisterhood of subtlety. Her body perfectly suited her work dancing in "beer and butt" joints. She strutted on legs long enough to support a superstructure and her own frame featured an ultra-slim waist, carved by surgically removing the lower ribs, and of course her famous killer-breasts. Tanya was a classic bombshell of near comic proportions. Her plastic surgeon had recently plumped her lips, and given the upper a heart-shaped cap. She saw Lee, waiting for her at the passenger arrival area, and puckered her new toys in his direction as if on a test run.

Underneath the potent exterior, Tanya was a loyal friend to her longtime lawyer. The big woman liked to think she was good at taking care of herself. Subliminally, she understood she was a bundle of little insecurities. Lee's confident manner made them all disappear.

Her husband had died seven years earlier, leaving her a young widow without insurance. The only thing he had bequeathed was his funeral bill, so she took up topless dancing, initially just to pay it off. After she became accustomed to stripping for drunks in bars, she continued for the money. Pay was good, so long as she looked appetizing. And, Tanya didn't just wet palates; she flooded them.

At thirty-four, Tanya had only one legitimate fear in life. Ever since her husband had been diagnosed with AIDS, she worried about receiving an HIV positive test reading. She checked her blood every six months. So far, results were negative. She knew Lee was aware of the circumstances surrounding her husband's death and Tanya expected that's why he never accepted her romantic advances. He was the one man who seemed immune to her charms.

*Perhaps*, she thought, *that's why I'm so heavily attracted to him.*

She went to Lee's side, planted a kiss on his cheek, and watched for his reaction. He didn't move to get away. Still, just like Lee, he wasn't taking advantage of the opportunity she would gladly bestow. He could take their relationship far as he'd like. She handed Lee the package she had brought him from Philadelphia, then sought his counsel with urgency.

"Legal question," she gushed. "You don't need tops on the beach, here, do ya? I just bought a new G-string."

Lee grinned. She could tell he remembered her magnificent boobs. Once, when he had met mob contacts in a dive where she worked, Tanya had performed for him. She wanted to show him those babies again but understood he wouldn't have time. Tanya also knew she wouldn't be lonely in Miami Beach. She always found—well, call it companionship.

She yelped to porters, who struggled behind her.

"Hey, hurry it up!"

Then, Tanya turned back to Lee and cooed.

"I have about a dozen bags, Sugar. Will that be a problem?"

A car followed Lee's Corvette from a safe distance. DEA agent Tillis and his partner had tagged it to tail him. The tag was easy to make. Since the 'Vette didn't have a trunk, the lawyer had strapped luggage on its back. The overloaded sports car moved slowly so nothing would fly off.

Tillis followed it across the Route 195 causeway toward Miami Beach. Off both sides of the roadway fishermen and fisherwomen bobbed in pleasure crafts. Tillis was oblivious to the aqua waters that attracted them; his eyes focused solely on his quarry. Keeping just far enough behind to stay out of sight, he stared intently as they entered Miami Beach.

Lee cruised through a traffic light just as it turned red.

"We're gonna lose them," Tillis' partner said.

DEA Agent Mercury was a younger, black man whose youthful appearance often helped infiltrating teen crack gangs that worked housing projects.

"I'm not losing anyone," Tillis declared. "Let me show you how to work a tail."

He slowed for the red light with his eyes focused wide, then accelerated through the busy commercial intersection.

An elderly woman, who was pulling a small shopping cart across the street, raised her fist, shook it, and yelled.

"That's a Goddamned red light, you asshole!"

Agent Mercury laughed.

"You pissed off someone's grandmamma big time," he noted.

Tillis had no patience for distractions. Doggedly, he trailed the sportscar, keeping back just far enough to avoid risk of exposure. At last, it appeared to reach its destination: it pulled up to main entrance of the towering Fontainebleau Hotel. As it parked in line at bustling check-in doors, Tillis stopped their car and peered. A trio of words escaped his lips, like air bursting from a pin-popped balloon.

"My friggin' God!"

Agent Mercury's baby face glowed. He, too, stared in erstwhile appreciation. Neither could take their eyes from the huge blond disembarking from the lawyer's tiny car.

Bellhops unstrapped luggage and scurried. The big woman directed them like a traffic cop at rush hour, waving her arms and pointing. The animated porters marched her bags into the hotel while the lawyer drove away.

As Tillis adjusted his sunglasses, the younger agent summed up their feelings.

"The counselor must live a charmed existence to hustle that blond and a brunette at the same time. What's he up to?"

"We'll find out," Tillis promised. "I'll come back later for her."

"She'll be easy to spot."

"I'll use a ruse and pump information from her. Then, we'll bury that slime ball lawyer and Agent Calero in the same body bag."

# Chapter Eleven

# Palm Trees and Concrete

LEE SENSED DANGER as he sat across from Frankie No Throat. The *capo* peered out plate-glass windows from Lee's office into a bright courtyard. Like so much of the Miami landscape, palm trees and concrete filled it. Lee wondered what the man was thinking. Though Frankie was a friend, he would turn on Lee fast if he felt squeezed. Frankie's boyish looks concealed the simple truth: he was a career criminal who killed as casually as you clean your ears. Frankie never broached the subject with his lawyer, but Lee had heard stories from corroborating sources. Some of his clients, who were Frankie's "business associates," had described his prowess with small-caliber, easily concealed pistols that were his trademark. The mob *capo* could also bring death subtly, as Lee had learned from the file Frankie burned in that dark South Philly alley.

Lee glanced at the package on his desktop, the one Tanya had brought. As Frankie took a seat, his eyes fell to it also, then rose to Lee.

"I asked you here to talk about Panama," the lawyer began.

"Is it me—or is it getting hot in here?" Frankie interrupted.

Lee trained his eyes on the package as he said, "Miami's always hot, Frankie."

He was ready to talk about his FBI meeting, explain his imbroglio, and enlist Frankie to help resolve it.

*This is a day*, Lee thought, *a lot of people are going to sweat.*

A single bead of perspiration glided down the small of a tawny back. Tanya's broad shoulders made the contour of her spine all the more remarkable with such a slender waist. Face down on a lounge chair, she tanned at the famous Fontainebleau pool. Roasting in the sun, Tanya wore only her G-string to avoid a tan line from a bikini back strap. She had ordered a piña colada from the pool waiter and wondered why it was taking so long to arrive.

*Just relax and enjoy*, she told herself.

Tanya listened to splashes from the iconic Fontainebleau Hotel waterfall as water cascaded into the swimming pool. Watching torrents pour down the manmade rock formation that was adorned with lush tropical plants, she came to a realization.

*It's an eternal fountain*, she thought. *Water will flow from that thing forever.*

Peering through Chanel sunglasses, she absorbed the sights. People at poolside reeked of big bucks. Vacationers came from around the globe, looking rich and smelling wealthy. She spied their designer bathing suits and fancy wraps. Sure, plenty of middle-class conventioneers booked the hotel, but most attended meetings at that time of day while better-heeled visitants enjoyed midday sun.

"Your drink, Ma'am," called a man from behind her.

"Put it on the table next to me," she casually answered, "and charge it to room six-fourteen in the North Tower."

Tanya turned her head and saw something was wrong. Looking from her low level, she first observed the man's scuffed dress shoes.

*Vinyl tops and cardboard soles*, she thought.

Black socks hung low on spindly ankles. Slowly, she peered upward. Centered on pasty limbs were a pair of knobby knees. Glancing higher, she spied a tacky print bathing suit that could have only come from a South Miami discount store during a closeout sale. Folding over its top, something alabaster jiggled, a three-keg beer belly. Higher still, like Brillo pads glued to porcelain, coarse and curly hair adorned a sunken chest.

She wondered.

Do I dare look higher?

Curiosity piqued so she went all the way. Tanya saw it: the face of an albino bull frog.

*If this guy doesn't layer himself in suntan lotion,* she figured, *he'll fry fast.*

"I'm Dave Tillis," the DEA agent offered. "I'm here from Minnesota for the cable-TV convention."

"Pardon me," Tanya responded, "while I pat down my goose bumps."

Either missing or ignoring her sarcasm, Tillis settled into his ruse.

"I heard you order the drink and thought maybe you could use company. The waiter let me buy one for you and bring it over. In fact, you looked thirsty, so I brought a half dozen. Mind if I stretch on the chair next to you and share some of these?"

Tanya studied the six tiny umbrellas in tall glasses, then focused on the heat and stifling humidity. The frozen cocktails looked too good to pass up.

*Oh, why not?* She finally told herself.

He looked harmless enough. The guy probably had a wife and six kids back in Duluth, stranded in snow drifts, while he attended his convention. Cable-TV conventioneers were running around her wing of the hotel looking for fun. Maybe she would give him some.

As she rose to lift a drink from his tray, Tanya watched the man's tongue drop. She'd forgotten that she wasn't wearing a top. Accustomed to his expression in her line of work, Tanya uttered the simple truth.

"Funny how two teats can make grown men look so goofy."

She slipped on a T-shirt and sipped her first drink. The frog had lots of questions, but he had lots of pina coladas, and became less appalling to look at with each one. Drinks relaxed her. She answered every question with simple innocence and without restraint. Tanya talked and he listened as they sipped one cocktail after another.

Lee had told his story. Frankie seemed to know about the tax evasion charges already. He looked at Lee almost as if he felt sorry for him, then spoke more earnestly than Lee had ever heard him.

"The feds are using those charges to jam you worse than you can imagine, Counselor. If you take the mission to Panama, don't count on coming back alive. My advice is to drop the whole thing, now. Your friends at the FBI can't help you there. Noriega isn't just a political leader run amuck. He isn't just a drug lord, either. He's the fucking Anti-Christ. If he says you're dead, it's just a matter of how they rip you apart.

"There's no law in Panama outside the areas controlled by the United States military in the canal zone. Noriega can even have you whacked inside 'the zone' if he wants. His agents kill just to feel alive. His intelligence network lets him know how far you squirt your morning pee, if he's interested. Go there and he'll have you scoped out from top to bottom. His operatives will learn about your FBI contacts. Then, it's over."

Frankie paused to catch his breath before continuing.

"Another thing. You can't count on your sweetheart to save you. You're secondary to the government's plan. They've probably decided you're expendable. The world won't miss a lawyer, who doesn't return from that place when the scheme goes bad. They'll plant a news story saying you were killed while you were dealing drugs there. The whole operation will be swept under the table."

"I'm not counting on their agent to keep me alive, Frankie. I'm counting on you to do that."

Frankie stared at Lee, then looked out the windows at the palm trees and concrete.

"I've already told you. I'm not going near Panama again, ever."

Lee studied his old friend. He had damned little chance of pulling off the mission and had to do whatever he could to increase his odds for survival.

"Frankie No Throat," he said, shoving the package between them toward the man, "look at this."

The mobster opened it and pulled out documents. His face fell. Frankie scanned investigation reports from the European police network Interpol, reports from the Philadelphia Police Department, records bearing the royal seal of Monaco, photographs, medical charts, hospital records, and death certificates. His open mouth let Lee know the hood was astounded.

"You kept a copy of these papers?" Frankie gushed. "The only thing that saved you from getting whacked by the boys in South Philly was my word that I torched them. There's enough here to reopen the Kelly mess."

"Two more copies of that file are in safe keeping, Frankie. One goes to my new friends at the FBI and the other goes to the press if something unfortunate happens to me, whether I suffer that misfortune here or in Panama."

Lee allowed Frankie time to peruse the file further. While he did, Lee looked around his office and compared it with what he remembered of Robert Sheppard's. No family photographs lit up the room. He yearned for what the government lawyer took for granted. Lee longed for family, stability, and roots. He had been deprived of those things too long. If he could get through the mission alive, he would make some big changes.

*Few second chances come in life*, he thought. Lee prayed for one as a long shot.

"What you've got, here, buries me," Frankie declared in an extended breath.

Frankie paused, then shot a cold look that chilled Lee. For an instant, it was as if Lee were laying again on icy asphalt in that Philadelphia alley. He could still see Frankie's heel smashing his knee, and still couldn't move out of its way.

"There's an old Sicilian saying," Frankie said. "Three can keep a secret if two are dead."

The meaning wasn't lost on Lee. Frankie, Lee and Kell had shared the secret of Grace's death. Frankie's people had buried Kell. The secret would be safe with Lee dead, too.

"Help me, Frankie, and I'll give you every copy of the file that exists. That's my promise."

Frankie sat silently as Lee continued.

"We'll go to Panama with our own agenda. The FBI has its plans. We'll have ours. I'm completing that mission and getting on with my life. I've spent the past three years in purgatory. You put me there and you're pulling me out."

Lee gave Frankie no more choice than he had himself. The hood rose and stared out the window.

"Fucking Miami," he said. "Nothin' but palm trees and concrete."

He turned back to Lee and spoke as if siphoned of all emotion.

"We'll need cash. It's mother's milk that nurtures friendships where we'll be going."

"Here's fifty grand."

Lee turned over a manila envelope with the Diaz brothers' cash.

"We need a million. Goddamn it! There's only one way to flip your cash into what we'll need."

"Flip it fast, Frankie. I have a meeting tonight that may bring the invitation neither of us wants."

After the second set of six piña coladas, it seemed like a good idea to take the party to her hotel room. Tanya's new frog-faced friend grew on her. She watched him sprawl butt naked across her green bedspread, looking like a flabby amphibian on a lily pad.

Tanya smiled and walked into the bathroom. She lined up twelve drink umbrellas as if they were parading, then changed. She ripped off her T-shirt and G-string.

"Goodbye, Tees and Gees," she told them.

Tanya pulled a slinky teddy from a hook on the back of the door and slipped it over her head.

"It's so wonderful to find a guy who listens to a chick," she called out. "Most men just want to blab."

She grabbed a towel rack for support, taking a moment to reflect upon the afternoon as she steadied her gait.

"And, you know something, after all we drank, I don't even remember what I said. Hope you don't mind if I tell you all over again."

Tanya poked around her cosmetic kit until she found what she needed. She had forgotten to take her morning medication, so she swallowed a handful of Premarin tablets in a single gulp to keep girlish. Then, she searched for KY Jelly to lubricate her plumbing.

When she returned to the bedroom, Tanya found Tillis snoring. Cocktails had marinated and sun had cooked all life from her frog. Already, a crimson sunburn glowed.

"Hey, wake up," she called.

She studied the man with grave concern.

"Later, you'll be in too much pain for lovin'."

"Bur-rib-bit," he snored.

Tanya sighed. "Oh, who cares? By then, I'll be too sober to want ya, anyway."

Tanya sat in a chair beside the bed wearing her flimsy teddy. Her eyelids grew heavy. Alcohol and sunbeams had made her slumberous, too. She closed her eyes to rest just a second. When she opened them, it was nighttime, and he was gone.

"Hey," she wailed woefully, "where's my frog?"

He had taken the twelve drink umbrellas and all traces that they ever met. Tanya walked to the window and removed her teddy. Naked and alone, she stared at the moon.

Frankie No Throat stood in somber solitude, under the palms, watching moonlight glitter on calm waters of Miami Bay. Even after dusk, the temperature remained high. Humidity stifled. He had enlisted in Lee's mission or, more precisely, the lawyer had drafted him. Lee had promised to give him every copy of the file that existed for his cooperation and Frankie could count on Lee to keep his word. Still, he wondered.

Will either of us come back from Panama alive?

He didn't like—hell no, hated—no, God damn it, feared returning there yet he had no choice. Yes. He would help Lee, but he'd see that the lawyer paid a heavy price.

*Never take a squeeze,* Frankie No Throat thought, *without squeezing back.*

He waited for someone, somebody who would help in the days ahead. He knew friendships in the drug world were only kept with cash. The job would take about a million dollars, he figured, and he needed it fast. Lee had given him seed money to set-up a scam. Frankie tapped his pocket and felt the manila envelope containing fifty "gee-whizzes." Lee had handed it to him without asking any questions. The fifty-grand ante had to multiply, and the hood knew how to do it.

He always felt a rush of excitement when he was about to take on a bank. It stemmed from grade school when a nun at Saint Bartholomew had asked every kid in his third-grade class what they wanted to be when they grew up. Incorrigible Frankie proudly stood before his classmates and announced he wanted to be a bank president. Sister Magdalene flushed that pipe dream.

"Francis," the miserable old crone said, "you can't even do your times tables. Stupid and lazy boys shouldn't have grand ambitions."

He never forgot his classmates' laughter. Frankie had been getting back at the habit wearing, bulbous-nosed witch ever since by scamming bankers. Usually, he outsmarted them without recourse. When they came after him, he secured legal help. After he and Lee had come to know each other, Frankie explained his favorite scam.

"I call it 'Banking 102'," he declared. "See the numbers next to the account numerals on this check."

Lee peered quizzically.

"Those are routing numbers," Frankie continued. "When a check's deposited into a local bank, it's sent to the Federal Reserve Bank for clearance. Local banks know that 'in-state transactions' take a max of three days to clear the Fed and 'out-of-state transactions' take a max of five days. If the Federal Reserve Bank doesn't return the check for any reason during the float time, the local bank assumes the check's good and pays on it.

"What I did was use a cigarette to burn a small hole through a routing number. The teller didn't think anything of it and accepted the check on deposit. She had no reason to be suspicious. I had run good paper through the account by passing the same hundred grand through repeatedly. You know, I'd deposit a check into the dummy account, cash it out after it cleared, then run it through other banks so I could keep depositing checks into the dummy bank—always with the same teller. After a few cycles, the dummy bank was comfortable with me.

"Anyway, I made my final deposit, and waited three days. The dummy bank assumed the deposit was good, just like the others, and paid on it. They didn't realize what the hole in the routing numbers would do. It took the Fed an extra ten days to route the check, even though the bank prints its name on the item. The Fed looks at routing numbers on checks, not bank names, until there's a problem. By working the 'float time,' I cleared a quarter-million-dollar check against a bogus account with five bucks in it.

*So much for treasured memories*, Frankie thought.

Now, he prepared to scam a mid-sized Savings & Loan institution in Hallandale that caught his eye. He had maintained accounts, just waiting for the right time to do banking. The cash Lee gave him in the manila envelope was his venture capital. The bulbous-nosed witch was motivation.

"Time," Frankie declared, "to invest wisely."

He'd break out investment duds. His navy-blue pin stripe, three-piece suit always brought luck: bankers like dealing with folks who look like them. After swindling the S & L, he would invest his earnings in the pharmaceutical industry. The dough would seed a coke deal: he'd buy powder to flip. That part of the plan was risky because he didn't have much time to check his buyer. Successful drug deals depend upon knowing everyone in the transaction and timing everything perfectly. Frankie couldn't do either.

He stood alone under rustling palm leaves, where even night breeze blew hot. Beams from a full moon reflected on rippling bay waters. The spectacle should have soothed but nothing pacified the ill-feeling churning the pit of his stomach. A sudden gust delivered damp and heavy air that tore through the palms. Slender leaves fluttered and whistled in the breeze, as if warning of havoc to come.

*Yet now*, he thought, *I don't have the luxury of trusting my intuition.*

Frankie knew he and Lee were in too far to avoid taking the sojourn. As he sweat under the moon, Frankie recalled how fate inextricably glued them together. Those memories rushed fast as the bullets fired when it all began.

# Chapter Twelve

# Little Quakers And Nittany Lions

*LIFE'S BREATH IS SWEET AND I'm about to steal it.*

So thought an even leaner, maybe even meaner, Frankie No Throat on November 10, 1966. That was when Jackie "Toes" Tosalero was the most feared man stalking the streets of the City of Brotherly Love. As a mob "collector," he and his crew collected protection money from pimps, scam artists, and assorted freelancers, who worked the Philadelphia crime family area of control. Jackie Toes was also responsible for paying off cops on the take: dirty work for a dirty man.

The job suited Toes. With hair that never found a straight part, and a face unevenly shaven, the stranger to showers and tubs emitted an essence akin to his name. When he came around, your nose smelled toes.

He collected from scumbags who couldn't complain. After all, how could a pimp tell police that Toes would have a prostitute's face rearranged if he didn't regularly pay the mob? Just as regularly, Toes paid off cops. A precinct commander's car would stop outside the newspaper store, which Toes maintained as a front on busy South Broad Street, and a cop would hustle into the store for a Daily News. Inside that newspaper was enough cash to pay every nightstick twirler in the precinct.

Cops have a saying: "Once you take mob money, you become one of them." They have another saying, too. "If you don't take mob money, you live in fear of what they'll do to you."

Like most forms of humanity, Jackie Toes was reasonable when things went his way. When doings didn't, his crew beat or whacked the offender. Notwithstanding a lack of socialization and hygienic skills, Toes was a good *capo*. Men on his crew were dedicated. That autumn day, Frankie No Throat was one of them, an up-and-coming young wise guy still "making his bones," who never thought twice when told take out a man.

The big boss had given Frankie special orders. Toes was skimming the take and the family Boss ordered Frankie to whack him. That's how it's done. Whenever possible, the job is given to someone close to the victim, so he won't see it coming. Frankie knew he would either kill his capo or the Boss would have him whacked for refusing. So, Frankie traipsed to the small store, where Jackie Toes stood behind a cash register that rarely rang a legit dime. The joint's tiny back room had a doorway leading to a rear alley for those who preferred a less conspicuous entrance. Frankie silently entered it, pulled out his .22 caliber pistol, and waited to pump Jackie Toes in his head with six rounds.

Frankie harkened to a sports wrap-up on the radio blaring in the main room. He bet heavily on football and Friday afternoons, he listened to weekend betting lines. Before killing Toes, he'd take down point spreads, then pick a half dozen pro and college games, maybe even a local high school rivalry.

Take the Nittany Lions of Penn State plus seven points, Frankie told himself as he went through the pick sheet he'd hand to his bookmaker. He considered their young, new head coach, Joe Paterno.

*Yeah,* he figured, *always count on a paison.*

After selecting weekend picks, he would wait for the store to empty and whack Toes. The plan was simple—shoot then leave through the rear door. Frankie just hoped he'd have better luck with his picks than Toes would have taking breaths.

He had to select hurriedly because there's so much to do after whacking a target. Well, you *gotta* bathe and wash your clothes so thoroughly. Gunpowder from a fired pistol leaves traces that cops can use as evidence. It lands under fingernails and everywhere.

*It's unfriggin' believable*, Frankie thought.

The only way to remove residue is to scrub with white vinegar. Afterward, you *gotta* bathe again to rid the odor. Frankie had an early dinner date and didn't want to go out smelling like a Caesar salad.

A sportscaster was announcing scores of high school football games in progress. Frankie listened intently as he peered into the main room. Jackie Toes had one customer. Soon as the guy left, Frankie No Throat would murder.

Across town in East Falls, a game clock ticked down. The Little Quakers of Penn Charter were losing by six points, 13-7, in the final quarter to archrival Germantown Academy. As one of the nation's oldest schoolboy rivalries, the football game had all the meaning of an Army-Navy classic for the faithful attending their homecoming match-up. With less than two minutes on the clock, the Penn Charter blue and gold varsity team would have to march eighty-five yards to score a touchdown. Lee Gunther huddled with the rest of the offense players for their final drive.

"Time to pull it all together!" their quarterback called out.

Lee realized the QB was looking around at their offensive weapons. Their two best receivers were out with injuries and Lee was still an untested commodity. He had the height but was underweight for varsity football. He had taken a backup receiver position to make the team in his junior year. He didn't have bulk to play other positions, but he had enough speed and excellent hands. If he could reach a ball, he usually held onto it. Coach Dooney had called him an overachiever, and Lee knew the more experienced quarterback was counting on him to mature as a player fast. On their last chance to move down the football field, Lee had just become the primary receiver.

Time for more overachieving, he thought, as their quarterback called the play. Eleven PC blue and golds positioned for the ball snap.

Lee looked into the stands, hoping his father had come to the game. Dad had said he would try, even if his work made him miss the first half. Lee was hopeful, but also realized that his father felt uncomfortable at the clubby affairs, especially for that homecoming game. Many kids at the school were "legacies." Their families had attended the prestigious school for generations. Most fathers in the stands had been PC students themselves and shared a comradeship that escaped parents of first-generation students.

Lee's dad had come up the hard way as the son of a Pennsylvania Dutch immigrant. His father's family had moved into a tough working-class neighborhood in North Philadelphia where his grandfather had labored a beer brewery. In the days of prohibition, his grandfather, like many poor German immigrants, even made beer for bootleggers in the family basement. Lee's dad had risen above humble roots by studying chemical engineering locally at Drexel University. Though he never obtained a college degree, he had found a good job at the oil refineries in South Philadelphia. He was leaving work early that day, if he could, to catch the biggest football game his son ever played.

His father's salary had afforded a private school education for Lee and his younger sister. Gwen was a fourth grader enrolled across the street from Penn Charter. She attended the Lankenau School for Girls, or as the Penn Charter boys referred to it, "Skank-in-all," in deference to a student body that seemed less than comely. Lee spotted his little sister in the stands but couldn't find his dad.

"Hup, one," his quarterback called out. "Hup, two!"

The quarterback called the play on the short count, and Lee ran a straight out. He juked to the left and darted toward the center of the field. The play worked. Defenders were playing wide-outside expecting a sideline pass. If the receiver ran out of bounds, the clock would stop to save precious time on their last-ditch drive. By going inside, the field was open. The quarterback tossed the ball toward Lee's outstretched arms. Lee felt the pigskin kiss his fingertips. The grab was good for eighteen yards before charging GA defenders in their black and red uniforms smothered him. The PC blue and gold had a first down. Lee picked himself off the ground and looked again into the stands. Still, he saw no sign of his father.

Back to the huddle, he told himself.

"Listen up," the quarterback said as he called the next play.

They changed formation and lined up in a "T."

What are we doing in a run formation? Lee asked himself.

Suddenly, it dawned on him. His quarterback still didn't have faith in him as an untested receiver; he had called a running play. Hope rested on their star running back.

On the ball snap disaster broke. Five black and red GA jerseys pounded the big running back. PC blue and golds suffered a short loss. Time disappeared from the clock. A signal came from their half-crazed coach on the bench and Penn Charter called its last time out. The Little Quakers hustled to the sidelines to meet with Coach Ray Dooney.

"Son," Dooney told his quarterback, "if you put the ball on the ground one more time in this drive, I'll put you in the ground."

Lee caught the older boy's reaction. He knew what their quarterback was thinking. Lee looked good in practice however he'd rarely played under game conditions, and never in a win or lose final drive. Lee looked again to the stands for his dad.

Coach Dooney sent the team back onto the field, all excepting Lee.

"Gunner," he said to his young receiver, "get your head back in the game. If you miss one ball because you're looking for some sweet thing in the stands, I'll bury you deeper than I'm gonna bury. . .."

Lee didn't hear anything else his coach said. He would be the "go to" guy on the drive so he'd concentrate on getting open and catching the ball. He'd think of nothing else. Lee wasn't just an overachiever as his coach called him; he was cocky, and he'd play the rest of the game with swagger.

Lee ran back on the field as the crowd in jammed stands roared. From the GA side fans called for "deee-fense." From the PC side cheers and clatter erupted. A bass drum pounded faster, and the piercing cry of an air horn shot across the playing field.

He didn't make the huddle, but knew the play called. Lee went wide left. On the snap, he ran long with all the speed he could muster. The quarterback tossed the ball into the air in a perfect spiral that arched at midfield and began its descent toward him. One defender strode along his side, matching Lee step for step. Another waited deep in a zone. Lee knew he would have to outmaneuver both to make the catch. If he didn't, a defender would intercept.

Lee concentrated on the ball, only on the ball, as it came down among the three players. He readied to leap for the pigskin while still in full stride. Breaths echoed inside his helmet. He could hear a cry from a defender who slipped to the ground. Everything happened as if they were moving in slow motion: his shoulder pads clattering, adhesive tape wrapped round his ankles for support tugging his muscles, his legs straining for more speed with each step. Lee's feet left the ground. His hands reached above the remaining defender.

*Concentrate*, he told himself.

Frankie No Throat concentrated. At last, he and Jackie Toes were alone. He approached the counter holding the .22 in his right hand by his side. With the counter to his left, Toes couldn't see the compact weapon.

"Jackie," he called out with a smile.

Jackie Toes looked up.

"Frankie No Throat pick me a couple of winners," he called. "Last week I got my tail kicked on games."

"No problem, Toes. I got something good for you, right here."

With that Frankie raised his right hand and shot Jackie Toes square in the center of his forehead. The slob didn't seem to feel it, so Frankie fired again and hit him in the skull with another small caliber round.

Toes took instinctive action. He pulled a loaded .44 magnum handgun from under the counter and fired wildly. He wobbled from the head wounds and Frankie easily ducked under a table, and out of the way.

"You no-good motherfucker," Jackie Toes screamed, "trying to do a hit on me with that little fucking pistol.

You can't take out the fagot ass on a queer rat with that thing!"

Just then, Frankie heard the bell over the front door jingle.

*Who would enter this place*, the thought flashed, *in the middle of a hit?*

Frankie glanced but didn't recognize the guy.

*Must be a bonafide bystander*, he thought, *hustling into the store to pick up something fast and go on his way.*

Frankie stood and held out his .22 in the direction of Jackie Toes, who woefully moaned.

"Eat shit, you smelly bastard," Frankie thundered while pumping the last four rounds from his handgun into Jackie's head.

Jackie slumped forward on the countertop. With the pistol dangling loosely in his hand, Toes managed to squeeze off a final shot. Frankie ducked to the floor again, not knowing where the bullet was going. When he got up, he saw Jackie lying dead over the countertop, blood seeping from small-caliber head wounds. Frankie also saw the bystander dead on the floor. He had probably entered for a real friggin' newspaper. The sorry bastard would be in the next edition.

It had taken six bullets to whack Jackie, and one unlucky shot to kill the bystander.

"Go figure," escaped Frankie lips as he mused.

He strolled to the rear door in need of a vinegar scrub down. The good news was he still had enough time to soak. Frankie felt content even though he hated seeing a civilian drop.

*What can ya do?* he thought. *It happens.*

Frankie walked briskly, rather than run, from the rear door, out an alleyway, and onto South Broad Street. Then, he juked right and left through heavy traffic, hoping to avoid cops called to the scene after the gun bursts.

Penn Charter had first and goal on the three-yard line. The Little Quakers had covered the length of the football field with passes thrown to the kid they had all started calling "Gunner." He'd caught everything thrown to him, and the moniker his coach had chosen became a badge of admiration. He had to keep catching the ball if he wanted to retain their respect.

The PC Little Quakers lined up and snapped the ball. Their quarterback threw the ball out of bounds to stop the clock with five seconds remaining. They had time for one last play and three yards to go for a touchdown.

"Give me the ball," their big full back shouted. "I'll stuff it in."

The wide-bottomed senior could bull his butt through defensive linemen. That close to the goal line, it made sense to go with his size, strength, and experience. Their quarterback turned to face their bench. Coach Dooney paced the sidelines, clipboard in hand, looking as anxious as everyone in the stands and on the field for the QB to make the call. The referee's whistle signaled resumption of play.

"We play-fake the run and throw a short pass," the quarterback said.

All eyes in the huddle turned toward Lee. It was up to him.

The QB pulled his arms apart wide and brought them back together fast, clapping hard, as he shouted.

"Break!"

Lee chugged along the line of scrimmage. Three defenders keyed on him. He couldn't do much to shake them. He would have to run within the ten-yard depth of the end zone, and he'd be triple teamed.

*We should change-off to a running play*, Lee thought.

He had no way to get open. Besides, if he was triple-teamed, fewer defenders would be on the line to stop a run by their star fullback. That was a perfect time to change the play. He hoped their quarterback was thinking the same thing as he lined up.

On the snap, Lee darted smack into the middle of the defenders. The move worked. Two of them bumped into each other and hit the ground. The ball was on its way to him, but it came before he could adjust from the collision. It sailed into the hands of the remaining pass-defender. Lee plowed into the bigger defender with all his strength. He saw the player fall backward with the ball in his hands for an interception. As the defender went down, Lee wrestled for the football. By the time they hit ground, the ball belonged to Lee.

"Touchdown, blue and gold!" a referee called out.

Lee was dazed. He ran off the field to the sidelines. The ball was still in his grasp when their field goal players kicked the point after touchdown, finishing the game 14-13, Penn Charter over Germantown Academy.

Teammates pounded Lee's shoulder pads, hooting and cheering. Spectators screamed and clamored to their feet as Lee anxiously peered into the stands, still searching for his dad, unaware his father lay dead beside Jackie Toes.

Frankie heard the news as he sat in an old-fashioned, four-footed bathtub, surrounded by empty bottles. He reeked of vinegar and scrubbed like a coolie on laundry day. A favorite old movie flashed on his black-and-white-screen portable TV. John Wayne was playing the Ringo Kid in a 1939 classic: "Stagecoach." Frankie had seen his horse-riding hero in the film so often he knew all the actors' lines by heart. So, he kept the TV sound off and listened to sports wrap-ups on his tiny transistor radio. That's how he learned.

"Damn," Frankie muttered.

The guy, who got whacked with Jackie Toes, was the father of a local football star at some rich-kid school. Frankie would never have known except the story hit the radio sports news. It was a heartbreaker even to the guy who had almost caught the bullet that Jackie meant for him. He would have to do something to make it right. But first things first.

He stood up in his tub and pulled the rubber drain stopper. Vinegar and water swished away as Frankie readied to refill for a second rinse.

After the shooting, Lee learned the meaning of the school motto: "Good instruction is better than riches." On Thursdays, the student body in the Quaker school attended a "Friend's Meeting." Members of the Society of Friends engaged in a peculiar form of worship: the small Christian sect believed that sitting in silence for forty minutes was a rewarding spiritual experience. Occasionally someone would stand, should the "inner light" of God strike, to pontificate. Lee used the time to reflect on his father's untimely death. As a form of meditation, the unconventional religious service helped sooth the pain of his loss.

Following Friends Meeting, Lee and his mother met with the school headmaster. Lee never liked him. The name "Quaker" had come from an early leader's admonishment to "tremble or quake at the word of the Lord" and the nervous little man seemed to tremble and quake at everything. Lee knew why they were meeting—his father hadn't financially planned for a shortened life. Tuition was overdue and the Gunther family couldn't afford to pay. After a few curt words, the headmaster ejected Lee.

*So much for good instruction if you don't have riches*, Lee thought, while accompanying his mother out.

A dark kerchief wrapped her head, blond bangs falling through the front, covering her forehead. He stared at her oversized black sunglasses, knowing they concealed weepy eyes. His mother was too young to be a widow and unprepared for financial hardship that befell their family.

"Don't worry, Mom," he told her. "We'll get through this. They're not turning me from gridiron hero to hobo."

Lee sensed their roles were beginning to reverse as he became man of the house by default. From that day, he would look out for his mother and sister as best he could.

"Your father always wanted you to go to college. We won't be able to afford it when the time comes."

"Mom, don't worry. Everything will work out."

Lee was less confident than he sounded but he wouldn't let poverty steel his swagger. Somehow, he would succeed.

He enrolled at Central High School for Boys, a public school with a reputation for fine academics. Lee still played football but not well enough to earn a university scholarship. His mother couldn't afford to pay for college, so the military draft was looking chilly. Upon graduation, the army would send him to Vietnam.

Lee sat in his bedroom tossing a football into the air and catching it. His senior year was almost over, and he had no plans, though friends were preparing to attend colleges that had accepted them. The telephone rang but he wasn't really interested. His younger sister received most calls; Gwen was just at that point in life. Unfortunately, at his point, life showed no bright prospects.

"Lee," his mother sang, "the phone call's for you."

He walked casually to the living room to talk to a buddy. With their senior prom coming, they'd make plans.

"Yo," he called into the receiver.

"Well," came the reply, "yo to you, too."

Lee didn't recognize the more mature voice. He just listened and fell into a chair. When he hung up, he remained dumbstruck.

"Who was that, Dear?" his mother called.

When Lee didn't respond, his mom rushed to him and spoke with greater urgency.

"Are you all right, Lee? There isn't any trouble, is there?"

Lee leaped and wrapped his arms around her. Freckle faced Gwen scurried into the room, attracted by their mother's call. Lee embraced her, too.

"Hey," she yelped. "You're hugging me too tight!"

"What is it, Lee?" his mother persisted.

"That was Coach Paterno from Penn State," he shouted. "One of his scouts has been following me. The guy saw me play at Central . . . and they're giving me a scholarship to play for the Nittany Lions."

His mother began to cry. Lee was in shock. College recruiters had told him that he had good hands, but he was still too skinny. Though he had enough speed for high school football, he was a step slow for collegiate level play. Someone had gone out of their way to get him a sports scholarship.

Lee wondered about the scout. He would never know it was his guardian angel: Frankie No Throat had pulled strings and his favorite *goomba* coach gave the overachieving kid a chance.

It was first and ten again in Philadelphia and Lee wore the white and blue uniform of a Penn State Nittany Lion. By his senior year, he put on weight. With hands that caught so many balls tossed his way, he was a marginal prospect for the pros. He wouldn't make professional football as a top draft choice, but he might get selected in lower rounds. The overachieving kid with the confident swagger hadn't let Coach Paterno down for giving him a scholarship. He had played his heart out to become one of the Lion's stars.

They were squared off against the Temple University Owls when it happened. The Owls played tough for a team that wasn't supposed to be particularly good. Lee lined up wide and ran a crossing pattern. When he sprinted into the middle of the field for the ball their quarterback had thrown, he saw the red and white jersey of a Temple defender barreling headfirst. Lee just concentrated on the ball. He knew he was going to get hit hard but he wanted to make the catch. Absorbing a hit on a crossing pattern is just part of the game.

Just as he firmly planted his left foot to cut back for the ball, a red helmet struck his left knee. He heard something in his body crunch and felt excruciating pain. Lee would never play football again. Surgery and physical therapy would restore movement, yet he would walk with a slight limp, only detectable when the injury flared. Still, he would keep his vow to never lose his confident swagger.

After the injury, Coach Paterno helped by finding Lee a partial scholarship to the Temple University Law School in Philadelphia. The rest of the money he'd need to complete his education would come from a part-time job the coach somehow found him in a South Philadelphia hardware and building supply store.

Lee was on his way to earning a law degree and though he didn't know, his guardian angel was earning a pair of wings. A single bullet tied Lee and Frankie No Throat together—its blast still echoing when their invitation to Hell came soft as a dove's coo.

# Chapter Thirteen

# An Invitation to Hell

VELVETY TONES COOED against a deafening backdrop while Lee and Jaime masqueraded as adoring disco desperados. It had been three months without an invitation the FBI scheme was calculated to deliver. Lee played their game, biding time, while praying for the plan to harmlessly evaporate like rainfall on a steamy Miami boulevard.

"Senor Gunther," again came the soft and respectful calling, "I wish to. . .."

Lee saw Jose Batista's lips move but couldn't hear him over pulsating dance music in Centro Espanol. The Miami nightclub presented a hallucinogenic mix of age and sexuality. Tanya came to mind as the place seemed more her scene than his anymore. Among the bustle of straights and gays, glamour queens and drag queens, he had agreed to meet his former client for a singular purpose. He leaned close as Batista's mouth approached his ear. When it was close enough to bite, the man began again.

"President Noriega's advisors have mentioned your name. Most favorably, I should add. He sends tidings with his gratitude for what you have accomplished. He also wants to discuss certain grave concerns of our nation with you." Brimming with self-importance, Noriega's emissary extended the invitation Lee dreaded.

"Come to Panama as his special guest."

The man never fully concealed his underlying nature. Within the quiet timbre of his voice, inside the doe-like softness of his eyes, lurked traces of a trained killer's shrewdness. Lee gritted his teeth, wrestling to conceal emotion. He knew Batista bore observing eyes and ears for Manuel Noriega, searching for any reaction he could report to his master.

"I'm too busy, right now, Jose," Lee said, not wanting to appear overly anxious.

"You know legal affairs trouble our President in the American courts. This is your opportunity to discuss those problems with him and work your magic."

"Don't know if I can get away."

"Perhaps I should have made something clear."

As Batista pressed, his quiet voice gained an edge. Fawn eyes transposed into a carnivore's form.

"The President will surely see that you are well compensated and entertained."

Batista's thin veneer betrayed more than a vicious underlying nature. Apparently, he was responsible for delivering Lee to his boss.

"Well, perhaps if I could take a young lady with me, I could combine this business with pleasure."

"Of course, you may, *Senor*. If she's the attractive woman I've seen you escort, she'll be well received."

Something in Batista's quick smirk alerted Lee. His cat-swallowed-the-canary leer let Lee know Batista enjoyed toying with a bird before he ate it.

"Of course, you'll make special travel arrangements due to the sensitive nature of these talks. Don't take a direct flight or sea passage."

Lee didn't like what he was hearing.

"Book a trip to Cancun. Use your lady friend as a cover. Say you're taking a Mexican vacation. Spend a few days in the Caribbean sun on Cancun beaches. From there, travel fifty miles south to a private air strip. One of our planes will fly you and your lady directly to Panama."

Lee's teeth ground. He sensed something wrong in a plan so wrought with subterfuge.

"You'll enjoy the hospitality of a gracious host," Batista offered earnestly, "but you must leave soon. President Noriega is eager to see you within the next week."

Drums pounded. Shrill trumpets blared in the crowded nightspot. Under lights flashing fiery red hues, bodies jostled, swirling in a frenzy on the dance floor. Lee strained harder to hear Batista's soft voice, and realized he was listening to a messenger deliver an invitation from the devil. So many thoughts raced through his mind.

As Batista outlined the dictator's agenda for their meeting, Lee wondered what had happened to his old friend. He hadn't heard from Frankie since they had met in his law office.

He must be hustling for our cash, Lee thought, suddenly realizing they needed it faster than either had anticipated.

Frankie No Throat cast his fishing line into the shallow waters around the air boat. With a plunk, the hook and bait sank. He peered into the water.

"Fishing," he groaned, "the most boring way in the world to drink a case of beer. I hope nothin' bites this damn line. Fish are slimy little bastards."

He lifted his baseball cap and wiped sweat from his brow.

"A climate with no breeze, one-hundred degrees, and two-hundred percent humidity. I've got the early stages of sun poisoning, my thirst is unquenchable, and my cheeks are glued to my underpants."

Frankie swatted swarms of bugs.

"Mosquitoes the size of hubcaps on a '66 Eldorado, animals that belong on another planet, and plants that look like they're man eaters. God, I hate the Everglades!"

Frankie wasn't a typical fisherman, yet he wasn't atypical of drug dealers, who dealt all over South Florida on land and water. He had done well enough in his banking venture to score a pharmaceutical acquisition and he was about to make a sale. Frankie took the last swig from his beer can and tossed the empty overboard.

"Hey, man," his indigenous American guide said, "be a little more environmentally conscious."

Frankie looked overboard pensively, and said, "Fuck the fish."

His head shook slowly from side to side.

"Four-thousand square miles of swampland covered with saw grass, snakes, wildcats, and alley-gators," he moaned. "This is one nasty place."

"Good place—for what you're doing," Jake the Seminole replied.

The native American didn't sweat a drop. His red skin dry, his eyes at peace, Jake found tranquil accord in the harsh environment. He had grown up on a nearby reservation and for a price, he guided drug dealers through the swamps.

Under the guise of being a sports fisherman, Frankie was going to deal: he had coke to sell. The cash he'd raise would be front money he and Lee needed to grease palms in Panama. The sale was about to go down and Frankie had a bad feeling in the pit of his stomach.

"Not enough time," he told himself repeatedly.

There hadn't been enough time to check out his buyer. The lure of cash they so badly needed had brought

Frankie there despite misgivings. He had stored the cocaine in waterproof compartments inside oversized pontoons that held the airboat afloat. They also carried a small arsenal of weapons and ammunition for protection. The extra weight made their airboat float lower and move slower. His buyer had stored one-million bucks in the pontoons of a matching boat. They would meet, check the goods and cash, swap boats, then leave in separate directions.

Frankie reeled in his fishing line. He readied to cast it again when he saw Jake the Seminole stare into the distance, then grow rigid.

"What is it, Chief?"

He marveled at the innate skills and abilities of the indigenous people and wondered.

*How'd the feather head spot what I can't hear or see?*

Jake's raised hand motioned for silence. To the guide's trained ears, Frankie realized, something was wrong.

"Two airboats," the Seminole said.

Frankie looked for his submachine gun. At just over two feet long with a folding stock, the Uzi stored nicely in his huge tackle box. The weapon fired at the rate of 600 rounds per minute. He had another in the box for Jake. He had stocked plenty of extra ammunition clips and a half dozen hand grenades. They were well armed, but if they had to run, their heavy boat would move slower than they'd like. Frankie would count on Jake's skills to navigate to a safe hiding spot, and realized the Seminole was about to have his abilities tested.

"Three boats, maybe four," the Seminole said.

"It's supposed to be a one boat deal," Frankie muttered under his breath.

He was freelancing so he couldn't bring any of his boys from South Philly as back up. The only way to pull off the transaction was to keep players to a minimum. One airboat was to meet him with no more than two guys aboard. That way, Frankie and the Seminole could handle any problem that might arise. More than one boat was a signal for trouble. He put binoculars to his eyes and peered across the swamp.

"Out there," the Seminole pointed. "Coming fast."

With so much shit on board, Frankie gave the order fast.

"Crank this thing up and get us *outta* here."

His buyer had either turned him in to the DEA or sent cocaine cowboys to kill them in the swamp and steal the joy powder. Straining through binoculars, he saw a man in the nearest airboat holding a radio handset. The guy was calling his backup. If it came from the sky, they were probably feds.

"Move this thing!" he screamed to the Seminole.

The fan on the airboat roared as they jetted away. Frankie sprayed a burst from his Uzi toward the two boats speeding from their rear. Far away, two more boats raced from their right. He fired again just to let them know he wouldn't go down without taking someone with him.

Bouncing over the water at the speed they traveled, only a lucky shot would hit anything. Their pursuers didn't return the firepower. Whoever was after them patiently waited for closer range.

Jake the Seminole steered their boat through saw grass, veering toward a thick cluster of high-growing vegetation and trees. The four pursuing boats gained on them.

"We'll hide in the mangroves," Jake shouted over the engine's roar, "and try sneaking out after dark."

They darted toward a winding water trail in the thickets. The force of air blowing his face tossed Frankie's baseball cap off his head and made his eyes tear through his sunglasses. He couldn't even read the warning signs, which were posted on stakes planted in shallow waterbeds, as they swept past them into the brush.

The Indian zipped one way, then another, down narrow waterways overgrown by tree branches and vegetation from both sides. Plant life formed a canopy, where they could avoid observation from above, and water trail bends would slow whoever was after them. The waters branched off from place to place, slowing their pursuers even more.

Jake steered their boat to a tree cluster, then shut-off the engine. Frankie tossed him an Uzi and picked up some grenades. They looked into each other's eyes, knowing what they had to do. Jake jumped into the shallow water first and made a dash for the thickets.

They'd disappear into dense growths of mangroves and pines until nightfall, then try running to the Indian reservation.

Frankie followed, hustling to keep up. He looked back over his shoulder for any sign of the boats that were chasing them and stumbled. He fell facedown into the water, then rose and spun all around.

"Jake!" he called out.

Where was he? Frankie froze in his tracks. The Seminole had stranded him in the swamp. Frankie didn't know which way to run. He was twenty feet from the boat, standing in the shallows, surrounded by tall vegetation. A heron swooped down, squawking through its long beak as if it were laughing.

Frankie spun around in a 360-degree search. Everything stood still—no ripples in the water, sawgrass standing straight, tree branches and leaves motionless. There was no sign of the Indian, nor any trace of which direction he had gone. Jake had deserted him.

"That crumby bastard," Frankie grumbled.

Like a typhoon materializing from nowhere, water whooshed all around him. An eighteen-foot alligator shot into the air with the torso of Jake the Seminole clutched between powerful jaws. The gator slammed the water surface with its mighty tail and took the Indian back underwater to drown and devour.

As bloody bubbles surfaced where the man-eater dove, Frankie spotted them. On the water bank thirty feet away, a dozen gators that had been lazily lying suddenly rose, attracted by the kill. They rushed to join the feeding and swam toward him fast. Frankie pulled pins from his grenades and tossed them as if throwing snowballs in a snow fight. Then, he desperately dashed through the shallow water toward the air boat.

Grenades exploded with ringing booms that sent shrapnel whizzing. Water, weeds, and gator meat flew through the air. Frankie kept churning his legs, lunging toward the boat. A feeding frenzy started behind him as alligators fought for the remains of the Seminole and the ravaged carcasses of their buddies.

One gator zeroed in on Frankie. Its powerful tail deftly propelled the natural killing machine. Frankie lifted his feet higher, trying to accelerate by high stepping over water that slowed his paces. As ferocious jaws snapped at his behind, Frankie leaped onboard the airboat. The reptile hissed and readied to lunge. Its unnatural stench gagged him.

Frankie aimed the Uzi and readied to blast the toothy bastard with a full clip. Two more gators swam toward the boat. He realized that the gargantuan reptiles could easily jump on board to devour him. They slowed as his heart beat faster and his mind raced.

*How many bullets,* he wondered, *will it take to cut one down?*

He watched them slink around him, positioning themselves from all angles.

Frankie speculated: *Will I have time to reload if they all attack at once?*

Overhead, Frankie heard a helicopter.

"The Goddamned feds," he wheezed, still trying to catch his breath.

The copter hovered, serving as a beacon to direct airboats to his location. He had no way to escape. Frankie could never outrun them in his boat, and he couldn't leap ashore to hide.

"There's enough coke stored in these pontoons to send me to prison for twenty years," he told himself.

Gators hissed, and readied to pounce aboard. The closest was an ugly fifteen-footer. Frankie aimed between its monstrous eyes, readied to squeeze the trigger, then lowered his weapon. An idea came to him. Ever so cautiously, he moved toward the waterproof compartments on the pontoons. With his eyes trained on the hissing reptiles, who eyed him back as their supper, he slowly opened the pontoon hatches, and pulled out plastic-wrapped bags of cocaine.

"Feeding time, you Motherfuckers!" he called to the alligators.

He tossed bags into open reptilian mouths and watched the gators devour them whole.

"Twenty years in jail, my ass!" he screamed wildly. He would feed them the friggin' evidence.

As the four air boats, which had been pursing Frankie, pulled into view, a voice on a megaphone called to him.

"DEA! Put your hands in the air, now!"

"Come and get me, Jerk Offs!" Frankie called out.

The agents feared coming close. They couldn't kill the lawfully protected species. They had to keep their distance and wait for the alligators to leave.

Frankie never stopped moving. He kept feeding the gators that surrounded his boat, making it impossible for DEA agents to approach. Agents with guns drawn watched helplessly, as Frankie fed one-million dollars worth of cocaine to his hungry reptilian pals.

"You'll sleep well tonight, you scaly bastards," he called to them.

When Frankie ran out of coke, he opened another beer. It was Miller time. He wondered what his lawyer friend would do. The coke was gone but Frankie No Throat knew the feds still had enough evidence to arrest, prosecute, and convict him. He also knew that his rap sheet contained a lengthy criminal history, including past flights from prosecution. They would never release him on bail.

Lee was on his own. The FBI couldn't help the lawyer in Panama and his friend didn't even understand how impossible his situation was. Frankie chugged his beer, tossed the empty can at the gators, then picked up another.

"Yep, this is one nasty place," he proclaimed loudly.

He relaxed as DEA agents inched toward him in their boats. They would lock him up, just as tight as fate would lock up his lawyer. Without his help, Lee and his lady friend didn't stand a chance. The truth fell trippingly from his lips.

"They'll die in Panama.

With an affable bar swarm mingling behind them under paddle fans, and the electric skyline of downtown Miami sparkling across the bay, Lee and Jaime soaked in atmosphere and supped on surf and turf at the Key Biscayne Rusty Pelican. They sat close, her head nestling on his shoulder as Lee spoke softly.

"The more I think about Batista's plan, the more I don't like it."

"We're leaving tomorrow," Jaime said flatly.

Lee shook his head.

"If we don't take a commercial flight to Panama, there won't be a record of our having traveled there. Passports won't be recorded on Noriega's private flight. And if we disappear in Panama, the last place anyone will have seen us is Mexico. U.S. authorities won't have any ground to allege the law's been broken on American soil. It will be virtually impossible for them to intervene."

"Supervisor Martin approved it. He knows what he's doing."

"Jaime, the arrangement totally protects Noriega, and leaves us no margin for error. I don't like it."

Her hand caressed his cheek.

"Stars," she said dreamily.

"What?"

"Stars in the sky are lucky for us."

Lee looked over the bay, then into a face that enticed and bewitched.

"You look both moral and exciting at the same time," he uttered, "without the appearance that it's a struggle."

As Jaime approached for a kiss, he asked a question that begged for an answer.

"Is this part of the role you're playing?"

She kept coming, as if her lips were prepared to tell something with their touch that she wasn't ready to surrender in words. Glistening and moist, like ripe promises to fulfill every yearning, they reached for his. But before they met, a kiss stealing voice interrupted.

"Mr. Gunther," the waitress said, "you have an emergency call from your office."

The young woman held a patron phone, which plugged in by their table. Lee and Jaime leaned apart, and he took the call. As he listened, his body grew rigid. He set the phone down and didn't speak.

Jaime said, "Something wrong?"

"We can't leave tomorrow. One of my clients was just arrested. I have to spring him."

"If it's one of Noriega's people, you can handle him with Sheppard before our flight leaves."

"It's a friend from Philadelphia. And, if Sheppard doesn't release him, I'm not traveling anywhere."

Lee's next words came carefully chosen.

"I've . . . known him for years."

Jaime's eyes narrowed and hardened, as if filled with hatred.

"Until this moment, I'd only guessed how close you are to the scum you represent. You're the shit that sticks to their heels."

Instantly, Jaime's eyes turned cold. Lee wondered, as he had when they first met, what ugly secret her beauty masked. Perhaps he would never learn.

Yet something else was certain. Unless he sprang Frankie, Lee could never embark on the journey to Panama she was so intent to undertake. He would take his chances in a courtroom, defending false charges he didn't have a way of beating.

A glance at the World

## Chapter Fourteen

# Friends and Relations

ROBERT SLAMMED A CLENCHED FIST into his desktop. Papers and files flew with the powerful jolt. Jaime sat across from him, venting every bit as much steam. Lee just sat in silence. Remarkably, she thought, Sheppard's family photographs had diverted the lawyer's attention. The threesome sat at odds and Lee was odd man out.

"What do you mean?" The Assistant U.S. Attorney screamed. "Why aren't you going through with the deal? Have you forgotten how many thugs we put on the streets to pad your credentials?"

"Then, it won't hurt to let one more guy fly," Lee responded.

"Noriega's scumbags walked because that's part of the operation. We're not cutting walks for every other skunk you represent. Look at this guy's rap sheet."

Robert held up a computer printout that unfolded page after page after page. His secretary had pulled it for them when Lee first entered the office demanding they release Frankie "No Throat" Cinelli from jail.

"Bank fraud, racketeering, money laundering, flight from prosecution . . .."

Robert gave up scanning the sheets.

"You've represented Cinelli for over a decade. The guy's your friend. Now, you want the bastard to take a free ride on a major cocaine bust. I can't take that to the DEA. They're already up in arms over what's happened to their cases involving Noriega's people. I'm not releasing your Philadelphia pal."

Jaime knew they were at an impasse. Robert didn't even have authority to release the hood. His prerogatives were strictly limited to cases involving Noriega's associates. She listened to Lee doggedly insist.

"I'm arguing Frankie Cinelli's bail application at three this afternoon before Judge Ramis. If my client is released, I'll be on the next flight to Cancun."

As much as he outraged Jaime, she was angry with herself. She thought she had known him better and realized she'd made a mistake falling for him. Her feelings caused her to miss character flaws she usually spotted. Those faults jeopardized their operation for the sake of a mob captain. Jaime had so much at stake, professionally and personally, she loathed Lee for making her have feelings for him, feelings she quickly abandoned. Jaime looked into his eyes one last time for a glimmer of hope. She didn't want that to be the end for them.

"Cinelli gets released or I don't go," Lee repeated as he rose.

"I'm opposing the application," Robert instantly responded. "This time I'll inform the judge that your client isn't part of any government plan. No federal judge will release a career criminal with Cinelli's record."

"Not unless someone arranges it. I'm counting on you, Robert."

"Count on Cinelli rotting in jail. Then, count on joining him. I'm sending your tax evasion charges to the grand jury, if you're not on that airplane."

Their standoff would quickly come to a head in Judge Ramis' courtroom.

Lee turned to Jaime. She looked away. As Lee walked out the door of Robert Sheppard's office, a piece of her heart went with him. They had become close and Jaime would never let it happen again. Momentarily, she peered at the framed photographs that had drawn Lee's attention.

"What are you going to do?" Robert asked.

He jolted her attention back to the unraveling mission.

"I'm meeting Supervisor Martin at noon," she said, "with someone else involved in the operation."

"CIA?"

Jaime didn't answer.

"National Security Administration?" Robert pressed.

Jaime bit her tongue.

*If he knew everything, he wouldn't play any part in this*, she surmised.

Robert was a straight shooter and they planned ducking around some dirty corners.

"There's a lot happening here that you're not a part of, Robert. I'm neither authorized nor disposed to discuss those aspects of the—"

"You have a personal stake in this operation, don't you? It isn't all professionalism, love of country, and apple pie."

Jaime didn't answer.

"Calero, you don't think they've told you everything, do you?"

Jaime hurried to make her appointment. She took a seat in the same stark room where they had interrogated Lee. A clerk popped his head in the doorway.

"Agent Calero," the young man said, "Supervisor Martin is running a little late. He'll be here shortly."

Jaime nodded. She waited alone and thought of where they planned to send her. As she leaned back and closed her eyes, memories of the place, thirteen years earlier, flooded her mind.

In 1975, Jaime attended her first society gala. The carnival party rollicked in the Panamanian seaside town of Colon where she was born. A full orchestra played on the stage. Sitting at a round table in the ballroom, the thrilled teenager watched well-dressed celebrants, dignitaries, and people of influence, sway on the dance floor and chatter at their tables.

She sat between her godfather, Doctor Hugo Spadafora, a robust and warm-spirited man, and her mother, a fair-skinned woman with chestnut hair. Jaime's older brothers sat on her mother's other side. The oldest, Juan, eagerly searched for a beauty to waltz to the dance floor. Pepe, who was closer to Jaime's age, simply stared in awe at the splendorous affair they attended as the doctor's guests, while Jaime cherished every moment by the man's side. Across from them Hugo's talkative wife chatted with an older companion, who like Jaime's mother had lost her husband.

In all of Latin America, the institution of *compadrazgo* creates an enduring bond between children and their godparents. The kinship carries moral, ceremonial, and religious significance. The relationship bears responsibility of the godparent to influence the child's welfare, so parents carefully select for their children.

In selecting Hugo as Jaime's godfather, her parents had chosen well. She felt deep affinity for the man who had been so close to her father.

"Doctor Spadafora," an older man called.

He approached Hugo with something grasped, almost reverently, in his hands.

"Would you autograph your book for me? It would be such an honor."

Jaime spied the cover of her godfather's autobiography, entitled *Thoughts and Experiences of a Medical Gorilla.*

As Hugo signed, Jaime's mother whispered into her ear.

"Aren't you proud? Your godfather's a national hero and your Papa was his right-hand man."

"Yes, Momma. I know all the stories."

"Well, I have the right to feel proud, too—proud that your father was also a hero of the people."

Jaime's father and the physician-revolutionary had fought side by side in the Portuguese Guinea guerilla war, which had raged through Africa in the 1950s and early 60s. They had gone there before Castro had even sent Cuban forces to the struggle. The Panamanian press glorified stories of Doctor Spadafora and his men. Their accounts were memorialized in the man's immensely popular book. Paradoxically, Hugo was from middle-class roots, educated with a medical degree from the University of Bologna and gentlemanly refined. Yet, he had become a hero of the people, fighting a guerilla war for the poor and oppressed.

"I never knew Papa except through your eyes," Jaime said. "You still love him, don't you, Momma."

"When your father was killed in the last days of the war, I made two vows to the Holy Mother. I vowed to never love another man—and to never lose my sons the way I lost their father. That's why we're leaving for the United States. There's no opportunity for your brothers in this poor sea town. And, your godfather's wild scheme to lead Panamanian forces, fighting for guerillas in Nicaragua, isn't going to steal your brothers from me."

Jaime's godfather had openly discussed his plans to wage another war. A masterful storyteller, she felt his enthusiasm for the venture.

*Surely,* she thought, *his ardent tidings will attract eager recruits.*

Northward in the Central American country of Nicaragua, his guerilla forces would join the Sandinista National Liberation Front. As he explained, the Sandinistas battled the oppressive Somoza government, which the United States supported.

Jaime's mother had often expressed her feelings when Hugo's cries to glory filled eager young ears. She feared Hugo's machismo would bring him an untimely end. Unlike Jaime's father, Momma had a serious comportment. The adventure her godfather planned would send many good men to their graves. She was taking her family away to spare them from such folly.

"You'll see," her mother said earnestly. "We'll all have good lives in New York. You'll finish school and someday attend college."

Momma wouldn't risk losing her sons the way she had lost the man of her life. Jaime's parents had built their marriage on a passion that had overcome the strict class barriers in Panamanian society. Her mother came from a middle-class background and was well educated. Naturally, her mother's parents had opposed marriage of their daughter to Jose Calero, a darker-skinned man from poorer roots. Being one of Hugo Spadafora's right-hand men didn't lessen the blow when her mother told her parents she had eloped with the handsome guerilla fighter. When the love of her life died, her mother dedicated herself to her children, raising a closely-knit family in strong Roman Catholic traditions.

Her brothers looked more like their father, dark complected and burly. Jaime favored both parents. She bore her mother's fair skin and refined features yet was tall and athletic like her father. Though Juan and Pepe didn't take well to schooling, her mother always vowed Jaime would obtain a college education. She would groom her daughter for grander things than the uneasy life she led as a widow in an economically depressed town on the Caribbean Sea.

Jaime had only seen her father in Momma's treasured photographs. His resemblance to her godfather struck her. The strong likeness in physical features and the kindness of her compadre made it easy for Jaime to think of Hugo Spadafora as her own father. Her godfather was the personification of Latin machismo: manly, fearless, and handsome. She always imagined her father to have been the same.

Fun loving Hugo danced almost every dance. When his wife grew weary, he politely escorted many attractive women to the floor. At last, he invited Jaime. She rose and took his arm. Jaime's heart glowed, almost with a schoolgirl's crush on the dashing older man. As she fancied thoughts of graceful spins around the room, a junior military officer stopped them.

"Doctor Spadafora," the young man said, "my commander wants to talk with you. Please join him at his table."

Jaime watched her godfather scowl, then shake his head. His reaction was uncharacteristically rude.

"Tell your commanding officer I decline his invitation."

The young officer's eyes bulged. Apparently, he was unaccustomed to rejection. He slunk across the dance floor and spoke to another uniformed man. Jaime's view of the officer was blocked by dancers on the crowded floor. For an instant, she caught a glimpse of a hideously pockmarked face on the short man staring at Hugo. The man's beady black eyes burned as if rage set them afire.

"*Compadre*, who's that?" Jaime whispered.

"An intelligence officer, Dear," Hugo replied. "It's nothing to concern you. He's the kind of man who's running the country, these days. We must learn to watch men like him very carefully."

"He looks mad."

"Truly. These days, few people have courage to decline an invitation from Manuel Noriega."

"I don't wish to dance with him quite so near the dance floor."

"Never run from anything, Jaime. Face your fears and they'll fear you."

Her godfather wrapped her in strong arms and swept her past other dancers, who seemed to disappear. Joyful music called without a care, softening Jaime's pangs of trepidation with every step they shared.

Weeks later, she fought the bustle of crowds through Tocumen International Airport in Panama City. Jaime's mother was flanked by her children as they readied to board their flight to New York. Juan approached his mother and hugged her.

"Mother," the oldest boy said, "I can't go with you."

Jaime's mother tore apart.

"What? Our flight's about to depart."

"I'm going to Nicaragua with Hugo. It's what Papa would have done. Please try to understand."

Tears welled in the woman's eyes. Creases formed in the hollows of her cheeks as if age had instantly taken a decade of toll. Jaime rushed to her side.

"You knew, didn't you," her mother shrieked at her daughter. "You all knew!" She looked toward heaven and cried, "I'm not losing a son to another foolish adventure."

"Momma, don't worry," Jaime soothed. "If we face our fears, they'll fear us."

Jaime's mother slapped her face with a single hard blow.

"Your godfather put that nonsense in your head. Thank the Holy Mother you're a girl—and will never die following foolish dreams of glory."

Momma turned to Juan. Rage replaced her sorrow.

"You'll die, my son. I will never see you after this day. "Momma!" Jaime gushed.

"I know what I see in widow's dreams. I've seen you, too," she warned her daughter, "perish horribly in my nightmares. Thank God we're leaving this country or you, too . . . would be lost."

Jaime looked up from her seat in the FBI white-walled interrogation room. A man entered the room alone. Unremarkable of build and plain of appearance, he wore a grey business suit and carried a metal briefcase. He set it on the floor and took a seat across from her. Jaime saw through his bland expression. The spook was ready to send her on her way.

# Chapter Fifteen

# Spooks

CLANDESTINE WORDS COVERED MURKY GROUND with a shroud.

"You have never seen me before, have you Agent Calero?" Unlike usual visitors the Bureau office, those kinds of people wore no ID. The spook bore all the substance of a puff of smoke, but his tone carried no room for doubt.

Jaime nodded her head.

"Verbal responses," the spook said, pointing to ceiling-mounted cameras and microphones.

Jaime cleared her throat. "I have never seen you before."

"You still haven't seen me. Is that clear?"

"Quite clear."

She had first met the people, who dreamed up those schemes, when she had taken training courses offered to Bureau personnel by the Central Intelligence Agency. They played dangerous political games for high stakes. Her credentials and unique background had intrigued them. She had met them again at the outset of the operation. Jaime realized she never fully trusted them.

"You'll spend three days with Noriega," the man continued. "We don't know where, but you've been briefed on his properties in Panama. You are familiar with each."

"I know their layouts."

"Your Bureau guidelines for professional conduct will not apply in Panama. During your stay, you are to be . . . cordial. We've found Noriega's eccentricities to be quite specific. Again, you have been briefed."

"I know the role I'm to play."

"Will ties to your homeland keep you from playing it?"

The spook raised Jaime's instant ire, causing her to fire: "This is my homeland! I'm a United States citizen since girlhood with more reasons to love this country, *my country*, than—"

The spook raised his hand to stop her then continued.

"If the lawyer does not talk Noriega into surrendering to United States authorities, you will execute the second part of the plan without hesitation. You will terminate Noriega's regime and extract yourself from Panama. That's correct, is it not?"

"As you say."

"Precisely as I say," the man insisted.

"Precisely as you say."

"The lawyer's life is secondary to the success of your mission. You understand that, do you not?"

"Precisely as you say."

"You understand my meaning."

"I understand what you've told me."

They locked eyes, silently conveying messages until the spook appeared satisfied with the stone certainty of her acquiescence.

"They'll search your luggage after you arrive in Panama. If you must implement the second part of the plan, our mole in Noriega's circle will deliver what you need. You'll find it in your cosmetic bag. After you deploy it, our friend will help you escape to the nearest United States military facility. Bases are principally situated around the canal zone. Know them all.

"There is one thing you won't know: the identity of the seed we've so deeply planted. If you were to be caught and tortured before you had an opportunity to exfil or abort yourself, you could endanger a valued resource while serving yourself no purpose."

"Understood. Precisely as you say."

"Any questions, Agent Calero?"

Jaime had but one.

"Is that the only thing you haven't told me?"

"Calero," the man spoke with eyes lowered, "I know you're extremely bright: it says so in the Bureau's personnel dossier. Consider yourself fully informed."

Then looking directly at her he pressed, "Are you troubled by anything I've said?"

She leaned back. "I have no troubles. No regrets."

The man nodded to her, then looked up to the cameras to nod again.

Supervisor Martin entered the room and Jaime wasted no time addressing him.

"Will you be instructing Judge Ramis to release Cinelli?"

Martin shot back. "Take your luggage with you on the way to the courthouse, Agent Calero."

Jaime rose to leave. As she reached the door, Martin called to her.

"Jaime."

The man paused. Uncharacteristically, he seemed without direction.

"Yes, Sir," she said.

"Oh, shit. There's no way to do this except say it. Your promotion didn't go through. I didn't want to tell you before you left but it's being posted. I wanted you to hear it from me, first."

"Decent of you," she said with a smirk. "How many breast-feds were up for the supervisory position."

"Don't give me that, Calero. You cover two of my minority bases."

Martin proved he could stare just as hard as her.

"I wanted this for you." Conviction framed his words.

"Top test scores, best record."

Her succinct commentary came without malice; the words were delivered as statements of fact.

"Don't push so hard," he said. "Some things come easier when you travel at the same pace as the rest of the world."

"Not where you're sending me."

Martin looked away.

Jaime turned to walk out but Martin stopped her again.

"Jaime," he said. "You deserved the promotion. Don't let it distract you. Good luck."

When she had gone, Martin's furtive allegiant pulled his briefcase from the floor. He set it on the table and addressed the cameras.

"Shut down the monitoring system and confirm compliance."

A voice called back to them from an overhead speaker. "Monitoring system off, Sir."

He inserted a key into his briefcase and turned it. A metal flap opened over a keypad. The spook punched numbers into it. Slowly, the briefcase opened by itself, as if it possessed a mind of its own, and was deciding whether to reveal its contents. A single manila folder and a cassette audio tape lay inside. The spook stared at them.

"Calero," he said, with a drawl absent of all emotion, "was born for this mission. Have you seen the CIA file on her godfather and brother?"

Martin's attention refocused from the door his agent had just walked through.

"Never completely."

"Here." The man pulled the file folder from his briefcase and slid it across the table with the audio tape.

Martin took the file, flipped it open, and nodded his head.

The spook let Martin read, then told him: "She has compelling motivation—stronger, perhaps, than our own. Remember that over the next few days. If you develop any doubts, listen to the tape."

"But what your Honor must understand, and what the government cannot ignore, is that. . .."

Jaime had to snicker despite herself. She sat in the oak-paneled courtroom, listening to Lee argue his case. He stood beside his mobster pal at the defense table. Two U.S. Marshal deputies waited in readiness behind them, no doubt aware that the defendant was dangerous. Across from them at the prosecution table, Robert Sheppard fumed. Stern determination plastered his face.

She watched Lee demand his client's release on nominal bail. The argument was difficult to make for Cinelli. The hood's record clearly made him ineligible. Yet Lee's quick mind popped loopholes in Sheppard's arguments. On one hand, for the defense lawyer, there was always the other hand. Lee was a courtroom octopus.

His ability to think fast on his feet impressed her, no matter what she thought of him. Jaime had heard he was a good lawyer and saw how he'd earned the reputation. As Lee sat, Robert leaped back to his feet. He reiterated the obvious. Cinelli presented too great a danger to the community and too great a risk to flee for the Court to grant bail in any amount. Then, the lawyers rested and waited for the judge to rule.

Judge Ramis used her right hand to sift through briefs presented by both attorneys and to study the defendant's extensive rap sheet. Her left hand held her chin, which she stroked as if the gesture might assist in evoking wisdom. At last, frowning gravely, she issued her ruling.

"Gentlemen, I have considered the arguments of counsel. The Court must heavily weigh the defendant's lengthy criminal record, which is documented on the government's rap sheet. Accordingly, I fix bail at three-million dollars."

Jaime could see a look of relief flash on Robert's face. She watched Cinelli whisper in his lawyer's ear, knowing what turned Lee's face down low. The Philadelphia crime family would never front that much cash to get the hood out of jail. She saw Lee place a finger to his lips to silence the mobster.

"However," Judge Ramis continued, "I see no reason why I should not allow the defendant to sign a personal recognizance bond in lieu of cash. Mr. Cinelli, you'll sign some papers at the Probation Department, and be released later this afternoon without the necessity of posting any funds."

Jaime realized Martin's message had been delivered to the judge, and watched the mobster wrap his arm around his lawyer. Robert slumped into his chair as Jaime followed her supervisor's orders. She raced to the defense table and grabbed Lee. She saw his astonished look when she planted a hungry kiss on his cheek.

"Sweetheart," she cooed, "we better run to the airport if we're going to catch our plane."

Lee would have been even more surprised if he had known what else she'd been ordered. They left the courtroom arm in arm under the admiring gaze of Frankie No Throat.

Frankie was ready to be processed and released. He knew the drill. Frankie also knew what he'd have to do. He had to retrieve the Kelly file from Lee and he only had one quick way to raise the cash they needed in Panama. He would get it from the boys downtown. They would have their own plans for both Noriega and the lawyer, who had freed him. Frankie would collect the cash and meet his lawyer in Panama. Yet, he knew Little Vinny would send him there with an agenda that wasn't what the lawyer was expecting.

*Time to clip my wings as guardian angel*, Frankie thought.

He would bring the lawyer down. For the first time, he regretted what he had to do for his family. But, one thing remained constant in his universe. Frankie always got a job done.

Jamie was duty bound. As she and Lee boarded their Cancun flight under the guise of lovers, he reminded her to act the part.

"Noriega's people may be watching us," he said.

Though he was probably right, she couldn't bring herself to feign affection. She sat far as she could from him in their adjoining first-class seats. Taking a last glance at the lawyer, Jaime closed her eyes and thought of what they had to do. Then, she remembered her godfather and his simple last goodbye.

Her compadre had come to the airport the day Jamie's mother took her to New York. She had kissed him and her brother Juan. Afterward, what Jaime had learned about the twosome had principally come from government intelligence files. She considered the lesson Manuel Noriega so openly bragged he had taught Doctor Hugo Spadafora.

# Chapter Sixteen

# A Lesson for the Doctor

DOCTOR HUGO SPADAFORA had energetically recruited his band of Panamanians to fight alongside the Sandinistas in Nicaragua. Ironically, the man Hugo most despised in his own government was designated as the Panamanian Chief of Operations over the struggle against Nicaraguan strong man Anasasio Somoza and his Contra forces. Hugo frustrated his Operations Chief continually, causing him to lose face by ignoring orders. That embarrassed Panamanian officer was Manuel Noriega.

The Sandinistas won the war when they overturned the Somoza government in 1979. Hugo returned to Panama with his men—Jaime's brother Juan Calero among them—poised to pursue another mission.

"Will you rejoin your family in New York, or can I count on you to remain with us?" Hugo asked Juan.

"To take on our own government?"

"To steer our homeland from corruption and dictatorship."

Stirred by jubilation of the moment and a strong sense of patriotic duty, Juan remained by the side of the guerilla leader to rid Panama of the cancer known as Colonel Manuel Noriega, who held his county's second highest rank en route to becoming both General and *de facto* ruler of the nation.

Through the 1970s and 1980s, Noriega manipulated U.S. policy to Panama, skillfully accumulating absolute power over the little nation that possessed a canal vital to United States interests. Hugo knew Noriega had skimmed funds from arms sales made by the Panamanian government to the Sandinistas, and that Noriega was using government pilots and troops in his own drug trafficking operations. Noriega had become a key player on behalf of the Medellin Cartel run by drug kingpin Pablo Escobar. Under Noriega's influence, Panama became a laundromat for drug dealers looking to clean and store their cash. His rule was marked by corruption and murderous persecution of political opponents.

Evidence Hugo collected on Noriega was the kind of dynamite that can explode in your own hands. He delivered his proofs to the Panamanian press, but editors were unwilling to publish articles critical of the man who had the power to shut down their presses. So, Hugo went to the U.S. Drug Enforcement Agency.

*Surely*, he thought, *the DEA will stop a drug operation that floods the United States with Colombian cocaine.*

Reasonable thinking can be flawed. Hugo never knew the CIA was protecting Noriega as its man in Panama and blocking DEA intervention. Finally, Hugo consulted former comrades in arms, one being Juan Calero.

"Hugo, you've drawn life-shortening attention," Juan counseled. Leave the country. Leave now!"

"To go where, *Amigo*?"

"Costa Rica if you must remain close, but the United States is safer. Right now, you're too great a hero for public execution, but you know what Noriega's people will do if you remain in Panama. You'll disappear."

"Nah. They can't make me disappear—not permanently. But they can detain me. Perhaps temporally relocating to Costa Rica is prudent."

"I'll travel with you."

"Juan, the journey will be dangerous."

Juan looked at the proud man who had been as much a father as he'd ever known.

"We'll leave tonight," he simply said.

Costa Rica stretches two-hundred miles between Panama and Nicaragua. Unlike many of its Central American neighbors, the small nation was renowned for democratic traditions. Wealth was more evenly divided among its citizenry and political freedoms were unparalleled in the region. It was a natural safe haven for Hugo, but he missed his adventuresome lifestyle and recognition from countrymen.

On September 1, 1985, Hugo asked Juan to return to Panama City with him. In the capital, he'd face Noriega in a showdown of political strength, calling upon the people to take down the dictator.

"They will be with us," Hugo promised Juan. "And, with the people behind us, the nations of the world will recognize our movement. We saw that happen five years ago in Africa. Dictator Idi Amin called himself 'His Excellency and President for Life,' while his people knew him as the 'Butcher of Uganda' before displacing him.

"The United States will be slow to act, but can be roused to oppose oppression, where their interests lie. Awakening the people: that's our key to freeing Panama. And I'll wake the living and the dead."

*Machismo so often drives Hugo*, Juan reflected apprehensively, *and an overdose of manliness spawns unsound decisions*.

He voiced opposition but Hugo was undeterred.

"We'll travel to the Panama by different modes of transportation to elude detection," Hugo schemed, "plane, buses, taxis. My brother will meet us at the Restaurant y Café Los Mellos along the border to help us cross."

Juan couldn't dissuade the guerilla leader, who—with such élan—relished cavorting on death's edge.

The night was blanketed by humid mist when they arrived outside the café on the border. Juan grabbed Hugo's arm.

"This is the most dangerous leg of our journey," he reminded. "Don't enter the café. You won't be safe until we reach Panama City, where your popularity with the people may protect you."

Hugo remained undeterred and adamant.

"I'm challenging Noriega head on. If the people are to follow me as a national hero, I can't crawl into the Capital."

Hugo studied the café then offered, "I'll go into the restaurant first. Then come inside, if you must, but keep away from me in case there's trouble."

Juan's cursory nod sent Hugo away. He stood alone outside until he could linger no longer. Apprehensively, he entered. The café was crowded yet the one man they sought wasn't there.

From across the room Hugo signaled for them to depart. Juan moved toward the door, then grimaced. The restaurateur stopped Hugo, pulling something from behind his back. A thought flashed through Juan's mind.

*Is it a gun?*

Then, Juan groaned, realizing the man carried a copy of Hugo's memoirs. With unbridled fanfare Hugo autographed the book, his ego overpowering sensibilities.

As Juan departed, he saw a waiter lift the telephone to place a call, perhaps the call Juan dreaded.

Smothered by darkness outside, he waited for Hugo, who strutted out with aplomb that Juan greeted tersely.

"Where's your brother?"

"He didn't show, and we can't wait," Hugo replied. We'll head to the bus terminal down the road."

"The army maintains checkpoints along the bus route."

"I trained you to fight on Costa de Mosquitos in Nicaragua. When did I teach you to fear?"

They reached a small rural bus stop and boarded a bus bound for the Capital at noontime. The driver eyed Hugo as they passed toward seats in the rear, where they opened their shirts in the battered vehicle that lacked air conditioning. Juan sweat while scorching sun and tightly packed bodies raised the temperature.

*Is my perspiration seeping from the heat*, he wondered, *or from unsettled nerves?*

As the bus was about to depart, a Panamanian army officer leaped aboard, and the driver whispered his ear. The officer turned toward Hugo, then took a seat up front.

Juan's words rushed out, "Recognize him?"

"Bruce Lee."

"Who?"

"That's what they call him," Hugo said, "more for his violent reputation than for martial arts skills."

"My God, that's him? He'll identify you to troops at the next checkpoint."

Juan glanced at his watch as the old bus started with a backfire.

"If this bus had departed on time," he observed, "we wouldn't be with him."

"The bus is leaving on time."

Hugo's eyes darted down as if he was embarrassed.

"I just realized our mistake. When we crossed the border from Costa Rica into Panama, we forgot to move our watches back an hour. That's why my brother wasn't in the café. We were early.

Juan's eyes widened.

"Too late to go back, now."

With a jolt the bus rolled. Juan felt for his knife. As a guerilla fighter trained on the rain-drenched Caribbean coastal plain called the Mosquito Coast of Nicaragua, he knew how to stalk and kill. The blade was strapped to his lower leg under his trousers. He'd wait until steamy heat put passengers to sleep, then slit the officer's throat, lest Hugo be turned over to troops manning checkpoints.

When Juan figured the first checkpoint was near, he moved toward the front of the bus, knife ready. The officer faced forward as Juan lunged to kill . . . but a strong hand grappled his wrist. Juan spun round, then froze.

Hugo shook his head from side to side and whispered.

"If I must die, it will be on Panamanian soil without a struggle."

Juan yearned to kill the officer, who had brutally slaughtered so many of their countrymen, but followed orders. No one on the bus muttered a word though Juan sensed every passenger, by now, recognized the popular hero, and understood what "Bruce Lee" could do to him.

When the bus slowed for the first checkpoint, brakes screeched, and passengers lunged back and forth. They watched the officer leap out and speak to troops on duty. Then, two armed soldiers entered the bus and checked riders' identity cards, including Hugo's. As the soldiers jumped off the bus, Juan let out a long breath and leaned toward Hugo.

"We made it," he sighed.

Juan closed his eyes, then heard commotion. Soldiers with guns now drawn jumped aboard and raced toward Hugo. Passengers lowered their eyes as troops led Hugo off the bus to a guard shack. Juan folded his hands in prayer until the bus backfired and its engine revved. As they rolled forward, Juan wondered what to do.

Suddenly, the bus braked. Soldiers placed Hugo aboard and Bruce Lee took the same seat. As Hugo walked to the rear of the bus, passengers cheered. Young and old alike leaned to touch him as he passed. Hugo beamed.

"God bless you, Doctor Spadafora," a man called, "we all know who you are."

Hugo roared for all to hear.

"I'm returning to Panama City to call for an uprising of the people—an uprising to wrestle our nation from President Noriega's control."

Impassioned cries rose.

"We're with you," an elderly woman pledged.

Hugo settled into his seat next to Juan.

"This is how it will be," he exclaimed. "The people will protect us. We have a thirty-minute layover at La Concepción, where there's an army garrison. Once we pass it, the battle to return our country to the people begins."

Juan rode uneasily, rocked by uneven roads, drained by heat and exhaust fumes, and devoured by voracious misgivings.

The narrow streets of La Concepción twist like a labyrinth. So they zigzagged until stopping at the bustling terminal. Hugo disembarked first to make certain they were safe. Juan waited, until Hugo held up his thumb, then disembarked and froze. Troops marched toward Hugo in two columns. They halted and Bruce Lee spoke to their platoon leader.

"Run, damn you, Hugo," Juan muttered under his breath. "Run!"

The soldiers broke formation to surround Hugo, who smiled confidently, and bellowed to the crowd in the terminal.

"I'm Hugo Spadafora. This officer is detaining me. Tell everyone you know. Doctor Spadafora has been arrested!"

As he held up his identification for all to see, Juan realized Hugo wanted witnesses so the government couldn't deny soldiers had taken him into custody. He wondered.

*Can popularity with the people save Hugo?*

Juan sensed celebrity would do little good in that remote region. Major Luis Cordoba, who commanded the local military garrison, bore a reputation as ruthless as the arresting officer. Juan remained transfixed as he considered his options.

*Should I run or risk being caught by tailing the troops that took Hugo.*

Mamma's impassioned plea to avoid danger filled his ears yet his father's blood flowed thru his veins: blood rich with honor, pride, and courage, all of which are oft perilous influences.

Then, rang a shout.

"That's him! The young one," Bruce Lee screamed. "Get the son of a bitch traveling with Spadafora."

Juan darted around a corner. He eyed a cantina, bolted inside, then stiffened at the sight. A half-dozen uniformed men drank at a small bar, while a dozen more sat at tables, some with scantily clad women on their laps. Juan had run into a watering hole for Noriega's troops. He could do only one thing.

"Rum," Juan called to the bartender. "Double shot."

He lowered his head, hands shaking as he waited for his drink. When the bartender delivered it, Juan raised his glass high and offered it as if in a salute to the troops, who had stopped talking. They stared at him as he downed the hearty spirits.

"Another," Juan called.

"Double again?" barked the bartender.

Juan nodded.

As the bartender grabbed the bottle, Juan spied a woman leading a soldier by the hand up a flight of stairs. The place was a whorehouse and Juan knew how to escape.

"*Senor*," he said as the barman delivered his second round, "I hunger for a woman."

The man smiled knowingly.

"Why not try the little number behind you?"

Women graced the cantina in all shapes and sizes, so he wondered what he'd find. A sip of cheap rum burnt his throat as Juan turned and froze. Every soldier had a weapon trained on him. Through heavy smoke a familiar face breathed inches from his own. Bruce Lee took Juan's glass and finished the drink in a guzzle.

As troops marched Juan away, he realized he could have escaped, if only he had instantly grabbed the opportunity. When they reached the regional military headquarters, Juan was relieved it nestled in a residential area. Children playing in the street were whisked away by a woman, who whispered in their ears. The setting seemed an unlikely place for harm to befall him and

Hugo. The neighborhood would fill with screams if soldiers tortured them, and it was unlikely troops would murder a hero of the people where they'd have to cart away his corpse in public view.

Once inside the garrison, Bruce Lee's men took Hugo and Juan to the Commanding Officer's office and sat them on the floor to be gagged with duct tape.

Major Cordoba, lean and fit for middle age, spoke into a speaker telephone.

"We have the rabid dog in our hands."

The reply came swiftly: "What does one do with a dog that has rabies?"

Juan recognized that voice from television and radio broadcasts. Hugo must have known it firsthand—the stone-cold voice of Manuel Noriega.

Major Cordoba lifted the telephone receiver to converse privately, then looked down at them.

"You'll enjoy my hospitality through the day," he said. "This evening, you'll meet someone who has special plans for you."

Soldiers led them to a windowless cell. Juan realized he had been right. Noriega's forces couldn't torture or kill them in the residential neighborhood without raising alarm. Elite troops would take them away.

Somehow Juan managed to doze, waking when soldiers entered their cell with a diminutive officer, who stepped forward and spat in Hugo's face.

"Move," the little man barked.

Hugo rose, spittle coating his eyelids, as the Dark Angel and his men led them into the night, shoving them in the rear of a canvas-covered military truck. Juan couldn't tell where they were going but certainly to someplace where they would not be heard, seen or found.

The Dark Angel spoke to a larger man he called Batista. As the twosome chatted, they studied their captives and grew macabre grins.

When the truck at long last stopped, troops scurried Hugo away, the Dark Angel departing with them.

Juan wondered: *Where are they taking him?*

Minutes later, Batista poked his rifle barrel into Juan's stomach, then pointed it to the rear of the truck. The young man lifted himself uncertainly, staring out the back at uninviting darkness. Batista's shove sent him into it. Juan hit the ground then looked but saw nothing. No moon, no stars, no signs of anyone except Batista and the six soldiers who led him away. They marched him to an empty field where Batista spoke in silky tones, the quiet timbre of his voice allaying Juan's fears.

"Lay on the ground," Batista cooed. "Face down."

Juan obeyed and kissed dirt moistened by an afternoon shower. He heard crickets transmitting their indecipherable messages. Then, a wild animal howled so loudly that even the crickets stopped. The shrill squeal chilled Juan's bones. Another hideous yelp broke the stillness of night. Suddenly Juan realized he was wrong. The inhuman cries were coming from Hugo as they tortured him.

Above Juan, Batista pulled a machete from a leather sheath.

"Holy father," Juan prayed aloud, "forgive my sins and receive me this night."

He felt a sting at his neck and gasped for air, realizing they'd slit his throat. Death delivered his silence before "Amen."

Children at play found a carcass in Costa Rica. Medical examiners later determined it was the body of Doctor Hugo Spadafora.

Someone had badly bruised his torso. Ribs were broken. Sharp objects inserted under his nail beds had removed all fingernails. His testicles were grotesquely swollen from prolonged bastinado. Neat symmetrical incisions had skillfully cut his groin muscles to ease homosexual rape. Repeated and violent penetration had grossly deformed his rectum. Someone had removed his head. Blood found in the stomach indicated his decapitation had been deliberately slow. Examining physicians opined that the doctor knew they were beheading him as his body swallowed its own fluids.

The head was never found, nor were the remains of Juan Calero.

# Chapter Seventeen

# The Fertility God

AS THEIR PLANE NEARED THE CARIBBEAN COAST of Mexico, Jaime thought of the brutal autopsy reports. She had also heard an audio tape from the CIA file maintained on her godfather.

An intercontinental telephone transmission to Noriega's chateau in France had been intercepted and recorded. Apparently, the dictator thought having an enemy tortured is more entertaining if you can listen. Intelligence experts believed the tape contained Hugo Spadafora's last howls, cries, and whispers. The spooks had played it for her without warning. They had fully prepared Agent Calero for her mission.

Jaime had no moral dilemmas. Noriega was a monster responsible for the misery, torture, and deaths of so many in the land of her birth. If required, his execution would spare many more the same misfortune. She could do it with the unshakable strength of her convictions. That, too, her father had instilled in his children's blood.

For the next few days, though, she would push the lethal business from her mind. Jaime watched Lee doze, then looked below.

From the air, Cancun is a peninsula, shaped like a sea horse, fourteen miles long and a quarter-mile wide. The daytime high temperature remains constant at eighty-eight degrees year-round and clear waters surround it for one-hundred feet. Limestone sand beaches are pure white crystal and unlike any other sand in the world, the uniquely fine-grained powder is never hot to the touch.

Once, the entire land mass had been sand, palm trees, and scrub brush. The Mexican government had first developed it as a tourist resort area in the 1970s so the hotels, which were mostly in the head of the sea horse, were new, immaculate, and waiting.

Jaime was enticed as they readied to land. She would enjoy a few days in the sun, and relish evenings at all-night restaurants and clubs. Jaime needed time off more than she wanted to admit. They were 560 miles southwest of Miami. In sixty minutes, her toes would touch that crystalline beach sand, water would sooth her senses, and sun would bake away tensions.

She looked at Lee again. A few margaritas would make him easier to stomach, too. They had three days before they would meet Noriega's pilot at a private airstrip fifty miles south. She intended to enjoy each of them. As a flight attendant came their way, checking passenger seat belts for landing, Jaime grabbed Lee's arm, drew close, and planted a kiss on his cheek.

Lee stirred with a jolt.

"Noriega's people will be down there," she whispered. "We won't know who they are."

Lee nodded.

"So, you're back into the role."

Jaime nuzzled, and set him straight.

"Don't say that, anymore."

A mustachioed man aimed a gun at Lee and Jaime. Cornered at their dining table, neither could escape. They could only watch him squeeze the trigger. Seventy-six - proof ammunition took its toll as Jaime gurgled every drop.

*Bandito* waiters, young men dressed as Mexican cowboys, slinging water pistols filled with tequila, had struck another gourmet with an intoxicating burst. Fellow diners cheered and Lee lifted his margarita. Then, every moment in Cancun blurred into the next.

Disco balls spun, strobe lights flashed, and music blared at Dady'O. To Lee, the famous discotheque seemed like an indoor football stadium—too big, too loud, and too much. As if driven to celebrate each minute alive, they rocked until dawn.

Sunrise didn't slow their pace. Splashing in multilevel-freeform swimming pools at the plush Fiesta

Americana Condesa Cancun resort hotel, wading in the clear Caribbean Sea, they found refreshing waters. They would have also found time to reflect, if either had paused for an instant, but they charged, swallowing good times in gulps.

Dusk again unleashed nocturnal energy that can propel vacationers nonstop. Dancers gyrated in a "foam room," covered by bubbles that reached from floor to ceiling. Lee and Jaime broke through the suds, her eyes locked on his, his harnessed to hers. They laughed as she wiped froth off his face, and he diverted onrushing spumes from hers.

Lee hadn't seen Jaime smile since Frankie's arrest. He grabbed her in arms that ached to hold her, their lips meeting, neither daring to open their eyes until lips parted. Earnestly, Lee whispered.

"I've had enough clubbing for a thousand lifetimes. Let's leave a day early to see the ruins of Tulum."

Jaime looked uncertain.

"The Mayan ruins? They're in the middle of nowhere, aren't they?"

"They're on the way to Noriega's airstrip. We can book a room nearby for the night."

Jaime's eyes flashed her answer as foam rolled like cascading surf, forming a cocoon where they only found each other.

A shuttle taxi furnished by their resort took them on the two-hour afternoon ride. Their elderly Indian driver had a small and heavily furrowed brow. Deep creases etched his auburn cheeks and framed the corners of his mouth. Dark bottomless pools seemed to fill his eye sockets without room for the whites of his eyes. Proud of his ancient heritage, he told them what they would find in Tulum, delivering words in a near whispered chant.

"Tulum was once a thriving city built on a cliff where thousands of people lived, worshiped their gods, and prospered. Two dozen structures remain. Of them all, you'll find your peace in the temple overlooking the sea."

"Peace?" Lee said.

They hadn't even spoken on the long ride. He and Jaime were too exhausted from late hours on the town.

He wondered: *What does the old man mean?*

"Chac will find you there," the Indian said, almost as if answering Lee's unspoken question. "He walks through the ruins and searches for the souls so long ago departed."

They drove in silence and arrived with the late afternoon sun beating down on the remains of the ancient city.

"I'll take your luggage ahead to your hotel," the old man said. "Will you need anything from your suitcases?"

Jaime stirred from her sleepy ride.

"No," she said. "I packed a small bag that we'll carry with us."

The driver moved slowly. He ambled out and held the door for them. As they departed, the old Indian studied them with the dark eyes that seemed to absorb their thoughts, then called to them. Lee and Jaime turned back for his simple words.

"You'll find your peace, here."

Lee and Jaime joined a small procession of tourists. A government guide escorted sightseers through the ancient city. The youthful woman, looking to be no more than seventeen, was native to the Yucatan. She had grown up just as tourism took its foothold. The Mexican government heavily invested in the once destitute area to build a better economy. Young people, who reaped the benefits of the development by working in the booming tourist industry, had grown distant from traditions of their people. The younger generation dressed, spoke, and thought in more modern ways.

"The Mayan civilization stretched from the Yucatan, here in Mexico, through all of Central America," their guide explained. "It prospered for one thousand years before the birth of Christ—until the Spaniards invaded in the sixteenth century. The people were harshly impacted but never conquered. Descendants of the Maya still practice elements of the culture and traditions that are more than two-thousand years old."

As they strolled through the decaying remains of once grand structures, the tour guide pointed to colored frescos and relief carvings that had withstood the passage of time. They passed remains of walls that had fortified the city from attack and ancient platforms once used for ritualistic ceremonies. Lastly, they approached the grand temple of Tulum. Built as a massive pyramid overlooking the Caribbean Sea, it evoked reverent awe that its builders, dead more than a thousand years, had intended to inspire.

"Here," their guide said, "the Maya worshiped gods that demanded human sacrifice. The gods needed human blood to become strong so they could serve the people. A priest would cut the heart from a live victim and offer it to a god with a solemn prayer. In turn, the god would bless the people with his favor and grace."

The young woman paused to focus upon the grouping before continuing.

"Often, they would sacrifice an enemy. If the victim was particularly wicked, they would eat his remains. Mayans believed this sacred form of cannibalism pleased the gods."

Tourists laughed uneasily at the gruesome detail, then split into different directions to explore the temple and its surroundings. Lee approached the tour guide with a question.

"Where will we find Chac?"

The young woman looked at him inquisitively.

"How do you know of him?"

"Our driver mentioned him," Jaime offered. "The old dude was *kinda* spooky."

Their guide smiled.

"Some of the old people still believe," she said. "You must understand the Mayan culture closely connected religion and state, like the culture of the Spaniards, who stole gold and jewels from their temples, and enslaved them. Invaders converted the people to Roman Catholicism four hundred years ago. They executed those who refused conversion, but some pagan religious practices persisted, handed down from one generation to the next. Even today, some believers worship Chac."

"The old man said we would find him, here," Lee said.

"You will. He's up there," the young woman offered.

She pointed to a stone mask adorning the top of a corner on the temple.

"Faces of the old gods decorate the buildings here. Chac is all over. You can always spot him by his elephant-tusk nose. The Maya were dependent upon rain for agriculture in their dry climate, so they prayed to Chac as a rain god and bringer of life. He was a very powerful deity. They say he was even the god of fertility. But I'm afraid you'll only find him carved in stone or painted in a fresco."

Their guide turned her head.

"Excuse me," she said, "I have to run. The tours are about to close for the day. This will be an empty place soon. Though," she added with a wry grin fast forming on her lips, "some claim to have heard the bustle of the dead walking these ancient avenues in darkness."

Lee and Jaime watched the guide scurry then continued taking in the sights on their own. Most tourists boarded buses headed back to Cancun. Others jumped aboard shuttles to the ferry that would carry them to the nearby resort island of Cozumel. Jaime pointed to the beach below the temple where a handful of vacationers still enjoyed refreshing waters of the Caribbean Sea: a sight too tempting for either to resist.

They descended the cliff and walked along the shore. Jaime set her bag on the sand and pulled out a beach blanket. Lee spread it while she stripped off her tank top and shorts, revealing a golden two-piece bathing suit, which shimmered brightly as Mayan treasure.

Lee admired Jaime's well-toned body as she darted into the waves. He ripped off his shirt and followed in shorts. Diving to meet her under playful surf, he spied her gliding and pursued as she swam farther from shore. At last both exhausted, they bobbed on the surface, treading water, while facing soft beach sands that beckoned. Without a word spoken, they returned to shore and collapsed on the blanket. After late nights in Cancun clubs, it felt good to rest in the late afternoon sun.

Lee woke and checked his wristwatch.

"Midnight," he whispered.

The beach was deserted, while above them Tulum was empty. He looked at the white stone temple high on the cliff above them glistening in moonlight and listened to the surf. When he turned to Jaime, he saw she had risen too, as if something woke them at the same time. She also stared at the temple. They turned to face each other under the moon and stars.

Jaime's words came slow and hushed.

"Do me 'til I'm done."

Lee ached to penetrate her with overdue urgency. Yet he didn't move, as if frozen in space and time, until her chest heaved with a deep breath and her words came in a rush.

"Do me 'til I'm—"

Drawn together by an inexorable force neither had ever known, they bound each other in arms that unremittingly clasped. Lee felt the sparked sensation of her bare breasts brushing against his firm chest. They shared eager sighs and savored the playful teasing of their tongues until something seemed to click.

As if time were playing tricks, Lee opened his eyes to see not her hungry lips but her raised nipple reaching for his outstretched tongue. Jaime's back arched upward. An impassioned sigh escaped her lips as he circled her breast with teasing nibbles. The tip of his tongue danced across her areola, first as if waltzing, then as if paired in a sensuous habanera, until again something seemed to click.

Magically, he withdrew to find his lips atop hers again. Intertwined as if they were one, he entered her slowly. She writhed beneath his frame, desire turning into frenzy, as passion of unearthly magnitude swept them to a dimension of magnificence.

Minutes later, hours later, how long didn't matter, as neither time nor words had meaning. They said nothing, consumed by enduring afterglow, resting next to the sea as surf kissed the shore. Naked on pure white sands, they came together for more and again something clicked.

DEA Agent Dave Tillis had an eyeful, a roll full, and a lap full. Their performance was worthy of the standing ovation that inflated his trousers. He had clicked and shot all thirty-six photos in his surveillance camera. Equipped with a military night scope and powerful telephoto lens, the camera could catch a pimple at three-hundred feet. Used primarily to collect photographic evidence in drug cases, the camera served a very special purpose.

Tillis had followed the couple to Cancun, looking for proof his agency needed. He knew something was awry when solid drug charges were tossed out of court. Tillis patted his camera. It held what he needed to take back to the FBI. He would turn incriminating evidence over its Inspection Division. The photos would initiate an internal investigation of a rogue agent who was literally sleeping with the enemy. Tillis resented Calero. She had stepped on him in Miami and he would smash her toes.

If she was selling out to the mob lawyer, he would have her put in prison. Even if she was working with the attorney on a legitimate undercover operation, he would still have Special Agent Calero off his back. He had thirty-six pictures of her breaking the FBI's "kiss only" rule. One way or another, the agent was history at the Bureau.

"So long to bad news," he whispered.

Tillis set down his camera and looked around. Nestled atop the cliff overlooking the beach, he had clear views of the sea in front of him and the ancient ruins behind. He had come without his partner to tail the unsuspecting FBI agent and her lawyer lover, thinking he wouldn't need backup. Alone in the night, he wasn't so sure. He felt as if he was being watched by eyes hiding behind him in the ancient city.

"Nah," he said to himself. "I'm just letting my imagination run wild."

A warm sea breeze blowing through the deserted ruins caressed him. As wind wisped by, he thought he heard murmurs. It sounded like a thousand voices all taking at once. Then, they left with the breeze, fast as they had come.

He looked back into the ancient city yet couldn't see anyone in the dark. Somebody was there. He was certain of it. Tillis picked up the camera and activated the ultraviolet night scope. Then, he put the camera to his eye and pointed in the direction of the echoing cries.

*Where*, he thought, *is it coming from?*

A faint draft rose, carrying the sonnet of a lone troubadour. It floated to his ears in a mystical tongue. Tillis pointed his camera toward the source of the lyrical call. As the breeze grew brisker a thousand-voice chorus joined. Tillis spotted something in the dark. He focused the camera lens as a face came into clear view, a hideously contorted face with an elephant tusk for a nose.

"I'm gettin' out of here fast!" he blurted.

Tillis scurried to his rented jeep, shoved the camera under his seat, and turned the ignition key. The jeep didn't start.

"Christ Almighty!" he wheezed.

Tillis turned the key again. The engine turned over, first with a putter, then with a roar as he floored the accelerator pedal. In seconds his tires touched the unlighted, single-lane highway stretching eighty-one miles to Cancun's airport. He was zipping all the way back to Miami. Tillis had what he wanted.

He also had a special date at home. She was flying into town for the weekend and he was ready for her. Something had lighted his loins as he watched the lawyer and FBI agent. Tillis was eager to find his own rapture with Tanya.

Lee and Jaime basked under a canopy of moon glow and starlight, massaged by gentle sea breezes and serenaded by waves lapping against the shore. Three times they made love on pristine sands, once hotly and physically, then more gently with richer passion, and finally with tenderness transcending anything they had ever known. They held each other through the night, consumed only by thoughts of each other.

Jaime's voice came in a wisp.

"The old man was right."

Lee raised only a single breath upon which a word could escape.

"Peace," he said.

As Jaime's warm body fit snugly into his, she completed his thought.

"Peace without a thought of tomorrow."

They found a world where only two existed. Eyes closed, secure in locked arms, neither considered what the new day was bringing.

*The Mayan Temple of Tulum*

# Part III

# Chapter Eighteen

# Milk Over Coffee

"I DIDN'TKNOW OUR FLIGHT PLAN until we were in the air this morning," the Panamanian pilot of the Cessna 172 said. "You're going down there."

Hands on controls, he craned a long neck, pointing his head toward the right side of the small single-engine plane.

From above, Jaime recognized the topography from the maps and aerial photos she studied of the dictator's properties. They were looking down at Noriega's Playa Blanca estate, a fortified mansion surrounded by lush grounds on the Panamanian Pacific coast. The beachfront compound possessed tennis courts, pools, main house, and dwellings for guests and troops stationed on the premises. High walls surrounded the property with guard stations strategically situated.

Lee peered and look of relief flashed across his face.

"Is that a U.S. military base?" he said, pointing to the facility below.

"That's where we land, *Senor*," replied the pilot. "It's the Rio Hato base of the Panamanian Defense Forces."

Jaime inspected the military base. The PDF had placed the formidable complex near Noriega's beach retreat. She recalled the place from a briefing on the dictator's real estate holdings. The plush compound was west of Panama City on the Gulf of Panama, which enters the Pacific Ocean.

The man owned many mansions and estates. Besides that forty-five-acre beachfront property, he owned a mansion in Panama City and homes in three other Panamanian provinces. He also owned properties around the world—a ranch in the Dominican Republic sporting a fortified bunker and airfield, a penthouse in Caracas, a house in Japan, a chateau in southern France, and an apartment in Paris. He traveled between them so enemies wouldn't know where to find him.

Noriega could well afford to purchase and maintain real estate that the CIA had appraised for more than $50 million. The agency estimated his net worth to be $722 million, not counting money he had stashed in coded Swiss bank accounts. The man, who had come from dirt poor roots, was a billionaire with an insatiable appetite to increase his wealth.

Jaime had hoped to meet the dictator somewhere near a United States military installation in the canal zone. Instead, they were about to land in a Panamanian military base close to the dictator's compound. The nearest American facility was Howard Air Force Base. She would have to travel far past the PDF facility to reach it. There couldn't be a worse scenario for what she would have to do if Lee couldn't convince the man to face criminal charges in the United States. Jaime had seen Lee think fast on his feet in the courtroom and hoped he could react just as quickly in the presence of the animal they had to snare.

They hovered over the PDF airstrip and prepared to land. For the first time, she questioned whether she should've accepted her assignment. Whatever transpired in Tulum had been unexpected. She had planned making love with Lee to flush him from her system, but something happened that confused her.

*Damn it*, she told herself. *Stop thinking so hard.*

Jaime cussed her self-doubts. Second thoughts like those could jeopardize the mission and her life.

Another airplane hovered in the eastward sky over Panama City. The commercial flight circled to approach Tocumen International Airport with Frankie No Throat onboard. He came with orders from his family. Frankie also carried his own agenda. He arrived for reasons his lawyer never contemplated. As wheels of the 727 touched ground, Frankie massaged his temples. Tension brought on a headache that came like an ice pick stuck in his brain.

He walked through the modern airport facility and spotted a long line at the customs desk that didn't deter him. Frankie walked past it and shoved his passport in the hand of a Panamanian customs official. The little man puffed with the authority his uniform commanded.

"The line starts way back—"

"International investment banker," Frankie curtly interrupted.

The man picked up an internal security phone. He spoke in hushed tones, then smiled. To show courtesy and respect, he tipped his hat. Frankie could pass without anyone inspecting his baggage. The job description was a pseudonym for money laundering. Frankie was a known drug player who was free to come and go as he chose.

"Welcome back to Panama, Mister Cinelli," the customs officer said.

He returned Frankie's passport with panache, holding it in his right hand and courteously resting it atop his left wrist, as if in deference to a special honoree.

"May I find someone to carry your bags?"

Frankie didn't bother answering. He walked his two large suitcases to the taxi station and grabbed a cab.

"Caesar Park Hotel, *rapido*," he called to the taxi driver.

As the driver reached for his luggage, Frankie stopped him cold.

"My bags travel with me on the rear seat."

Frankie flopped in his seat and looked out as the cab rolled. He hadn't seen the place since midget marines had ripped off six-million hard. He still had bad feelings about Panama City but at least he was staying in its best hotel.

While his driver chugged through congested traffic, Frankie tried to shake his headache by taking a few deep breaths. His nose filled with a third-world fetor that reminded him of where he was. The scent was hard to place, but familiar, like the smell of gunpowder he had often scrubbed away after doing a hit. Something almost sulfuric tainted the air. He whiffed again. The stench came close as he could imagine to brimstone.

"I'm back in friggin' Panama," he complained aloud.

He would unpack and prepare for his midnight meeting at the Hotel El Panama rooftop discotheque. With a striking city view from the dance floor, affluent Panamanians, well-dressed foreigners, and gilded youth frequented it. There, he would find his contact. They wouldn't view the scenery. His meeting, as always, would convene at the pissers.

A PDF officer courteously escorted Lee and Jaime from the small plane to a waiting black Lincoln limousine. A miniature Panamanian flag adorned the hood. While riding from the military airstrip through the PDF base, they observed a tense atmosphere. Troops drilled on the parade ground. Shots rang from a nearby firing range. Noriega's forces were fine tuning.

Jaime turned to Lee.

"This could be a good sign," she offered. "If Panamanian troops have been placed in readiness, Noriega is afraid of an American incursion."

Lee's eyes didn't leave the drill field.

"Could also mean Noriega would rather fight on Panamanian soil than voluntarily surrender in Miami."

The big car bumped along the rough road leading from the PDF base to the Playa Blanca compound. As they traveled, Lee looked out at the faces of the poor, the common people of the country from whom the dictator had risen. Children in tattered clothing walked barefoot along the roadside. They stared at the shiny limo while it kicked up road dust. No doubt the dictator's personal vehicle, the car came fully equipped with telephones, television, video player, and a well-stocked bar.

*What must the man think,* Lee wondered, *as he passes his impoverished countrymen in the luxury of this limousine?*

Their limo pulled up to Noriega's imposing compound and stopped at the main gate. Four pickets in dress uniforms manned it. More soldiers were stationed at a nearby guard house, all heavily armed. Canine squads policed the perimeter. The well-armed troops with German shepherds patrolled both sides of the twelve-foot high walls topped with barbed wire. From the air, they had seen guard towers spaced at regular increments. From the ground, Lee looked up at the nearest one. Its darkened glass concealed whoever stood inside from view. The gate opened and they entered the sprawling property.

Lee let out a long breath.

"I've visited clients who are jailed less securely in maximum security prisons."

On the winding road to the main house, cautious troops stopped them again. At last, the main house came into view. Pillars rose three stories high by the front door. It was a fortified Tara by the sea—as if someone had taken the stately mansion in *Gone with the Wind*, placed it near an ocean, and fortified it like Fort Knox. Armed troops patrolled. Two servants, likely packing weapons, opened the limousine door as a genial attendant raced toward the car.

"Oh, hello," the nattily attired man called.

He wore a summer white-linen suit without a shirt. A single golden chain adorned his neck, from which a small pendant dangled atop a hairless chest. With glistening dark hair slicked back and a heavy accent, he seemed at first glance to be the personification of a Latin lover.

"I'm Enrico Herrera," he said, introducing himself with a smile that displayed a mouthful of perfectly capped, Hollywood bright, upper and lower teeth. On closer look, he was slightly built with delicately chiseled features and near feminine deportment.

Jaime took control. "*Buenas noches*," she said, wishing him a good evening.

Enrico looked pleased to hear she spoke his language. "*Tuvo a tenido buen viaje?*" he politely asked.

"*Muy bien*," she lied. The trip had been anything but good. The flight had been slow and uncomfortable in the small Cessna.

Their greeter turned to Lee and spoke in English.

"Please call me Ricki. I'll be your host until General Noriega arrives. He has business in the capital today, but he'll arrive later this evening. We often dine late to accommodate his busy schedule," Ricki offered sheepishly.

He led them inside the main house while servants carried their bags. The front door opened to a two-story foyer where a long, winding staircase swept to upper floors.

"I've planned a formal dinner for one o'clock in the morning," Ricki said as they trekked up the stairs. "This will give you time to relax and grow accustomed to your quarters. Our master chef is sending you something special to tide you over until dinner."

Lee and Jaime followed Ricki down a dim hallway. No uniformed troops were inside the house, but male and female white-uniformed domestic attendants silently roamed. At least one large man could have served as a bodyguard. He studied Lee and Jaime as they passed, which wasn't the obsequious conduct of a servant. Lee pegged him as a Noriega operative, planted in the house to keep an eye on them.

Ricki stopped in front of an oversized door, which opened to an elegantly appointed living room.

"I believe you'll be comfy, here, in the East Suite," he said with his hands raised high in the air.

He slowly lowered his arms as if proud keeper of the house showing off its lavish decor. With a smug smile, Ricki stretched both arms to point toward matching single doors, one on the right and one on the left side of the living room.

"There are separate bedrooms, should you wish, and of course separate baths. Please make yourself at home. Refreshments will arrive shortly. If you desire anything at any time, tinkle on the ting-a-ling. Just dial the operator."

Ricki flashed his Hollywood whites, pausing to allow Lee and Jaime soak in the grandeur of their surroundings. He moved toward the door as a food server rolled in a tray table holding delicacies under sterling silver plate covers. Ricki stopped the man. Gently, he raised the covers for quick inspection. Then, he lifted a champagne magnum from an oversized ice bucket, glanced at the label, nodded his approval to the servant, and departed.

The server opened champagne—Taittinger Comtes De Champagne Blanc De Blanc the label read—then poured a spot into a crystal glass for Lee. Though not a sommelier, nor even a wine connoisseur, he nodded satisfaction with the bubbly libation, which he recognized as kind of yummy and seriously pricy, allowing the waiter to pure and serve two glasses.

"*Gracias*," Jaime offered.

Without a word spoken, the servant then removed plate covers to reveal a trove of sea foods before bowing and leaving them alone in the room.

Jaime turned to Lee.

"Last night," she began. "Last night . . . was to get you out of my system."

Lee sipped hard, both hearing and sensing abrupt distance from her.

"I'll take the bedroom to the right," she said.

Lee ambled slowly toward the other bedroom, as if awakened by her coldness to the jeopardy of their situation. So cold and suddenly it struck him.

*Everything*, he realized, *culminates here and now.*

Frankie cruised through the Hotel El Panama rooftop discotheque. His eyes didn't glance at the glittery city vista from windows by the dance floor. Nor did he survey the wealthy Panamanians, influential foreigners, and advantaged youth, whose fashionables proved how fine a line separates style from ostentation. Frankie pushed past them all—the chic and the garish—to enter the men's room.

"Midnight at the pissers in Panama," he announced. "I can lead a world tour of these venues."

He took his place in front of a urinal. Jose Batista entered and walked up to the one next to it. As they spoke in earnest whispers, Frankie somehow realized he would never see that spot again. Frankie had three days to get in and get out. He and Batista had much to discuss and little time. Batista knew where to start.

"Money, Amigo." his soft voice reminded. "My bank is waiting for money."

"My people will wire a half million into your Cayman Island account in the morning. They'll transfer another half million when the deaths are confirmed and I'm safely out of here. That's our deal."

"The terms have changed. You want to free forty-million dollars of your family's money locked in Panamanian bank accounts by red tape. You want the big man dead. You want the *abogado* killed. I'll get you what you want but the price has gone up. One million dollars finds my account in the morning . . . another million for them to die and a million more if you wish to get out alive—paid in advance."

Frankie fought to conceal rage as well as fear. "Friggin' Panama," he muttered. "Everyone has an angle."

In Miami, Supervisor Martin and his spook counterpart made a tireless duo. They convened again in the FBI interrogation room. The spook had news.

"We intercepted two items the lawyer placed into the Mexican mail before leaving Cancun with your agent," he said. "One was a package that's being delivered to our friends in Philadelphia. The other was a letter to Miami we let pass."

"Miami?" Martin's eyebrows arched. "What business does the guy have, here, that can't wait?"

"Inconsequential. But, the package to Philadelphia gave the mob what it wanted. We're passing it along to them and they're in the process of repaying their debt."

"Can we count on them?"

"They have people who can reach Noriega. That'll insulate us."

Martin nodded in agreement.

"It's the same old game," the man reflected. "We help them and—well, you know—they help us. Won't be the first time we've gone to these kinds of people. Kennedy," he mused, "Castro. Oh, hell, you know where we've been with them."

Martin understood. The government and the mob sometimes shared more in common than he liked.

"Pragmatism," he offered, "has a way of turning black and white into grey."

The man sitting across from him leaned back in his chair. "We simply have jobs to do," he said. "Honorable professional tenants are never soiled by the dictates of duty."

Martin acceded with a cursory nod, then turned the conversation.

"How's Calero?"

"She's under the eye of our guy inside Noriega's camp," answered the spook, pausing before adding almost casually: "You know she probably won't come back."

Martin turned away.

"That's always been the understanding," he said, "but our extraction team is ready. They'll at least make an attempt to retrieve her when the time comes."

"It's a matter of how smart she plays it," the spook said. "We told her what to do."

At one in the morning, Jaime walked from her bedroom, ready for their dinner date with the dictator. She saw Lee waiting with a filled wine glass in his hand and admired his appearance in a white dinner jacket. Everything looked right about him except the stunned expression on his face. That would go after he grew accustomed to her transformation.

Jaime had cast away her virtuous comportment. She wore a sheer gown that fit like a second skin, low-cut at the top, slit up both sides to her waist. Slinky undergarments bestowed lift and fit with minimal coverage. Four-inch high heels screamed, "hump me."

Something else really dazed him, though. Platinum tresses completed the metamorphosis for her new role. A full and flowing blond wig transformed her into a different woman.

She took the glass Lee held with his eyes trained on her tresses. He couldn't speak so Jaime explained.

"Our host prefers milk over coffee," she began, unable to look Lee in the eye as her story unfolded. She conveyed some, but could not bring herself to reveal all, of what she had learned in briefings.

The CIA knew Noriega's outspoken tastes, his predilection of light-skinned beauties with fair hair over darker skin toned and dusky-haired playmates. "Milk over coffee," he called it. They had known him as an eager CIA volunteer in his military academy days and as their man in Panama for so many years. They knew of his attraction to prostitutes and the kinds of games he liked to play. The dictator was married and showered his wife and children with luxuries his station in life afforded. Yet, the time he spent away from their family home, combined with power and wealth, allowed him to indulge in very specific sexual proclivities.

Lee studied the sensuous creature standing before him. Nothing was subtle or innocent about her look.

Holding the tips of her blond hair, Jaime said, "This will help me get closer to him."

"How close do you plan to get?"

Before she could answer, a sharp knock sounded on their door. Lee opened it to find the burly servant who had caught his eye when they had first arrived. The man pointed to Jaime, then Lee. Without expression, he beckoned them to follow with a wave of his hand. The gesture wasn't servile. He had come to take them like a mute zombie in the night. They wouldn't be free to move through the house on their own.

Jaime grabbed Lee's arm aggressively. Then, they followed the big man. She seemed to move with forceful determination. As they rounded the winding staircase to the foyer, another large man, also dressed as a servant, stood inside the main door to the house. He appeared permanently stationed there and watched as they passed. No one could enter or leave the doorway without passing him.

Lee looked up and observed surveillance cameras in the foyer. He had probably missed them in the halls. They walked through a grand living room appointed with lavish antique European furnishings, then passed through an archway into the formal dining room.

A long mahogany table was set for four. Ricki was already seated. He greeted them with a smile too wide, like a jackass just goosed. Sitting at the head of the table was a man in a military dress uniform, his head lowered. Everyone in the room froze, waiting for his direction. Finally, he looked up and peered through two black pinhead eyes. Pallid was his flesh. From close vantage the pockmarks on his face were craters. Without expression his mouth opened to display yellow teeth.

"You know who I am," said Manuel Noriega.

With his nod, white-jacketed servants held two chairs across the table from Ricki, who gestured to Jaime, indicating she should sit closest to the dictator. Lee took the seat to her other side. They sat without a word spoken. Awkward silence followed as Noriega's head slunk low again. Then, as if arising from some transcendental psychic state, he lifted his face and clapped his hands. Waiters jockeyed to place the meal before them, serving large bowls that landed heavily on the tabletop.

Lee looked down. His soup had a fish head floating on the surface, bloody entrails dangling from where it had been severed. Its eye, identical to their host's beady peepers, stared as Lee's spoon entered the bowel and he raised it to his mouth. The taste of bitter broth lingered on his tongue. Nausea grew in the pit of his stomach, his heart pounding faster.

## Chapter Nineteen

# Beady Eyes and Bad Bouillabaisse

LEE WOKE WITH A THROBBING HEAD. Thirst ravaged him but he couldn't rise from bed to quench it. His sight, taste and equilibrium clashed; all his senses fought him, and he lost. Lee held his hands over his eyes and groaned.

"What in God's name happened last night?"

He remembered sitting at the dining room table, but nothing else. Thinking hurt. He massaged his temples and tried recollecting.

"Beady eyes!"

The words escaped his lips.

"Beady eyes and bad bouillabaisse."

The beady eyes of their host had shot through him. A single eye had also stared. Just as piercing had been its glare.

"The fish head," he said to himself. "That's the last thing I remember."

The third eye had floated atop the bouillabaisse, a highly seasoned stew that contains bits of fish and shellfish indigenous to local waters. The appetizer had left a bitter aftertaste. A day later and too late, he realized his host had it spiked with something that knocked Lee cold.

He remembered Noriega clapping his hands for waiters. Something in his gestures must have told table servers which guest was to receive the only bowl with a fish head floating atop. Lee rubbed his temples trying to recall more.

"Yes," he blurted. "It's coming back to me."

Noriega had sized up him and Jaime, then elected to deal one-on-one with the attractive young woman who knew the dictator preferred milk over coffee. Whatever had laced the soup worked quickly. Lee remembered nothing after the first few sips until he struggled to open his eyes.

Sunlight cascaded into the room, flashing too brightly for the splitting headache that confined him to bed more securely than chains.

*Jaime*, he thought with a start. *Where is she?*

Lee staggered into the bathroom, peered in the mirror, and almost didn't recognize his face underneath a heavy growth of beard.

"How long was I asleep?"

He dragged a razor across his face then jammed a toothbrush past his lips to scrub three times before his mouth felt like his own. Dressing casually in sport shirt and slacks, he was ready to trudge into the living room of their suite to check on her.

*Not here*, he thought. *She must still be in bed.*

He called into her bedchamber, "Jaime!"

Lee entered to find the room empty, the bed made. Suitcases and every trace of her had vanished, while everything remaining was neatly in place. The little mestizo maids, whom he'd seen wearing white uniforms, must have cleaned the room after removing Jaime's belongings.

*Where is she?*

He went to the main door of the suite, thinking he might find someone to answer his questions. Lee twisted the doorknob to find the door locked.

*The telephone*, he conjured.

He lifted the receiver.

"Hello, hello," he called out. "Damn, it's dead."

He ambled to the windows, and saw they overlooked a lushly landscaped courtyard that centered around a spurting fountain. Hidden under a canopy of heavily clustered palm trees was a large swimming pool. The beautiful view was one he would only see from that vantage point. The windows were fixed panes of safety glass, thick and probably bulletproof. Lee checked edges of the glass for weak joints where he could try prying the glass from its encasement.

*Damn*, he thought, *none.*

The suite was on the second floor so the drop to the ground wouldn't be too high, even with his bad knee, but it didn't matter. He couldn't get out.

Lee wondered why their host had installed bulletproof glass in the window. The mansion, like many fine Spanish-style houses, surrounded a courtyard that wasn't open to outsiders. Lee couldn't escape the house even if he climbed out the window. The only way in and out of the mansion was through the main door. His host didn't install the thick glass to protect anyone in the suite from intruders or dangers. Its sole function was to confine guests to their quarters.

Lee walked back to the main door. When he had worked part-time in a hardware and building supply store during law school, he'd learned a few tricks. Lee could jimmy most household locks. He knelt on his good knee to size it up the way a rooster appraises his opponent before a cockfight. Though secure, he could take on that lock with a safety pin. That would be the easy part. Harder, would be determining what to do when it opened.

His thoughts turned to Jaime. Something in her look had told Lee she would be open to Noriega's advances. She was up to something. He couldn't figure out her plan, but she was there to do more than merely act as his interpreter. For the first time, Lee realized she had her own mission. Suddenly, jealousy ate at him.

*Jaime, what are you really here for*, he wondered, *and how far will you go to get it?*

She slithered atop the coffee table wearing so little: sky-high pumps, panties slit in front, and a bra with apertures flaunting her nipples. He stared at her longingly from the couch. A tenor saxophone wailed to carnal Latin-rhythms as she manipulated herself with her hands. Perfectly manicured red nails caressed the length of her well-toned body.

"Choke your chicken," she called down to him. "Look at this body and choke your chicken for me."

His hands invaded his trousers. She pinched her nipple tips into cement-hard pleasure centers that broadcast a thousand nerve-rich sensations throughout her body. Her moans joined his in chorus.

At last, he leaped to his feet, slammed her to the carpet, and pinned her knees to her ears. Tears filled her eyes as he plunged deeper than she could take it. Orgasmic cries of the saxophone harmonized with theirs, while relentlessly he stoked their fire with a steel rod. Time and again insatiable concupiscence propelled them to sweat-drenched ecstasy.

Spent to physical bankruptcy, he rolled aside, fighting for breath.

*She's killing me*, he thought.

Her trick pelvis could drain his sac until he sang soprano. That's why Frankie No Throat always found the petite prostitute when he came to town. Carmella Ruiz made Panama special.

Within minutes of his call, she had arrived at the hotel. For twenty years, Frankie had called upon the sexy little hooker, whose talents elevated his lustful instincts like celestial inspirations. God, how he yearned for her. They had developed feelings for each other that transcended the libidinous business he always returned to savor.

Frankie counted on Carmella as something constant in his life. In her he found the closest he had ever come to a wife. Sure, he lived with Jimmy Picardo's old lady as an accommodation to his crime family. He never thought of the obese woman as his own, nor did she. She was married to Jimmy, for better and worse, and her marriage was on an upward spiral. Jimmy lost his murder conviction appeal but was getting released anyway. Life in prison never really means a lifetime under Pennsylvania law. He was eligible for parole. Frankie would gladly return the guy's wife with her virtue intact. That had been their unspoken understanding, though his cronies always assumed he was milking her famous udders.

Frankie studied Carmella with devoted eyes. They had been together so long he had seen her age, not badly, but they both had. Thankfully, she kept trim and shapely. She didn't have any grocery-market defects: no cottage cheese on her ass or Jell-O dangling from her underarms. She stayed fit in a business where beauty and youth were everything. Carmella had Indian blood and her dark features were ingrained in his mind as indelibly as the same lucky numbers he played each week for thirty years.

She removed her lacy garments and snuggled naked by his side.

"You came back for me," she said. "Over all the years you always come back for me, my Frankie No Throat. You're meant for me."

"Is that something your voodoo tells you?"

She kissed his cheek and scolded softly.

"Those who believe see many things you wouldn't know."

Frankie began to stir.

"I have to get dressed and do some business."

Carmella hugged him. Tenderly, he removed her arms and kissed her forehead.

"This business can't wait."

Lee jiggled the safety pin that had become his makeshift lock tool until he heard a click. Gently, he pulled the door open and entered the hallway. He didn't move with catlike stealth. Someone must have bounced his bad knee into something as they carried him unconscious from the dining table to bed. He limped, each step sparking pain.

Oddly, no one patrolled the hallway. He descended the large circular stairway to the main foyer. No one stood by the front door either.

*This is too easy*, he thought.

He knew he shouldn't be able to roam freely and figured someone was monitoring him. Security cameras, no doubt, transmitted his movements to a surveillance station.

Lee considered leaving through the front door, but where to go? Through thick windowpanes, he saw troops marching in formation. Besides, he wanted to find Jaime. He was compelled to find her, and something told him she was still inside the mansion.

"Where?" he asked himself. "Where can she be?"

Lee only knew that he wouldn't leave without her.

He entered the living room he had strolled through on the way to dinner. No one was in sight. He peered into the dining room. It, too, was empty. He decided not to pass through the servants' doorway to the kitchen. Someone was apt to be working there and he didn't want to press his luck.

Instead, Lee returned to the main foyer where he had seen another door.

*Must lead to something,* he figured.

He tested the handle. It turned smoothly. With a slight push the door glided open.

*Too easy*, he again told himself.

As he cautiously walked through the doorway, he heard loud voices nearing the foyer. Suddenly armed troops came into view. Swiftly, he shut the door behind him. It closed with the sound of a hermetic seal, as if he had walked into a vacuum-tight enclosure that was impervious to outside influence. In absolute silence and darkness, Lee searched for a light switch.

He wondered: *How can this room be so dark on so bright a day?*

His hand traced the wall by the door until he felt a switch and lights flashed. It was then he observed why the room had been so black. It was windowless. He looked around and stood transfixed. Shocked. The room was a bizarre showplace dedicated to a fiendish memory. Decorated with German World War II memorabilia, Lee's eyes scanned Nazi flags, small arms mounted in glass cases, German uniforms and helmets. An Iron Cross, the Nazi medal of honor, hung on resplendent display beneath a glass-domed enclosure.

Suddenly, Lee's head jolted back. A painting above the fireplace riveted his attention. On the oil-colored canvas a face stared down at him. The artist had given the visage the same tiny eyes that had haunted him at the dinner table. Noriega's unmistakable dark and beady peepers were painted into a portrait of Adolf Hitler. The room was a shrine to *der Fuhrer's* memory.

The portraiture hypnotized and held him hostage. Finally, as Lee's gaze fell, the same beady eyes stunned him again. They were cast in the face of Noriega, who had been sitting in the dark in a tall-backed chair that bore more than faint resemblance to a thrown. Dressed in a yellow jump suit with slippers, the diminutive dictator's feet didn't touch ground. With legs swinging backward and forth, apparently, he'd been waiting for Lee to find him there.

Noriega clapped his hands together and motioned for Lee to take a seat on the couch across from him. When Lee complied, he observed the tyrant had carefully chosen the seating arrangement. The couch was lower than Noriega's chair. Lee had to look up to the smaller man, who opened his mouth to address him for the first time.

Frankie No Throat headed toward the main door of his hotel suite to leave. Carmella rushed to him, wrapped her arms around his neck, and wouldn't let go. Her words came earnestly.

"Take me somewhere not here!"

"What? You've never asked me to take you anywhere, Darling."

"Take me somewhere far, my Frankie No Throat. Somewhere not here."

Frankie stared into her eyes. "You see something, don't you?"

"I've foreseen many things for you . . . over the years."

"And sometimes you've even been right."

"You shouldn't tease. When the peoples of this land mixed, they combined ancient knowledge and beliefs that came from Western Africa with the slaves, from the native Indians, and from the Roman Catholic Conquistadors of Spain. This is a land where people feel things that others never see. What my people call black magic, your scientists call medicine when they search our jungles for rare leaves to make drugs—the same leaves my ancestors used to make potions for thousands of years."

Frankie saw heartfelt concern stenciled across her face. That bothered him. Many Central Americans dabbled in voodoo, but Carmella was a true believer. Often, she had premonitions. She claimed voodoo gods and spirits of her Mayan ancestors sent them.

"You want me to take you somewhere to save me from something, don't you? Something that could happen in this place."

He paused, trying to figure it out.

"What do you see, Carmella?"

Standing on her toes, she clung tight, but said nothing.

Frankie reflected.

*Perhaps it's time*, he thought. *to get out of this business.*

The problem for guys like Frankie was the customary ways out were jail or death. The mob didn't sponsor a retirement plan and his work didn't qualify him for social security benefits. Sure, he had made a lot of dough, but he never saved any. What came in always went out. There had just been too many two-thousand-dollar dinners with the boys and too much life in the fast lane. He always thought when the time came, he would just pull one more scam to stash cash in some offshore bank.

*Maybe there is a way to pull it off, now*, he conjured.

He contemplated one last scam, the biggest of his life: scamming the money earmarked for Batista. He could have the Panamanian serve his purpose, then rip him off. The boys from downtown would never know what happened to the cash if he did it right. It would take precise planning but maybe that was his way out. Frankie looked down into Carmella's eyes and decided.

"Yes," he declared. "That's it."

Afterward, he'd take Carmella somewhere far, somewhere not here.

He pressed his lips to hers, then hurried from their suite and through the lobby of the grand hotel. Though luxurious by any standard, third world or five star, Frankie smelled staleness as he scampered. Like the odor that lingers in a morgue or settles in a funeral parlor, the stench of death filled his nostrils. Frankie didn't have time to ponder it. He was anxious to hit the streets before his time ran out.

# Chapter Twenty

# Inferno

"I AM THE WAY INTO THE CITY OF WOE. I am the way to a forsaken people. I am the way to eternal sorrow."

Noriega had flashed his saffron-toothed smile as he recited to Lee.

"Is that how you see me, Mister Gunther?"

Lee was still in shock. He hadn't realized the dictator could speak English so fluently. Apparently, he spoke the language well when it suited his purpose.

Noriega spread his arms wide.

"Abandon all hope ye who enter here," he intoned.

A hideous guffaw somehow escaped his lips though they barely parted.

"Dante," Lee said.

"Of course. Do you read the classics, Mister Gunther?"

Lee realized the well-read dictator quoted from Dante's *The Inferno.* The thirteenth-century tale told of the poet's journey through God's three kingdoms of the afterlife. He had traveled through *Paridsio*, heaven as we know it, the middle ground of *Purgatorio* or purgatory, and the dark realm Dante called *Inferno.* The poet's nightmarish vision of Hell was a land of torment and lamentations, severe punishments and hopelessness.

*Yes*, Lee thought, looking at Manuel Noriega. *I see him as Lucifer and this place is the vestibule of Hell where the quotation is inscribed.*

"I assure you I am no monster, Mister Gunther," said Noriega. "Panama is paradise, but I am a man with many enemies. The United States government yearns to bring me down. Do you understand why?"

Lee didn't answer, sensing it wiser to allow the dictator to direct their discourse.

"It's not me they are after," Noriega continued. "Your government covets this country. Panama is like a thin-waisted woman: everyone wants to fuck her. She's lush and beautiful. At her thin waist a canal stretches from the Atlantic Ocean to the Pacific Ocean, making this the most valuable real estate in the hemisphere.

"First the French, then the Americans, tried building that canal. When the United States succeeded, it spread Panama's legs and every foreign power raped her resources. Now, the United States is after her again. Our

Canal Treaty returns complete control over the waterway to Panama in the year 2000. The United States is attacking me for one reason: so it may continue to enforce colonial rule over so precious an asset."

The man pumped his arms as he spoke, as if flexing muscles adrenalized his vocal cords. At last, he brought them to his side. His feet resumed swaying underneath his chair while he looked into Lee's eyes.

"You are here to shelter me from their grasp, *Abogado*. Tell me your plan."

"That's why I'm here. But, first, I must know the whereabouts of Miz Calero."

Noriega smiled.

"Oh, she's enjoying the leisure pleasures of womankind. There are many diversions for idle minds and bodies on this estate."

Noriega paused. His feet stopped swinging.

"It was unfortunate you took ill over dinner," he continued. "I found your companion to be a clever conversationalist."

He lingered over his words.

"Perhaps . . . too clever."

Lee felt uneasy. Noriega's suspicions could spell trouble.

"Surely," Lee offered, "you're not a man who is intimidated by an intelligent woman."

"Me?"

Noriega cast a look upward, as if searching for his answer. The pause grew so pregnant, Lee became anxious of what words might be delivered.

"No, Mister Gunther. The President is never intimidated. A beautiful woman with a brain is like a beautiful woman with a club foot. Nothing more."

His eyes lowered and settled on Lee.

"On the other hand, this beauty could be something more than she seems."

Lee instantly sensed the intensity of his host's natural distrust.

"To business, Mr. Gunther. What's your recipe to place this unpleasantness behind me?"

Lee was relieved to direct their discussion away from a topic that fueled the dictator's paranoia. Still, as he opened his mouth to speak, one thought consumed him.

*Where's Jaime?*

Jaime rested on a lounge chair by the pool. The sun was too bright even through her sunglasses, causing her to perspire in a way that dips in the pool didn't cure. She sipped freshly squeezed lemonade. Ice cubes clanked against her glass, but the drink was tepid on her tongue. Wiping her brow, Jaime couldn't remember any day in Panama ever so torrid. Something about the place was wrong. No longer was Panama the land of her memories.

*My God*, she thought, *it's miserable here.*

Ricki walked close and took a seat on the lounge chair beside her. She wondered why the heat had not melted the grin spread wide across his face. Then, he spoke simple words that told her what she had been waiting to hear, and what she needed to know.

"When the time comes," he promised, "I'll be there."

"So, it's you," Jaime said. "Has Mister Gunther spoken to the President, yet?"

"They're in the study, now. And, I might add, it's getting hot inside there as well."

Jaime shut her eyes in the sun.

"If Lee doesn't talk him into surrendering by evening, I'll need the vial. I'll have to use it tonight when I see Noriega. Afterward, you'll have to get me out of here."

She looked up to see that the delicately structured man had disappeared quickly as he had arrived. Perhaps he would return with news of the meeting in progress. If he brought the deadly toxin to lace Noriega's drink, she would know what happened and what she would have to do. The silent zombies patrolling the property had already searched her bags. Ricki would place the poison in her cosmetic case so she could spike Noriega's drink. Then, he would lead her to Martin's extraction team.

She was ready, but something bothered her. Jaime had no qualms about killing that monster: exterminating the despot would be her catharsis. What bothered her was more fundamental. To do it, she would have to give the dictator "milk over coffee." Noriega had invited her to another late dinner. If he didn't agree to surrender himself, one of them would die before the next dawn.

Jaime thought of the blond hairpiece perched on a wig stand in her room. The coiffure had given her an alter ego, another personality that allowed her to act without shame. She could do whatever it took to get a job done. Yet without the wig, she felt humiliated and ached with contrition for pain she knew she caused Lee to suffer.

With eyes closed under burning sun, something else also raced through her mind. As a well-educated American, Jaime understood she should pass it off as folly. She couldn't, though. Where she had been raised as a girl, those kinds of feelings were embraced on a more spiritual level. Jaime had to accept what she knew to be true. Life stirred in her belly. She had so quickly sensed it since Tulum. There would be no physical signs, for a while, but she was carrying Lee's baby.

Frankie strolled through the heart of Ciudad de Panama. The province was home to the country's major municipality and capital, Panama City. A large portion of the canal zone ran through it. He looked like any tourist soaking in the charm of a lovely square where French military buildings once stood. All that remained of them was a dungeon that had confined prisoners. Nearby, the architecture of the French embassy bespoke an old-world ambience. For him, the embassy building was like a lighthouse with a beacon that welcomed ships from troubled seas into the safety of a calm harbor. It called to him.

*Perhaps*, he thought, *France is the place.*

Quiet country cottages in the south of France had once caught his eye. Perhaps that was somewhere far, somewhere not here. If all went well, he and Carmella would be on their way by midnight.

He turned to find statuary preening before him. An obelisk topped by a proud French cockerel had been erected in the heart of the square to honor French workers who had contributed to digging the canal. It lamented the many dead—those who had died of tropical disease and construction mishaps—in a way that made him think of those who would die so soon.

Martin's agent was waiting. He imagined her, anxious for the poison to arrive, poison he held in his pocket. Frankie No Throat was delivering it to one of Batista's men. They would transport it to Noriega's compound.

The mob had promised to cooperate in the operation. They expected the United States government to discontinue certain investigations into their activities. They also expected favorable treatment for their boys in some upcoming criminal trials. His family expected a lot for seeing that Martin's agent had venom when she needed it. Frankie was their delivery man. Familiar with the country from his money-laundering jaunts, he was their natural choice. He would see that the government operative had ingredients to mix a Borgia cocktail for Manuel Noriega.

The Feds would try to extract their agent. How she would get out of the country was not Frankie's concern, nor was Lee's plight. He knew Lee had kept his end of the bargain. The Philadelphia mob had received his Kelly files. Finally, they had destroyed all the evidence that implicated him in the deaths. Frankie was grateful but his days as a guardian angel were over . . . and he was consumed by critical undertakings.

First, he had to deliver the poison to Batista's man. Only after it reached Noriega's compound could he flee. Only then, could Frankie seek safe haven at a U.S. military installation. And, he would have to get there before Batista learned what happened to the money.

*I'm scamming Batista*, Frankie reflected, *scamming him good.*

The cash that was supposed to be wired into Batista's coded bank account in the Cayman Islands wouldn't be delivered. Frankie had paid off a bank officer to make a "mistake" in the wire. The funds would appear to transfer into Batista's secret account. Instead, a second wire transaction would send the money to Frankie's own account in Switzerland.

Batista probably wouldn't learn of the wiring error for twenty-four hours. That was Frankie's "float time" to flee the country. When the bank alerted Batista, he would hunt for Frankie with unabated enmity. The soft-spoken man, who was an Indian himself, would come for

Frankie's scalp with all the forces he could muster. Getting out of Panama alive with Batista's cash was a gamble Frankie willingly undertook. The three-million dollars was his retirement fund. He had even arranged for Carmella to meet him in the canal zone so she could disappear with him.

Frankie ducked into a restaurant that was nestled on the square. Under the vaulted ceiling at Casco Viejo, he placed the poison vial on his dining table and arranged a napkin atop it. He waited for Batista's man while sampling fine French luncheon cuisine. A savory appetizer of *ensalada de camarones*, an exquisite shrimp salad, preceded a main dish of a local delicacy. Spaghetti and meatballs, it wasn't. Still, it was excellent dining. Frankie appreciated good food and wanted the best, knowing the slightest flaw in his scheming would make the meal his last.

His waiter approached. The man was a *mestizo* like Noriega. They were a mixed breed of Black, Indian, and Spanish blood, a little this and little that—all little. They were tiny, dark people, who for generations had found themselves cast at the lower stations of Panamanian society. He spoke with eyes low.

"Is everything to your liking, Sir?"

"The conch," Frankie complained, "is a little salty."

"We make our *conchas nego a la provencial* from a highly seasoned recipe."

Their eyes met, aware that the scripted conversation confirmed they had found each other.

"I've soiled my napkin," Frankie said, "Please take it and bring me another."

He had just delivered the vial close as he would ever near Noriega. When Batista received the false confirmation of a cash transfer, his people would place it in the American agent's cosmetic kit.

Frankie considered the turmoil that was about to break loose: a nation in tumult no matter the outcome. With Noriega dead or alive all-knowing participants would be scampering for cover. He weighed the dangers, calculating risks all over. The odds weren't comforting, but a streak was. Lucky most of his life, he just needed to stretch that run a few more hours. Frankie No Throat was rolling dice for the biggest stakes of his life. He had always been a clever gambler, but bettors know one thing for certain and the thought struck him hard.

*You can't roll sevens and elevens forever.*

Lee looked to Noriega for a response. He had outlined his plan and they sat in silence. It seemed like he had a better chance of obtaining a reaction from the fisheye that had stared lifelessly from the bouillabaisse. Suddenly, the tyrant erupted.

"That's your fucking plan for me!"

Noriega jumped from his chair and fell forward on his face, having leaped so fast that he'd forgotten how far his feet had been from the ground. Lying face down on the carpet, his fists tightly clenched, he smashed his right hand hard against the floor. He did the same with his left, then pounded one after the other like a weepy child in a tantrum. The door sprung open. Three guards rushed into the room with their guns drawn.

"Get out!" Noriega screamed to them.

Blood vessels surfaced at his temples. Facial flesh vibrated. Loud and rapid breaths wheezed through his tightly clenched teeth. In his fury he'd forgotten to speak in his native tongue. Troops looked at each other uncertainly.

"*Largade de aqoui!*" he repeated.

They fled hurriedly.

Lee cleared his throat and tried again.

"Carefully consider what I've said. The United States is preparing for a military incursion that will overwhelm your forces. I can cut you a plea bargain, now, that you'll never negotiate if American troops lock and load. I can swing three to five years tops, maybe do better, possibly avoid jail altogether, if you resign from political office and provide meaningful assistance that dismantles the operations running drugs through the canal. I have already spoken to cautiously receptive officials, who can help put this into play for us."

"Whom you have not identified."

"My assets remain my own, Sir. That is my value to you. That and my knack for tipping the American scale of justice in favor of my clients . . . as your people have already vouched."

Lee peered around the room and considered the opulence at the estate.

"This shouldn't be a hardship for a man of your means. They'll seek substantial fines, restitution, and forfeiture of property, which we will resist. Ultimately, you'll grant major concessions, but you'll remain a wealthy man."

Lee had relied upon a more-or-less direct and honest approach. He could have lied, telling Noriega they could simply buy American justice a blind eye, but Noriega already knew that was impossible. Instead, Lee relied upon a nearer variety of truth, albeit embellished to suit his purpose.

Noriega rose. He walked around the room, settling in one chair, then rising to find another more to his satisfaction. The man, who lived under so many roofs, looked ill at ease in any one spot. Finally finding cushioning of his liking, his body faced away from Lee, while his neck craned back around. His words came slowly, as if chosen with marked deliberation.

"I'll . . . lose . . . my . . . power. You fool! Don't you understand. I am not relinquishing control over my Nation!"

As he raved, his neck muscles forged seams that drew tight, compelling him at last to turn his body as well.

"My men will escort you to your room. If I must battle the United States, *Senor* Gunther, you and your lady friend shall be the first casualties. Get out of my sight."

Noriega climbed back into the oversized chair. His legs began to swing once again, first briskly then more slowly until they settled still beneath him, feet not reaching the floor. Finally, he closed his eyes, and returned to the trance-like state in which Lee had first seen him.

Lee realized, too late, that the dictator had wandered so far from reality that he would never accept any realistic appraisal of his predicament. Still searching for an elusive miracle, Noriega had made it clear that he would not voluntarily appear in the United States to face criminal charges. Instead, he would wage a pointless war.

Above the dictator hung the portrait of another monster who had never surrendered. Lee wondered if Noriega would follow the example of the Nazi leader, who had committed suicide inside a surrounded bunker to avoid capture in the waning days of World War II.

Lee surveyed the strange chamber one last time. Uneasy in the morbid shrine, which was dedicated to monstrous brutality, he left to find Jaime and a fast way out of Panama. As he walked into the foyer, four of Noriega's armed troops met him.

"I'm looking for *Señorita* Calero," Lee offered in a voice generated without its usual strength. Uncertain of the soldiers' purpose and fearful of their response, he silently cussed his inability to vociferate.

*I've lost my damned courtroom voice,* he thought, *and my swagger.*

Wordlessly, they escorted Lee back to his suite and locked him inside. Through the closed door, he heard an officer bark orders in Spanish that he easily followed. Guards stationed outside the door were told what to do if the American should enter the hallway.

"*Tirar*," Lee heard.

Then he picked up something else. The command had been gruff. If Lee walked into the hall again, the guards would shoot to kill.

# Chapter Twenty-One

# Potent Cocktails

JAIME SAT AT HER MAKEUP COUNTER, preparing for a date with a dictator. All too soon, they would pick up where they had left off and she wouldn't be able to resist the man's advances. Jaime knew what comes on his date plate.

As a young cadet at the Chorrillos Military School, Noriega's CIA file revealed, he had beaten a prostitute who refused him when he couldn't afford her price. The incident was serious enough that the school readied to expel him. But, working even then for the CIA, his handler was alerted, and reviewed the incident with an Agency supervisor.

"Pineapple Face," the senior man said as he paged through the cadet's file. That's what they call him?"

"Well, the handler mused, as a child his siblings called him *Cabecita*, meaning Little Head, in deference to a tiny noggin. As he matured, acne permanently scarred him. Kids, being pretty much the same everywhere, bestowed the new moniker. Since he became a cadet, few dare use it in his presence."

"For God's sake, what use do we have for an operative in a military academy?"

"Oh, no current value. It's the promise of tomorrows. Noriega has everything we want in a young recruit."

"Meaning?"

"He's intelligent, willing to work cheap, and lacks morality."

"All right, write up the incident for his file and see that the academy keeps him."

Later, when Noriega was a young military officer, another prostitute—not knowing who he was—spotted something frightening. Claiming he had "the eyes of a killer," she couldn't bring herself to bed him. Noriega beat her much more savagely. Again, his CIA handler memorialized the incident with a file notation, making it apparent that inflicting pain provided their operative gratification akin to sexual fulfillment.

Light raps on the door drew Jaime's attention. Ricki entered without waiting for her to answer.

"The President rejected Mr. Gunther's advice," he said.

Jaime's eyes slunk. She knew what she had to do.

"Your dinner date is set for the President's bedroom suite at midnight," Ricki reminded.

With a skittish grin, he pointed to the blond wig. "You're to wear that thing."

She knew how the dictator wanted her.

"And I suggest you don't try any tricks," Ricki blithered. "I heard about what happened last night. Telling a man, '*Su pene. Esto es demasiade grande!*' Really, Dearie, he's not that big and you won't get away with that twice." Ricki winked and added, "This will be a special night, won't it?"

Jaime poured herself a glass of wine from a bottle on her makeup counter. Then, she looked at the small purse beside her. When she had returned to her room from the pool, she had found the vial of poison in it. At midnight she would lace Noriega's drink and wait for Ricki to lead her to Martin's extraction team. Jaime would do it if she could just bring herself to put on that damned wig one more time.

"Yes," she agreed. "Tonight will be very special."

Frankie No Throat loaded his pistol. He would carry a .22 caliber handgun. The small weapon was like an old friend, a pal that had seen a lot of action with him. Concealing his tiny buddy was easy even if it didn't pack a heavy wallop. He placed extra ammunition in his pocket and faced a mirror in the living room of his hotel suite. The compact revolver tucked nicely into his belt, concealed from view by his shirt flaps.

"Dressed for success," he told himself.

"Drink this," Carmella called, as she walked into the room carrying a large pitcher and a glass.

Frankie stared suspiciously. "What's in it?"

"Sweet Seco Herrerano rum. It's made from sugar cane. Drink it all."

Frankie took the pitcher. The weight surprised him. Often, he forgot how strong she was. The well-toned muscles on her wiry arms had gentle curves. He looked at the glass, then shrugged his shoulders and tilted back the entire pitcher like it was a big beer mug. The brew was thick and pungent. Frankie gulped, then wiped his lips with the back of his hand.

"There's something stronger than rum in this," he said. "Man, this packs a buzz."

"Drink it all, Frankie."

He raised the pitcher high. The concoction froze his nostrils and his brain. Setting the pitcher down, he leaned against a table to steady himself, and collected his thoughts. They had a lot of ground to cover before he hit the streets.

"We'll leave our belongings, here in the hotel," he began. "Noriega's people watch the lobby and we don't want to attract their attention. I'll leave first. There're still some things I *gotta* do. Meet me at the Mira Flores locks inside the canal zone at midnight. You'll be safe, there, if I run a little late."

He looked into her eyes to make certain she understood. Fire danced in them in a way he'd never seen. He had to be certain she could make it. Leaving with Carmella had become the focal point of a life that had no other purpose.

"Are you sure," he pressed, "that you can pass the zone checkpoints to enter after curfew?"

"I'll use my cousin's ID card and say I'm a housekeeper who's been called back to work on an emergency."

Frankie nodded.

"The U.S. Army South Headquarters is close to the locks," he said. "They're expecting me. I can get you in and we'll be safe. The FBI made arrangements with my family to place me on a military flight to Patrick Air Force Base in Florida tonight. We'll take that flight together. Tomorrow night, we'll fly from Miami to a place I know."

The fire in Carmella's eyes burned brighter. "Somewhere not here," she said.

"Somewhere far," he agreed, "with money that's already in my Swiss bank account. We have to disappear fast. Soon as Batista learns he's been ripped, he'll look for me."

"This man, the one called Batista, is feared by my people. He comes from tribes in remote northwestern regions of our country. Like many with Indian blood, he joined the PDF hoping to escape poverty on the reservations. Some like Batista cling to old beliefs. They have ways that are cruel. Be careful, my Frankie. Batista is dangerous."

Frankie swigged again from the pitcher as Carmella helped him tilt it back.

"Blood lust," she whispered, "is at the center of his soul. Drink, my Frankie. Drink for the strength you'll need tonight."

Jaime set down her wine glass. A knock on the door told her time had come. The blond wig weighed heavily on her head. She moved uneasily. A brawny houseman, scrubbed and sterile in his white jacket and black pants, met her at the door. Without expression he called her along with the wave of a hand, and Jaime took her first step toward a dinner served by fate.

Suddenly, she stopped. My God, she thought. She had almost forgotten it—the vial of poison in her purse on the makeup counter. She ran back for it, the houseman following close behind. Suspicion was stenciled across his face as she grabbed it.

"*Lapiz m de labios*," she gushed. "I'll need my lipstick and—"

The big man took the bag from her and peered inside. One at a time, he pulled out each item, holding them up to the light of a makeup lamp. Carefully, he examined each, starting with a lipstick. The houseman lifted off the cap and twisted the glossy-red stick all the way out.

"*Rojo vivo*," she said, indicating that Noriega preferred lips bright red.

The houseman set it down and pulled out a small hairbrush. He ran his fingers across the bristles and put it down when he saw she couldn't use it as a weapon. Then, he looked at the small vial of liquid in an ornate container. He held it up to the light, studied it, and turned to her.

"Perfume," she said.

The houseman accused her of lying with a glance casting disbelief. Trained to be distrustful, as a vigilant guardian of his master, the man opened the container and sniffed. He pinched his nostrils, letting her know he didn't like what he smelled, and set it on the dresser. He put the lipstick and hairbrush back in her purse, but the perfume was to stay in her room. The houseman returned the purse to her and pointed to the door. Jaime left under his watchful eye without the perfume container. As the servant turned and locked the door, Jaime realized she couldn't return on her own. Then, the houseman led her to Noriega's chambers.

They entered his suite where Jaime anxiously surveyed a table set for two in the living room. Apparently, the dictator intended to gorge himself before picking up where they had left off. She envisioned a distended naked belly on the short, pocked-faced man, and wondered how she could go through with it. A glass of champagne beckoned at the table. She sat and sipped under the gaze of a frozen-faced waiter, another zombie, who knew well as she, what was slated for the last course.

Bumping through the night, Frankie No Throat traveled in the rear of a taxicab. Tired shock absorbers rammed his bottom into the seat as the old cab bustled north on Avenida Gaillard toward the locks. The night was warm, moist, and without a breeze. Mosquitoes, so abundant in Central America, swarmed like armies of bloodsuckers. The air conditioner in the old car gave out and Frankie felt sticky night air blow through open windows as he slapped buzzing pests. He looked out longingly as they approached the U.S. military base. He would be home free if he had his driver drop him off, but Frankie wouldn't leave Panama without Carmella. Memories of her swaying on the tabletop sharpened his resolve. He read the sign posted at the front gate: "U.S. Army Headquarters South," and called to his driver. "After we pick up my friend at the locks, we'll come back here."

"Have you ever *zeen* the canal locks, *Senor?*" The driver asked in heavily accented English.

"Yeah, I've seen 'em," Frankie groaned in the heat.

"It's an amazing sight," his driver offered.

Locks eased ships through the canal. Because water levels along the eighty-kilometer canal varied with the tides, engineers had designed a series of three locks. Ships entered them, towed into position by small trains called *mulas* or mules. Gates to the locks closed behind the ships. Water then filled or emptied the lock to raise or lower the ship to the water height on the other side. On average it took a ship twenty-four hours to pass through the canal. Half that time was usually spent just waiting to enter.

By day, tourists converged on the Miraflores locks. A viewing area provided an unobstructed view of canal operations. They listened to commentaries announced over loudspeakers on the passing of each ship. In English and Spanish, they heard about the vessels, their ports of origin, destinations, and cargos. At night the speakers were silent, but Frankie wasn't going as a tourist.

He spotted the small white lighthouse that served as a landmark along the way. A sign pointed the direction to the locks. Nearly there, his heart raced for her. At the zone guard gates, Frankie's ID quickly passed them through. They pulled up to the deserted tourist area and Frankie directed the driver to stop. As his eyes scoured for Carmella, his driver picked up the handset to the taxi CB radio and put it to his lips.

"What do you think you're doing, *Amigo?*" Frankie curtly said.

"Calling in my location to the dee-spatcher so I can get another fare after I drop you off, *Senor.*"

Frankie pulled out his small pistol and raised it to the driver's head. He cocked the trigger and issued a warning he wouldn't repeat.

"Put that motherfucker down or I'll blast your eyeballs out of your fuckin' head."

The driver dropped his handset fast with hands shaking. Frankie kept half an eye on him as an American war vessel being pulled through the locks by two mules diverted his attention. The electric locomotives guided and stabilized the ship they tugged with thick steel cables. Although a smaller class of aircraft carrier, the U.S.S. Tarawa dwarfed the trains that tugged along its side. Frankie jumped out of the car to watch. He waved his handgun at the driver, so he'd do the same. After the vessel was all the way into the locks, gates would close behind it. Then water—millions of liters of it—would pump into the locks.

Frankie noticed a contingent of U.S. Marines on the carrier deck. They stood on the near side of the ship beside a helicopter, looking ready for a practice mission. Ever since Noriega had become so thorny a problem, United States forces had entered a state of near readiness. Practice operations and maneuvers intensified in a cat-and-mouse game with the Panamanian dictator. U.S. armed forces intended to make their Panamanian counterparts nervous as much as anything else. Even civilians were growing accustomed to all the U.S. troop activity around the canal zone.

His driver called, "Is that who you're waiting for, *Senor?"*

Frankie turned and saw Carmella. A contingent of six canal zone police escorted her. Their uniforms made them look like cavalry coming to his rescue.

"I've never been so grateful to see cops," he said.

Canal police enforced U.S. laws in special American courts. Once, canal police had all been American citizens, but the strong presence of a foreign force had offended the citizenry. Natives demanded and received Panamanians on the unit as a concession in the canal treaty.

Frankie was glad to see them with Carmella. They had safely escorted her through the zone. Maybe he could even talk them into accompanying him and Carmella the short distance back to the U.S. army base. He waved to her, but she didn't wave back. Just that suddenly a thought flashed.

*These guys aren't canal zone police!*

He stared harder and saw Batista walking close behind Carmella, probably with a gun trained on her back, as his men shoved her along. Frankie reached for his pistol under his untucked shirt. As he went for it, the cab driver's accented words punctuated his intent.

"Put *zat* motherfucker down or I'll blast *yer* eyeballs outta your *fuckeen* head."

Frankie spun around. The driver, smirking from ear to ear, pointed a pistol at Frankie's face.

Another of Batista's men, he realized too late.

Frankie had laid everything on the table for the biggest gamble of his life, tossed the dice, and saw them land. He knew what he had done.

"I rolled fuckin' craps."

Jaime and her pock-faced dinner partner sat under the watchful gaze of a waiter who anticipated their every need. He poured water and wine when either diner sipped thrice from a glass. He brought fresh utensils after every course. They finished their meal with coffee laced with Tia Maria. Jaime watched opportunity disappear with each sip Noriega drew. She peered into twin pin eyes that reflected torment and death brought by the man's hand, then turned away. Something in those dark pools wasn't human and she didn't have strength to face it. Her focus darted downward as she recited her lines.

"Let's go to the bedroom."

The bitter taste of those words sickened her.

"Bring a fresh bottle of champagne with glasses. Tonight, I want to accept all of your manhood."

She couldn't look at him. Jaime knew what reaction she evoked from the man who preferred milk over coffee. She reached for her purse.

Noriega's hand grabbed hers as she went for it.

"Let me see what's in there," he said with apprehension resounding in suspicious tones.

"Just a hairbrush and lipstick," she said. The tip of her tongue caressed her lips invitingly. "I'll freshen for you."

He took the bag and peered inside.

Those eyes, she realized, nothing passes them undetected.

Noriega lifted his head. The purse was still in his hands. His eyes widened.

*Milk over coffee*, she thought, *milk over coffee.*

She repeated the phrase in her mind like a mantra, afraid the monster would somehow find the key to her psyche and spot the vengeance in her heart.

Jaime ran her fingers through long blond hair, then lowered her hands to playfully tug at her golden necklace. Bright-red fingernail tips contrasted atop milky-white flesh. Noriega's lips parted, exposing yellow teeth ready to nibble on her. He returned the purse and pointed to the powder room outside the master bedroom.

She rose awkwardly under the dictator's intense gaze, her heart pounding wildly. She staggered with her first step from the table and the waiter moved toward her, until she waved him off.

"Too much wine," she said.

Noriega didn't flinch. His eyes sexually penetrated her with every step she took.

*Why has all my strength left me?* Jaime asked herself.

The waiter grabbed her arm. As he reached for her purse, she pulled away fast, knowing she had to regain composure.

"I'm alright," she slurred. "*Gracias*."

She entered the bathroom and closed the door. Looking at herself in the mirror, she was aware—no matter what happened—that would be last time she would ever see herself under the wig. She pinched her cheeks.

"I've grown so pale," she whispered. "What did they put in my food?"

Jaime was entering a dreamlike state. She had to act fast. She opened the lipstick, redid her lips, then twisted the bottom of its cylindrical case, twice around clockwise.

*Even the slightest touch there, now*, she reflected, *will dispense poison. The bastards didn't find it.*

She returned it to her purse and walked toward the bed chamber where she would meet Noriega to execute her orders. She entered the room slowly and leaned on a wall for support. Whatever had peppered her food kicked hard. A feeling of euphoria filled her, as if they had intended to reduce her inhibitions rather than render her unconscious.

Noriega waited beside a mahogany chiffonier with a mirrored top, where a servant had placed a bottle of champagne in an ice bucket beside flute glassware. She joined him to set down her purse and watch as he filled one champagne glass, then another. She avoided eye contact with him and staggered ever so slightly under his watchful gaze. When she regained her balance, he poured a third glass of champagne. Jaime puzzled until she looked toward the bed.

There, clad only in scanty pink-pastel panties with white lace fringe, Ricki waited. His pearly-white teeth gleamed through lips painted red as hers.

"I told you when the time came, I'd be ready," he called to her.

"N-no," she stuttered. "This can't be what you meant."

Noriega laughed as questions rattled her brain. *Did I misunderstand Ricki at the pool?*

She watched Noriega remove his dinner jacket and place it over his arm.

*Did Ricki mean he'd extract me or isn't he Martin's man after all?*

Noriega crossed the room to drape his coat over a boudoir chair, all the while keeping eyes trained on her. She waited for a better moment to pull the lipstick tube from her purse.

Opening his belt, Noriega's smile widened in bemused anticipation.

As her knees weakened, Jaime fought to reinforce her resolve. She focused on what the success of her mission meant: sparing lives of American servicemen and women by obviating the need for an incursion . . . and sparing further misery to the Panamanian populace.

Ricki smiled impishly and patted the bed in a welcoming gesture, a movement that evoked Noriega's hideous guffaw.

Her deceased brother's face shot to mind while her godfather's words, spoken years earlier, echoed: she fought for strength to face her fears.

Yet, through the drug-induced fog, Jaime realized only one thing was certain.

*It's time for me to join them.*

*Miraflores Locks of the Panama Canal*

# Chapter Twenty-Two

# A Lesson for the Lawyer

UNSETTLED IN BED, EYES OPENED UPWARD IN darkness, Lee knew he wouldn't sleep that long night. Too many thoughts skittered through his mind: *What happened to Jaime? Where's Frankie when I need my old pal so badly? What's Noriega have in mind for an encore?*

Thumps on the entrance door to the suite interrupted a cognitive process that was spinning wheels but going nowhere. Louder they came, as if announcing the presence of a messenger with news so dispiriting it could arrive no other way.

Lee turned on a night table light, rose, and headed into the suite living room. Before he could reach the door, it opened, and a diminutive officer entered. Wearing a sharply creased uniform, the man strode confidently.

Whoever he was, he was accustomed to command, delivering words in swift staccato as if he were ordering a soldier to charge.

"Report to the dining room at noon," he said.

"Where is Miz Calero?" Lee called back.

The officer walked to a mirror, checked his reflection to straighten his necktie, then licked his fingers.

Lee reached for the same strength of voice he found whenever he barked "objection" in courtrooms.

"Where's Miz Calero?" he bellowed.

Moistened fingertips slicked down the man's eyebrows. Lee didn't know why but the man chilled him. Then, executing an about face as if in close order drill, the officer turned and departed. Lee heard the door lock from outside and listened to footsteps grow fainter.

Frankie No Throat stood rigidly next to the pistol wielding cab driver. Batista and his men approached. Dressed in canal police uniforms, no one had stopped them from moving freely through the canal zone with Carmella in custody. Frankie peered over his shoulder toward the U.S. aircraft carrier inside the locks. He wondered if he could somehow jump aboard for safety.

"Make a run for that ship, and you know what we'll do," Batista said, pointing to Carmella. "You know how we can treat a woman."

Frankie had heard stories. He could do nothing for fear of what would happen to her.

"Let the woman go," Frankie said.

"Oh, we will," Batista replied, "after she sees what happens to you."

Batista came closer. His hand raced from his back pocket and a silver streak flashed as he ushered the tip of a long knife to Frankie's nose, then poked its sharp point up a nostril.

"Suppose we trim this beak," Batista taunted.

Frankie fought the instinct to flinch.

Batista pulled back the blade and laid its cutting edge on Frankie's cheek. Blood surfaced as Batista pushed, directing Frankie's head to face Carmella.

"Look at your woman," he said.

Batista's men flanked Carmella, gripping her arms tightly. One held her head from behind, forcing the small woman to watch what they were doing to her man. More men grabbed Frankie's arms, and walked him to the edge of the canal. The lock gates were closed for water that pumped inside to lift the warship.

Frankie's physical sensations numbed, while his brain spun from the potent cocktail Carmella had served. He recalled what he'd been, and where life had taken him.

*Once upon a time*, he thought, *there was so much time to live.*

Memories raced as he reflected upon all he had done, while honoring vows sworn to his crime family so long ago. Frankie recalled the day he had whacked Jackie "Toes" Tosalero. A stray bullet killed Lee's father and he vowed to look after the kid. His mind stayed there until a veritable realization escaped his lips.

"When I stopped being a guardian angel, my luck ran out."

Batista looked him over, and spurted, "What are you talking about?"

Grace Kelly and her councilman brother raced forefront in Frankie's remembrances. Ironically, murdering the princess never brought the mob what it wanted. The crime families from Nice and Philadelphia never scored a foothold in the Monte Carlo casino. Instead, her demise had strengthened Prince Rainier's resolve. The nobleman confronted the mob as a tribute to the woman he—as well as his countrymen and countrywomen—cherished.

"All this started with a scam that floundered," muttered Frankie.

Batista grabbed a handful of Frankie's wavy hair and stared into his eyes.

"You're on something strong," he said in tones intense as the soft-spoken man ever uttered, "but this will rouse you. Look at me, *malditos tus ojos!"*

Frankie peered through insentient eyes.

"You have one chance to save yourself. My bank told me there was a 'mistake' posting your funds to my account. Know what I think? I think you scammed me, *Amigo*. I'm only going to ask you once. Where's my money? Answer!"

Frankie turned to the woman he loved, knowing any answer he furnished would end their discourse the same way. Through a violet mist that colored the world into which he slipped, he envisioned every atom of Carmella's flawless form.

She swayed to the call of a primal rhythm, the dark hollows of her thighs beckoning, the fragrant essence of her womanhood intoxicating him with lust. His mind burned with the sensation of penetration, then with the moist grip of tender folds massaging. Eager thrusts scorched as intemperate cries erupted from her heart, soul, and every fiber of her being, all in rhapsodic harmony with his own. For them alone, passion raced from the depths of Hades to the peaks of paradise. They were sacred unto each other. Then, in stillness, he dwelled deep within her, both drained of breath. They found Eden, a place somewhere far, somewhere not here.

"Bank this, Frankie No Throat," Batista barked.

The knife dug deep into Frankie's belly. He didn't flinch. Terror didn't seize his last earthly moments. Entranced in the peaceful realm, where Carmella had taken him, he cradled her under the purple dawn of a new day. Their lips met to ignite a vermillion cloudburst.

The knife gouged again. It scooped to carve a wider and deeper cavity.

Frankie felt no pain; he felt only the electric charge from Carmella's kiss as her lips swallowed his, forevermore.

Batista clenched something in his bloody fist. He held it to Frankie's face, but the loyal mob soldier never saw it. Frankie drifted peacefully to sleep.

Batista's men pulled cinder blocks from the cab, strapped them to Frankie's waist belt, and tossed him into the canal. The lockage continued to fill. Water, fifty-five million gallons, surged as Frankie No Throat sunk out of sight.

Jaime gazed at the two men, who stared at her so luridly. As Ricki patted the mattress, still beckoning, her senses grew more detached.

*Fight the drugging*, she told herself.

With Noriega engaged fully disrobing, Jaime was ready to make her move.

*Time*, she told herself, *to freshen my lips*.

She pulled lipstick from her purse and applied a fresh coat in front of the chiffonier mirror, then passed the tube bottom over the filled champagne glasses while releasing lethal poison. In her fog, she was unsure if she'd laced one or two or perhaps all the flutes.

Ever so slowly, Jaime carried the three glasses to the bed. She handed Ricki one then noticed for the first time how much his hairless body mimicked a woman's physique: shoulders rounded and soft form lacking muscular definition. She handed Noriega the glass she had earmarked for him. As suspected, his belly protruded with extra girth from a meal so glutinously devoured.

What shall we drink to?" she rang out.

"To what is about to come," Ricki coyly replied.

The dictator's hand met her backside and stroked as Jaime raised her glass. She laughed nervously, trying to conceal angst that was nearing transparency.

"To what is about to come," she said.

"To what is about to come," repeated men so ready to ravish her.

Ricki tilted his flute back, drinking fast and hard.

Jaime saw Noriega was waiting for her to drink. She hesitated, uncertain if the glass she held was free of poison. Then, Noriega raised his own glass and brought it toward her as if saying: "I'll drink only after you swallow."

*Now*, she told herself. *Do it.*

She swallowed as quickly as Ricki had gulped, realizing if she had screwed up by giving herself poison, she could count on dying fast rather than slow. Champagne bubbles tickled her throat. Jaime's pulse raced as she waited for any reaction to materialize.

Noriega looked into her eyes as he at last allowed his own glass to touch his lips.

*Such vacant pupils*, she realized as she returned his gaze, *utterly inhumane.*

Suddenly, the dictator dropped his flute glass.

*My God, why?* Jaime wondered.

Her query was instantly answered as Ricki convulsed spasmodically on the bed. Glossy lipstick accentuated the twisting corners of his lips as they curled with anguish.

Facial contortions creased the hollows of his cheeks. Short, loud breaths were followed by a long groan.

"*Biatch!*" he screamed at her. "The pain. . .."

Ricki rolled from side to side, both hands clutching his stomach as he regurgitated. White foam spewed across black silk sheets. His frame shook. In seconds, the spasms subsided, his bladder voided, and pungent gas emitted from his rectum. Then, Ricki was still.

Noriega studied Jaime, his jaw agape. Before she could speak, he screamed, his wails echoing for guards in the hallway.

Jaime fought the paralyzing grip of panic.

*What can I do?* She thought.

Jaime glanced at Ricki's motionless body. Martin's man was dead, and she would never find the extraction team on her own.

"No way out," she told herself, knowing they would torture her until her final breath was agonizingly drawn.

She didn't want to die like her *Compadre*. Jaime went for her lipstick. She'd kill herself. Better to perish like Ricki Herrera than meet death at the hands of Noriega's tormentors.

Her thoughts flashed to Lee. Just as Noriega's men had taught Doctor Spadafora a lesson, they would surely teach the lawyer one as well. She shuddered, knowing what they would do to him. Too late, Jaime realized, she loved him. Riddled with self-reproach, she posed her life's final question.

"How could I have not warned him?"

With Noriega's wails filling her ears Jaime hustled. She emptied the remaining poison into her champagne glass, while considering life that stirred in her womb—life that would have no chance to nurture. Then, she lifted the glass high and announced.

"To what is about to come."

As the crystal touched her lips, a fist bashed her skull. Champagne flew across the room and Jaime reeled to the floor. Above her, an officer stood in a crisply pressed uniform.

"Planning to leave us so soon?" said the same man, who had entered Lee's chamber.

Jaime massaged her cheekbone. Unable to stop her lower lip from trembling, she bit it. The face terrified her. She had seen the man's photograph in Bureau files. The Dark Angel had come to do his master's vile bidding.

She looked toward Noriega and struggled to speak, words coming faintly. "You're insane," she offered barely above a whisper.

Noriega calmed; his composure was restored by the presence of loyal troops. Dimples emerged on pockmarked cheeks as he mused aloud.

"It was an American author, Poe I believe, who wrote: 'The question is not answered yet, whether madness is or is not the loftiest intelligence'."

Carmella Ruiz stared into the canal. She had seen what they'd done to Frankie. The ancient ritual was well known to her people. Batista was also of Maya origin, and had extracted his revenge with blood lust. He'd killed Frankie in the way the Mayas had sacrificed victims to the Gods a thousand years ago—by extracting his innards while he was still alive.

Surely Batista had wanted to cut out her man's heart. Without time to sate the yearning, he'd cut into Frankie's soft belly with a circular motion that exposed his guts, then, ripped out a handful of intestines, like so many blood worms, and held them before his victim's eyes.

Carmella had seen Batista's startled reaction when Frankie showed no sign of fear or pain. Batista turned to her, his startled look conveying recognition of her as the voodoo witch that she was. She had given Frankie a potion to ease the suffering she apperceived would come to her man.

Batista and his men knew better than to harm her, so they left Carmella standing alone, when they vanished into the night. All their eyes spoke it: They knew she practiced sorcery. And, perhaps she had. No matter, for a true believer like herself. Black magic had strengthened the man for whom her very being was meant.

Carmella spied no sign of her Frankie No Throat in the water beneath her. Tired and mournful, she entered a self-induced trance. Spirits of her ancestors danced in her head until the sun rose. Only then, a single salty tear caressed her cheek. She could cry no more . . . no more at all.

*Just another day in Noriega's Panama,* she realized, *another day when more will die.*

# Chapter Twenty-Three

# The Party's Just Begun

AT NOONTIME, JAIME FOLLOWED A LARGE houseman from her bed chamber. That time she left the blond wig behind. The servant glided zombie-like through the mansion to the dining room, where she spotted Lee in the same chair he had taken on their first night there. Her heart raced to him, but she braked, uncertain of his feelings toward her. They hadn't seen each other since Noriega's men had dragged him unconscious from the dinner table. Jaime caught his eyes raising to hers and she turned away.

Unfamiliar emotions cast a thousand stones. Questions hit just as hard. Did he know what she had done and how far she'd been prepared to go? Struck by an overwhelming sense of shame and guilt—driving forces she had never known—words she never intended uttering escaped her lips.

"What do you see when you look at me now?"

Lee said nothing.

It was more than the bedroom activities that brought on her misgivings, she realized. The mission itself left her feeling . . ..

Jaime caught herself mid thought and studied Lee, who still said nothing.

*Sometimes there is so much to say that there is no way to say it*, she realized.

When he rose and lifted his arms for her, Jaime didn't hesitate to reach for his embrace.

"*Buen día, Senorita*," Rodolfo Angel called as he entered the room, "and good day, *Senor!*"

Lee and Jaime never touched. Commotion intervened as the room quickly filled with the Dark Angel's troops. Soldiers dressed in jungle fatigues, little men like Angel, perhaps ten of them, were armed as if prepared for a combat patrol. They carried M-16 rifles and handguns. Hand grenades clung to their duty belts. One toted a field radio.

Angel stood among their midst. First, he leered at her then at Lee. The glint in his eyes reminded Jaime of Noriega's infernal gaze. Her heart double pumped as a thought rushed to mind.

*Is this how they came for my brother and godfather?*

And, though she maintained a calm appearance, she could not keep more words from involuntarily passing: "God, help us."

"Time for a country ride," the Dark Angel declared. "Your host will not be saying *adios*. Business in the capital demands presidential attention. So, he's placed you in my charge."

Angel lifted his arms high, bizarrely welcoming them to the realm of his jaundiced imagination.

"Let me deliver you to a place I know," he said, "a place where flesh and bone are potters' clay for making tortured souls."

Disdain for his victims etched his deep-set eyes while scorn encrusted furrows lining down-turned lips. Casually, he pronounced, "Take them."

Angel's troops maneuvered like eager goblins. Dwarfish hands snapped handcuffs around their wrists. The cuffs pinched yet tiny hands squeezed them tighter. Slender fingers wrapped duct tape around their heads to cover their mouths. Ankle bracelets locked in place, joined by chains to restrain their gait.

"You won't need your belongings for our sojourn," the Dark Angel declared. "Ah, but you, my sweet darling," he crooned to Jaime, "will need something. This!"

Angel dangled the blond wig like a playful puppet to the delight of his men. They laughed as he held it above her head, then danced around her, holding the hairpiece in his arms as if it were his partner in a madman's tango.

"My men will video record you, My Darling, so the President may, at last, have you as he prefers. You'll give him 'milk over coffee'."

Angel commanded his troops: "*Abandonar!*"

Soldiers dragged Jaime and Lee outside, their leg chains rattling. Under fiery afternoon sun, swarming pockets of mosquitoes sucked blood. Troops shoved them toward a military truck with a canvas covered back. They opened the rear flap of the truck, then lifted Lee above their heads and tossed him inside, where they propped him on a wooden bench running along the truck's side. Next, they raised Jaime. Boisterous troops took liberties fondling her as they tossed Jaime on the bench beside Lee.

"Sitting together, my two lovebirds?"

Jaime turned to see the Dark Angel peering.

"Batista!" Angel called out. "Sit between them. Later, you'll help me make our love birds sing."

Batista climbed down from the cab of the truck, and jumped into the rear, where his eyes studied Jaime. She realized he was relishing contours of a body they would soon rearrange. Then, he turned to Lee, cooing in his soft voice.

"You don't look so *fuckeen* smart now, do you, *Abogado*?"

Jaime had studied files on Angel and Batista. The CIA had documented what they knew of all special officers in Noriega's Battalions of Dignity. Though his dossier was sketchy, it was clear that Batista had a reputation as a skillful tormentor. If Angel wanted Lee and Jaime to sing like lovebirds, Batista could harmonize their cries. She shuddered as the monster sat between her and Lee. As the engine started, Angel joined the driver in the cab and troops grabbed seats wherever they found them.

The truck lunged forward, causing all to sway back and forth. Jaime peered out the rear, where the canvas flap had been left open to circulate air, seeking her bearings. They passed the Panamanian Defense Force base, then turned onto another highway. She sensed they were traveling northwest into the barren countryside. Noriega's men had committed many atrocities in the less populated areas of the country, where no one would hear a scream or find a telltale carcass.

Northwestward were lands where the Guaymi lived. In the vast and sparsely inhabited region, the Guaymi Indians remained in semiautonomous communities, subject only to their tribal law, and living by their ancient traditions. While some engaged in rudimentary farming, most existed by hunting and fishing, using techniques mastered vast centuries ago by their ancestors. There were many places where only the Guaymi roamed and no one would find their bodies.

As the day grew on, Jaime found herself struggling to think. She felt the road grow bumpier as the truck traversed over unevenly paved surfaces of rural highways. Before long, she surmised, they'd bounce over roadways made of dirt.

With every kilometer the roadway roughened, delivering Batista nearer home. Many of his tribe had never left those sacred reaches. His mother was pure Guaymi while his father was of mixed blood. In Central America, where so many bloods intermix, ethnicity is often determined by language spoken and customs practiced, rather than by pure racial lineage. Batista regarded himself as Guaymi and cherished customs of the people he had forsaken. He'd given up much to live in the outside world.

Their truck stopped at a check point manned by PDF guardsmen. Batista knew they would be fast on their way, especially fast when the guards saw who was sitting in the cab. The Dark Angel had an unholy spirit that struck fear into the hearts of foes and friends alike.

As they moved on again, Batista tilted his head back, tired from the long night in the canal zone. While resting, he felt a meager sense of pacification as they rolled from the world under Noriega's rule. He had left his home to experience the outside world, joining the military under Noriega's wing. And, Batista served his master well. He had risen through the ranks and had even managed to stow away some money, but not the fortune he'd tried clipping from the mob's man.

After this detail was executed, Batista wouldn't return to the outside world. He was rejoining his tribe. Perhaps in time he would tire again of the simple life but for the moment, his only thoughts were of finishing his last detail and finding a measure of harmony with his indigenous people.

Batista knew what President Noriega intended for the lovebirds beside him. It required special skills and tolerances. The woman and man were to learn a lesson as others before them had. The President was said to be a believer in voodoo, and had special victims, like them beheaded. The superstitious believe a victim can't come back to haunt their killer if the head is severed from the body.

He wondered if there was merit to that notion. Some claimed a recurring dream haunted President Noriega. In it, a headless torso chased him, and he was unable to escape. Loose lipped servants claimed that Noriega often woke in a deep sweat, screaming at what was after him—the torso of his strongest enemy, Hugo Spadafora. Those, who knew, referred that nightmare as "the doctor's revenge."

Batista wasn't well-versed in those notions, nor was he a dabbler in voodoo. He was a disciple of Nacom, the ancient Mayan god known as the executioner. Batista inflicted suffering to receive the grace of his god, just as the Maya had tortured and killed sacrificial victims centuries earlier. Soon he would offer more blood. Agonizing cries would reach the domains of all the gods of the upper and lower worlds.

Batista recognized the hills as their truck neared the destination he had chosen. So soon lifeblood would spill again. The sun was growing short. After it set, he'd make his sacrificial offering.

Batista chanted softly as a prelude to dark tributes he would tender to his god. Some of the battle-dressed troops, also of Indian descent, joined, chanting in their native tongue.

Lee saw their hands had turned blue. The bastards intentionally fixed the handcuffs too tight to cut blood circulation. He wondered how Jaime was holding up to it. His fingers throbbed. He held the handcuffs up to Batista and gestured with his head, thinking his former client might loosen the cuffs for old times sake. Batista simply offered his soft and hollow laugh.

After dark, the truck decelerated as they left paved roadway and traversed over rough outback. Lee sensed they were approaching their destination. Batista and the others stopped humming and the troops gathered up as if readying for disembarkation. In dark overgrowths of the Panamanian countryside, he and Jaime would s learn what Noriega had in mind for them.

Then, they stopped.

"*Sal del camión!*" Batista intoned with a voice that barely rose above a hush, nonetheless, ordering troops out. Men, who had been humming with Batista, were last to rise. One snatched Jaime and another grasped Lee, forcing them off the back of the vehicle.

Lee's legs were unsteady from the long ride, and slow to move with the weight of chains. His bad knee had swelled, and he was careful with each footstep. A jab from the butt of an M-16 hastened his pace. They marched through narrow trails and dense vegetation. Despite the glow of a near full moon, Lee stumbled in the dark thickets and struck his swollen knee. He groaned through the gag. A soldier raised his rifle butt to nudge him to his feet and Lee hobbled along.

At last, they reached a clearing on a hilltop that surrounded a simple one-room adobe hut. Lee and Jaime were shoved inside. The walls were made of clay, the roof of woven grass. There was no door, just an opening for the entrance and two circular holes in the clay serving as windows. Far from anything so civilized as electricity, troops lit kerosene lanterns, hanging them above a table centered on the dirt floor.

Lee watched Angel place three items on the tabletop: the blond wig, a video camcorder, and a surgery kit. Opening the surgical instrument case with care, Angel looked like a physician about to perform an operation. He examined stainless steel devices under lantern glow. Lee wondered what use there was for a scalpel, and why Angel so intently examined it. He had yet to learn how an instrument of the healing arts can implement agony.

As if to demonstrate his intentions, the Dark Angel approached them. Soldiers grabbed Lee by both arms, then forced him to bend over the table. Angel placed the scalpel inside Lee's thighs and ran the dull side of the blade along his inner legs as if preparing to make an incision.

Why would he cut me there? Lee wondered.

The troops laughed heartedly, understanding, as Lee did not, that the Dark Angel would sever groin muscles to facilitate homosexual rape.

They tossed Lee to the dirt floor where he laid. From that vantage point he observed as Batista took half the troops outside, perhaps, he surmised, to be stationed at security posts.

*What could be out here*, he thought, *requiring security measures? There haven't been signs of human life for hours.*

Five soldiers remained inside. They leered at Jaime, speaking in Spanish and laughing in eager anticipation. Lee longed to comfort her. Duct tape covered her mouth, like his, yet Lee could see her face was frozen, if not in terror, at least in horrific realization.

The night was cloaked in silence, broken only by the buzzing of mosquitoes and the mechanical hissing of the lanterns hung above Angel's bizarre operating table. Batista returned, and nodded to Angel. It was time. Lee could tell it was about to begin. The Dark Angel came forward and addressed Jaime.

"You are a beautiful woman, my Dear," he said without expression.

Jaime appeared to squirm.

"You're the kind of woman who makes a man hard."

Men beamed approvingly, all too knowingly.

"I'll show you how we treat a woman who makes men so hard."

Lee studied the creature, spying a demon rather than a man.

"And you," he said turning to Lee.

Lee continued to stare, intensely glare, unable to muster more.

"Yes, you—the *abogado* sent to the Dark Angel. I will be your schoolmaster: a stern schoolmaster, you will find, to teach you a lesson in respect."

*This is the realization of Hell*, Lee thought.

Lucifer's words from Dante's verses rushed to mind: "Hope not to ever see Heaven: I come to lead you to the other shore; into eternal darkness."

"Remove the tape from their mouths," Angel barked. "Time to for their serenades. Where shall we begin?"

Two soldiers approached Lee. Two more went toward Jaime. While one man held Lee from behind, the other roughly tugged on the tape, then ripped hard. Lee thought his lips were coming off with it. Jaime cried out as they did the same to her.

"Singing your sweet song already?

Angel smirked.

Chirp for me again," he called to Jaime. "Make *musica* for my ears."

Angel approached Jaime and slapped her until she shouted again. Lee yearned to intercede, yet shackled and held, he was helpless when they started on her.

# Chapter Twenty-Four

# No Survivors

COUNTRYSIDE SLUMBERED UNDER NIGHT SKIES, as if the earth were blanketed for bed rest. Batista had stationed four soldiers around the adobe, two-hundred feet out, spaced at compass corners, then anchored one at the doorway.

As a sentry on perimeter guard gazed into the night, the howl of a wild animal pierced nocturnal serenity. Again, it came, a louder wail lifting fine hairs on the back of his neck.

"How inhumanely," he observed, "a human can cry."

The sentries listened intently to detect whether the howls emanated from wilderness or came from the hut. Each had volunteered for service on the Battalions of Dignity, some for freedom from prison, all for extra pay and a spirit of malevolent élan associated with Noriega's special force. Each had served on torture details and were acquainted with cries beseeching mercy. Unanswered prayers always confirmed torture ensued. Yet, the howls they heard that night were somehow different, arriving as if delivered by something neither man nor beast.

On the north corner of their perimeter, a sentry released the safety lock on his M-16. He tapped the magazine to assure he had chambered a round. If a wild animal was at large, he would cut it down. A twig broke. Instantly he raised his rifle into firing position and called out.

"*¿Quién está ahí?* Who's there?"

Clouds drifting across the moon made it impossible to see. He squinted, as if narrowing his focus would somehow light up the night.

*Perhaps a wounded animal*, he thought, *or maybe a—*

The sentry went down, grabbed from behind. His head twisted and his neck cracked as it broke. Eyes bulging, his tongue reached out, then laid still, like a salamander asleep on the side of his face.

The crack of fractured vertebrae stung the ears of the sentry at the door. He craned his neck to position his head high and peered into darkness as black clouds slowly passed overhead. Again, an inhuman cry filled the air.

The remaining three guards on the perimeter went down simultaneously. With a whimper, one announced the sensation of a nine-inch combat knife piercing his kidney. Another, crawled, gasping for air through a slit trachea. His hands played a desperate game of patty-cake, slapping over his open air hatch as he suffocated. Another soldier laid front down on the ground, head twisted clear around, face pointing like a contorted beacon to the sky.

The same long and lonely cry pierced the night.

The sentry by the doorway knew only that something was amiss. He scurried into the adobe where a rifle barrel greeted him with a lead burst.

Smoke rose from the weapon held by one of Batista's Indian troops. Another Indian soldier trained his M-16 on Angel. Batista stood over the corpse of another soldier, who had fallen to a knife wound. He pointed his pistol at the remaining goblin loyal to the Dark Angel, making him remove handcuffs and leg restraints that bound Lee and Jaime.

When he was freed, Lee rushed to Jaime, and took her in his arms. She bled from the corner of her mouth where Angel's blows had broken her skin. Then, he shook his wrists, trying to circulate blood. His hands were numb, and his fingers wouldn't move.

"Blood circulation will return," Batista told his *abogado*, "for you, at least."

Batista's pistol roared. As smoke cleared, Angel's remaining soldier sprawled on the dirt floor of the adobe, moaning. Blood spewed from his head wound like an open spigot. Batista signaled one of his Indian troops by running his right hand across his throat. The Indian went to the mortally wounded soldier and eased his pain by slicing his jugular.

"No survivors," said Batista in his gentle voice, which emerged so incongruously to the violence he dispensed.

The Indian soldiers bound Angel's wrists with the handcuffs that had secured Lee. As they wrapped duct tape around his head and over his mouth, four Guaymi tribesmen entered. They wore blue jeans and traditional multicolored shirts made of cloth woven on Indian looms and carried M-16s taken from the dead guardsmen. Their hair was long, straight, and black; their faces were dark, clay like, and expressionless. One let out the shrill cry that had filled the night air as a diversion to cut down the guards. Another addressed Batista.

"So, my Brother, you are ready to come home."

Batista nodded. "It's time," he softly intoned, "that I rejoin the people."

Then, he approached Jaime. Lee placed himself between them. Batista stopped, and spoke to her.

"I'll lead you to your extraction team. They're not far, but we've got to hurry. A second truckload of troops is on the way. They're overdue, now. When they arrive, they'll come looking for us."

"So, you're Martin's man," Jaime said.

"No longer."

Lee suddenly understood. They had sent Jaime to Panama with a prearranged escape route. Batista and his band of Indian tribesmen would lead them out of the God forsaken place.

Lee saw horror etched in Angel's eyes as Batista attached a dog collar to his neck and affixed it to a leash.

A tribesman called from the doorway in a strange language or dialect Lee had never heard. Batista turned to Jaime.

"The second truck's been spotted," he said. "We must move fast."

Batista led Jaime from the hut, as his men dragged Angel along.

Lee wondered: Why aren't they killing him with the others?

They ran into the night, Lee last in line. His knee had swollen and locked, making it difficult to keep up. They hadn't run far when he heard the shouts of Noriega's troops, who had found their fallen comrades. Loud voices and gunshots rang out.

"They're after us," one of the Indians called to Lee. "Move faster."

Batista picked up the pace and Lee saw distance stretch between him and their band. They dashed into thick underbrush for cover without slowing their pace. As the Indian soldier ahead of him took a sharp bend, a low-lying tree branch caught Lee's ankle. He stumbled to the ground. Sharp pain radiated from his leg to his brain. He moaned and held his knee. It felt just as it had when he'd gone down in Philadelphia, ripped apart again.

"Yo!" he called ahead on the dark trail.

No one answered. No one returned. Lee struggled to rise but soon as he put weight on the leg, ground rushed to his face, and smacked his lips. Lee couldn't see above the high grass, so he lay in pain, desperately listening for any sound from Batista or his men.

"Frankie, you were right," he groaned. "I am expendable to the Feds' plan. But what difference does it make? Die here or return to face twenty-five years in prison on charges manufactured by your boys from downtown?"

Brush stirred along the trail. Lee forced himself partway up to call for aid when he realized. The noise came from the wrong direction. Noriega's troops had spanned out, searching.

Mosquitoes swarming overhead descended in a cluster, blanketing his face and arms. Lee pulled back to swat them, then stopped.

"You guys only suck warm blood," he told them. "So long as you're feeding, I'm still alive."

Noriega's men called to each other, voices growing louder as they neared. Lee's head spun as he scoured for cover, dragging himself off the trail to avoid capture. With each inch he crawled, Lee realized he was making it impossible for Batista's men to find him, if they bothered returning. He settled into thickets and looked upward, searching the stars as if they held some answer.

Fitting words of the English poet Blake mulled in his mind: "There is no heaven without hell, for how would you know one from the other." Lee closed his eyes, knowing he'd die in hell. Heaven had eluded him.

Then, his hands clasped, never more solemnly joined.

Jaime spotted a helicopter ahead of them. The U.S. Navy chopper sat in the center of a clearing. As they approached, Kevlar helmets sprouted from high grass. A squad of eight camouflaged U.S. Marines leaped with weapons ready. They spanned around the bird. Someone wearing combat fatigues waved from inside. Jaime ran faster toward it.

"Move, Calero," the man called to her.

She hustled to the bird where a marine helped her jump aboard.

"Where have you been, Jaime?"

She looked at Sheppard. She had never seen the Assistant U.S. Attorney wearing anything other than a business suit. The big marine reservist well filled his combat fatigues. She was glad to see him, but too exhausted to answer.

The marines surrounding the helicopter ran back toward it, ready to board and lift off.

Batista rounded up his men. One held Angel on the leash while another jabbed him with his rifle barrel.

Then, they disappeared into the countryside that the Indians knew so well.

"Where's Lee?" Jaime called out.

"Take us home," Sheppard called to the pilot.

The copter blades spun.

"Wait a minute!" Jaime shouted. "Where's Lee?"

Sheppard looked out from the helicopter into the dark.

"He's not on my priority list," the big man declared. "My orders are specific. I'm to get you out of here and I'm to do it without any hostile contact with Panamanian troops. The White House doesn't want an incident. They can't give Noriega anything to garner sympathy with Panama's Latin American neighbors."

"Send your men back for Lee. He's out there, somewhere," Jaime said pointing into the dark.

Sheppard looked at her sympathetically but gave her an answer she didn't like.

"Calero, I'm a Marine reserve officer. Know what my MOS is? I'm not a commando. I head a motor pool. They sent me here because I know about the operation and I can identify you. I'm not sending a patrol out there, looking for this guy, when I have direct orders to avoid Panamanian forces."

Jaime stood at the open doorway and a thought flashed through her mind: *Maybe Batista's men can go back for Lee.*

She scanned into the night, but they were gone.

"We're out of here," Sheppard called to the pilot.

Whirling blades lifted the helicopter.

"Bullshit, Buster!" Jaime screamed. "I'll find him myself."

She jumped out. Her feet hit the ground hard then she rolled in the grass to absorb the impact. Dust blowing from the chopper blades made her eyes tear as Jaime looked around to gain her bearings. She would head for the thickets, knowing Sheppard couldn't let her go back alone.

"Set us back down," Sheppard screamed to the pilot. As the bird touched down, he turned to his marines.

"Sergeant," Sheppard barked at the squad leader, "take two of your men. See if you can find a damned defense lawyer out there somewhere. Follow the trail. If you don't spot him in five minutes, come back without him."

Then, he called to Jaime, "Stay here. I not losing both of you."

Reluctantly, she waited beside the helicopter as the marines ran to the trail that twisted through dense overgrowths. Jaime saw Sheppard check his wristwatch, and knew he meant what he said. In five minutes, they would take off with or without Lee. She looked toward the sky and saw cloud cover had parted. Moonlight would make it easier for Sheppard's marines to find Lee . . . but it would also be easier for Noriega's troops to spot him.

She bowed her head and offered a prayer, one that she had said as a girl, then stopped when she remembered. It was the same invocation she had recited every night for the safety of her brother, Juan, whose body had never been found. Yet, she knew better than to resist instinctive spirituality. Her eyelids lowered until Sheppard's call roused her.

"Get ready to lift out!"

She saw the marines returning. One ran fast toward the helicopter, the other two moved more slowly behind in the dark.

"We're *outta* here," the first man called.

Jaime's heart sank. They hadn't found him. Then, she looked again at the two marines picking up the rear. They were dragging something between them. Shots rang through the air.

"Noriega's troops found us!" Sheppard called.

Small arms fire clacked.

Sheppard shouted to his men in the field: "Move it! Move it! Move it!"

Jaime could see him. Lee was between their arms, hobbling on one leg. More shots rang and dirt kicked up around the two marines dragging Lee. They were still a hundred feet away.

"Lay down cover fire!" Sheppard shouted to his men.

They fired back from the chopper over the heads of their comrades as the helicopter blades spun. Two marines jumped out and helped lift Lee onto the copter. Jaime dove back in the bird with the marines. It lifted off as Noriega's troops entered the clearing, firing their M-16s at the helicopter in full bursts. Bullets whizzed, ricocheting through the chopper cabin.

"Heads down!" Sheppard called.

"I'm hit!" screamed the pilot.

His groans filled their ears as the bird twirled back toward ground. The copilot wrestled at the controls but couldn't stop their descent in time. Tail rotor blades hit treetops. Leaves flew as blades thrashed branches.

The pilot slumped in his seat. Blood from a chest wound seeped through his flight suit.

"Lift us up," he moaned to the copilot. "We won't be able to maneuver this bird if we lose the tail blades."

An explosion roared beneath them. Tree limbs flew in all directions.

"Mortar," Sheppard cried. "Lay fire over there," he directed.

Two men at the open door of the bird raised their M-16s. Fully automatic bursts rang. Flashes of small arms fire answered from the ground.

A deafening blast from another mortar shell rippled beneath them. Its impact flung them upward. The bird rose above the trees. Their copilot yanked on controls, trying to steady the helicopter as they spun around in a 360-degree circle.

"We're missing a piece of the tail blade," the copilot cried.

He pulled back on the controls and lifted them higher. The chopper weaved as he tried to keep course, heading westward toward the aircraft carrier that had passed through the canal.

"I don't know if we can make the Tarawa," the copilot called out. "It's too far into international waters.

Sheppard moved to him and shouted, "Can you reach the coastline?

"Maybe," the man called back.

Sheppard shook his head.

"We can't land on Panamanian soil, not even at an American facility. If we can't reach the carrier, call in a Mayday and ditch us at sea.

"Mayday over open channels may attract a Panamanian cruiser, Captain."

"Keep to our encrypted frequency and fly us close as you can to international waters," Sheppard ordered.

"Carlson," he called to his corpsman, "check the pilot."

He squeezed out of the way as the medic pushed past. Then, Sheppard turned to his marines.

"Grab life rafts and your bikinis, boys! We may take a swim."

Jaime studied Lee. His hands clasped his knee as her eyes cast a concerned expression.

"Will you make it," she asked, "if we drop down in the ocean?"

"Don't worry about me," Lee said. "I brought a G-string."

The near full moon lit the Panamanian night with a surreal glow. More platinum than silver, it lent quiet reverence to the ritual. Batista and his men had traveled fast and far. They knelt on sacred ground in the heart of Guaymi lands. Warm earth under their knees seemed to sense why they were there. Trees enveloping all sides of the meadow, where they prayed, were their only witnesses, for no one else would find them. Swaying branches waited for them to begin.

The man, who had tortured and killed to feel alive, was securely bound. The Dark Angel shook, whining and weeping through his gag. Four stakes had been securely set in the ground, spaced nine feet apart. Strong ropes were tied to them. The cords bound Angel's arms and legs, extending him spread-eagle, face up. They had centered a large rock between the stakes. Angel's back arched painfully atop it. The rock heaved his chest upward. They removed the duct tape from his mouth so his sobs would reach the upper and lower domains of the gods when they turned to wails. Batista knew cries from one so evil would please Nacom.

The Indians stood around the Dark Angel in a circle for the divine rite. They began to chant, soft and slow. Batista raised his arms toward the sky. The hallowed song of his men grew louder. The pace hastened. They chanted feverishly, swaying their heads in fast circular motions and rocking their bodies back and forth. Time had come.

A traditional stone knife was placed in Batista's hands. He brought the implement to his lips, kissed its tip, then raised it to the moon. With a cry to his god, Batista brought the stone blade down hard and fast, striking the Dark Angel between the ribs on his left side, just under the nipple.

Blood curdling wails echoed through the night. They came from the Dark Angel, unearthly caterwauls that tingled their eardrums. Batista's soft voice whispered in reverent awe.

"Never have the Gods heard such cries."

He plunged his hand into a cavernous wound and pulled out the heart. He held it before the Dark Angel's horrified eyes. It was the last thing he would see in the earthly world. His savage wail transformed into an infant's whimper. One of Batista's men held a stone plate. Solemnly, Batista placed the heart on it, while the Dark Angel let out his final horrific moans.

The bodily organ, still warm and pumping, lay before a stone relic carved by their ancestors. The idol accepted their reverent gift as they resumed tribal chants. They anointed the twisted stone face of Nacom the executioner with the Dark Angel's fresh blood. Chanting louder, they reached into Angel's open wound and wiped his warm blood through their hair. As it cooled, the blood began to cake. Their heads looked like red-clotted mops as they feasted upon the Dark Angel's severed remains.

His face stained from giblets, Batista peered toward the upper world where his god lived. The moon shined over the far reaches of their lands, letting him know what they had done was good. Their reclamation of indigenous power pleased Nacom.

## Twenty-Five

# Kodak Memories

HIGH ABOVE THE BROAD OCEAN SCAPE and waters cascading down manmade falls into the iconic Fontainebleau Hotel swimming pool, a hastily discarded wedding veil started a trail that blazed through the bridal suite. It led past white stiletto-heeled pumps, around a crumpled tuxedo, and over a hastily strewn wedding dress. It passed under a hanging banner bearing "Congratulations" and through the doorway to a bedroom where a light flashed like a discotheque strobe. The path led to the light source, a camera mounted on a tripod that flashed automatically, and finally to the bridal bed where heavy breathers embraced. He moaned in his sleep, as if mortally wounded by contentment. She sat upright—head spinning from everything that had happened so quickly—and pronounced her new married name with pride.

"I'm Missus Tanya Tillis. Hmm," she observed, "nice initials: I'm T 'n' T!"

Her husband acknowledged with a snore.

Tanya and DEA Agent Dave Tillis had become a hot item fast. He had proposed marriage and sought her answer before she could think twice.

"Shouldn't we get to know each other better first?" she asked.

"Sweetheart," her albino amphibian replied, "What else is there to know? We love each other. That's enough, isn't it?"

The big blond had reflected a moment. She had grown fond of the gruff man, who doted on her, and he would be a good provider. Her answer came decisively.

"Works for me."

They had opted for a ceremony in Denmark, which had just legalized the world's first same-sex unions in the form of registered partnerships but returned to honeymoon where their relationship had begun.

As her new husband slept, Tanya shut down his camera. They had focused it on the marital bed to preserve the wedding night. Automatically, the camera had clicked through their torrid love feast. She peered into the camera case that contained so many lenses and nifty things. At the bottom, Tanya spied a pack of photos in an envelope. She opened it and peeked at the pictures.

Rage filled her. Her words emerged with dagger points on the consonants and venom in the vowels.

"What's my frog doing with another woman?"

They were on a beach making out. She looked at rest of the photographs.

"Oh, my God!" she groaned.

He was doing more than making out.

Tears welled in Tanya's eyes. Why did he keep the pictures? Did her new husband love someone else? She took the photos into the living room for brighter light. Tanya glanced at the woman. She was a looker.

*God, how this hurts*, Tanya thought.

She studied her frog in the pictures, then realized.

"Hey, that's not my frog!"

Her eyes strained for a better look.

"Lee's got a birthmark on his butt."

Tanya set down the photos. Why would her frog have compromising pictures of the man who had saved her from trouble so often? She thought about what she should do with them. Immediately, Tanya decided and declared: "I'll look at 'em again!"

DEA Agent Dave Tillis walked down the long white corridor of the FBI Miami field office. Supervisor Martin and an Assistant U.S. Attorney expected him. He was seeing that Jaime Calero received her due. The meeting was a prelude to an interview at the Office of Professional Responsibility, where special agents exhaustively investigated all allegations of misconduct by FBI employees.

Calero was history at the Bureau. Tillis had heard rumors about her involvement in a mission with the lawyer. Still, that wouldn't excuse her for flagrantly breaking the Bureau "No Kiss" Rule while she remained under agency jurisdiction in Mexico. He had photographic evidence to lift her badge.

The receptionist conveyed a cordial welcome to the fellow federal law enforcement officer. Tillis followed a young man to the same interrogation room where Lee once sat. He waited anxiously for Jaime's boss and the Assistant U.S. Attorney.

Supervisor Martin entered first, closely followed by Robert Sheppard. They settled into their chairs quickly and began. Martin conducted the interview.

"Calero is on maternity leave," he said.

Tillis responded flatly, "I don't care."

"You know she's been promoted."

"Don't care. I literally caught her in bed with the enemy."

Sheppard set the record straight.

"Lee Gunther was cleared of the tax charges pending against him. His old mob buddy had people in Philadelphia send us a package that exonerated him."

"The lawyer even closed his law office," Martin added. "While he was in Cancun, he wrote for a new job. Now, he's an adjunct professor at the University of

Miami Law School, teaching criminal practice and legal ethics."

Sheppard jiggled. "Legal ethics?"

"Sometimes we teach what we need to learn," Martin said. "From what I hear, he's as sharp on his feet in classrooms as he was in courtrooms."

Tillis didn't care.

"Are you going to do something about this or not?"

He slid a package of photographs to Sheppard. Tillis saw the man's eyes blaze. The Assistant U.S. Attorney studied each one. Some pictures he turned sideways. Others he held up to the light.

Martin looked anxious. He grabbed the photographs from Sheppard's hands and did the same.

"What do you want us to do with these?" Martin finally said.

"Do what you have to do," Tillis responded. "Bureau rules apply to all agents."

"So what?"

Martin slid the photographs back to Tillis.

"I thought you might say that," Tillis said smugly. "That's why I sent a copy of these photographs directly to the OPR office in Washington."

"Why?" Sheppard said.

Anger surged through Tillis. They could play games, trying to save Calero's skin but OPR wouldn't be so forgiving. As he took the photos back, Tillis noticed something strange. The one on top looked like a picture of three boobs. On closer inspection, he recognized his bald spot and two very familiar breasts cresting atop. Rapidly, he scanned the rest. Someone had switched the photographs from Cancun with Kodak memories snapped on his wedding night. A bridal smile lit them all. His mouth formed one word.

"Tanya!"

Martin and Sheppard walked out the door.

"Thanks for the show," Sheppard called over his shoulder.

Lee perused correspondence on the sofa. Lecture notes surrounded him, just as trial briefs once had. Jaime came close and sat beside him.

"What came in the mail?" she said.

"Letter from a Swiss law firm," Lee said without looking up. "Apparently, I was named as a beneficiary in Frankie Cinelli's will. The estate's being divided equally between me and a woman in Panama."

"Big estate?"

"Probably just a token remembrance. For all the years Frankie scammed, he never had much. We'll receive an accounting in a couple weeks."

Lee looked up at the television. News cameras focused on American soldiers wearing camouflage-painted faces and Kevlar helmets. He turned up the volume with a remote.

"It doesn't seem much like Christmas to the twenty-five thousand American troops on the invasion force, here, in Panama," a reporter observed. "But the combat is over. It lasted just one day. An interim government has been appointed pending free elections. For the first time in thirty years, one-man rule in Panama, most recently under Manuel Noriega, has come to an end."

American GIs had become the largest, best armed, and most unusual posse in history to hunt one man—Manuel Antonio Noriega. Operation "Just Cause" was in full swing. When they had landed, Noriega ran for cover. The devil himself had fled to the Vatican embassy in Panama City seeking papal protection. Monsignor Jose Sebastian Labota, the Vatican ambassador to Panama, had appeared for a press interview to discuss his problematic guest. He seemed more like a hotelier or warden than a nuncio. Not only was he housing Noriega, but some of the dictator's ruthless accomplices were leaping over the embassy walls to beg for papal protection.

Outside, American troops afforded the embassy soil its diplomatic autonomy. Americans wouldn't enter without an invitation. They also knew the Vatican wouldn't expel a soul seeking refuge, so psychological operations intensified. Blackhawk helicopters constantly buzzed by the Vatican embassy close enough to rumble glass in its windows. Armored personnel carriers repeatedly pulled up to the embassy back gate. American troops with binoculars focused on the window to Noriega's bedroom. Supersensitive microphones picked up his every whisper.

Comically, rock 'n' roll music blared from loudspeakers pointed at the building. Noriega rose every morning to a chorus of "I Fought the Law and the Law Won." They cut off the former dictator's air conditioning. A priest removed the telephone from Noriega's room. Nuns emptied the embassy liquor cabinets.

At last, on January 3, 1990, Lee and Jaime heard the bulletin. It was delivered to them on a late-night television newscast as they lounged on the sofa in their family room.

"Make it louder," Jaime called out, when she saw the backdrop: Panama.

Lee grabbed the remote by his side.

"At eight forty-four this evening," the newswoman reported, "General Manuel Antonio Noriega surrendered to United States authorities. Drug enforcement agents bound the former Panamanian dictator using wire handcuffs. With hands lashed behind his back, they took him into custody."

Jaime watched relief sweep over Lee as the details enfolded. She was pleased to see it in his face, and envied his reaction, as if an elixir had vanquished the tensions from their mission that they both had brought home.

*Yet*, she wondered, *why don't I share that feeling? Where's my damned closure?*

Perhaps it wasn't yet time for her memories of those events to fade. She glanced toward Lee, as he sorted through holiday greeting cards on their coffee table. One seemed to stand out from the rest. Lee lingered over a note that came with it.

"Who sent that one?" She said.

"Paul Cameron."

"From Atlantic City?"

Lee only nodded vaguely, as if captured in thought.

She knew the younger lawyer's troubles. They had discussed the possibility of Lee rendering further assistance and it bothered her to think he might be drawn back into the affair. His former associate from Philadelphia had relocated to the New Jersey seashore, where he opened his own successful law practice by the boardwalk.

Jaime studied anguish that surfaced in Lee's expression. This could be a call for help that he had to answer, no matter how reluctantly.

Paul always walked the thin line separating zealous advocacy from lawlessness. Working with the Mafia family in the gambling mecca, he may have crossed it by a mile. Charges mounted. Lee had handled preliminary matters in the case, despite his keen reservations. Now, she realized, he was being implored to undertake the trial defense.

"Getting ready to I dust off your courtroom suits?" She queried.

Lee paused before he answered.

"Do I still have enough fire in my belly for a homicide trial?"

*Bellies*, Jaime thought.

She moved close to peck his cheek. It was strange to see him this way. She was the one, who found herself caught in pensive moments these days.

She took his hand, placing it on her tummy until they felt the baby stir.

"The fertility god in Tulum did his job," she said.

Lee smiled.

"I'd like to go there again," Jaime declared, "in about six months."

At the Mira Flores locks, Carmella Ruiz set a bouquet of opalescent blossoms on the ground where Frankie had been killed. She sprinkled a powder over them and recited a silent prayer.

A tourist looked on. She elbowed her husband and asked.

"What's that little woman doing?"

He lifted his baseball cap to scratch his scalp. As Carmella mouthed a slow refrain, the woman nudged him again.

"Now, what's she up to?"

He pulled down his hat and shrugged his shoulders. They gawked until a canal worker, wearing blue overalls, approached. He stopped next to the nosy spectators and wiped his brow with the back of his hand. With his back to Carmella, he warned them in hushed tones.

"Best not to stare."

Covering his mouth with his hand, he spoke in hushed tones and the twosome leaned closer to hear.

"They say she's a voodoo woman. Comes here once a week to pine over a lost love. Some even believe she's cast a curse on those responsible for his death."

As Carmella peered back at the laborer and sightseers, they moved away uneasily to avoid her gaze. Those, who knew her story, understood she did more than mourn. Carmella carried her flowers to the waterway. One at a time, she dropped them into the canal. As they fell, she called to her love.

"No one has ever seen the monsters who took you from me, my Frankie No Throat. No one ever will."

She cast another flower and uttered the simple truth.

"Justice takes many forms . . . and finds ways to reach us all."

As always, when the last blossom kissed the water, Carmella studied petals floating on the surface. It's then that her heart pours open. Carmella always cries when she thinks of her Frankie No Throat. Her tears fall freely in a land that is no longer Hell.

The Washington Post

FINAL

# U.S. Forces Crush Panamanian Military; Noriega in Hiding as Fighting Continues

## Noriega Headquarters Leveled; City in Chaos

### Americans Taken Hostage

*Days after senior President Bush orders the invasion of Panama to arrest Noriega on U.S. drug trafficking charges*

# Epilogue

*or where are they now?*

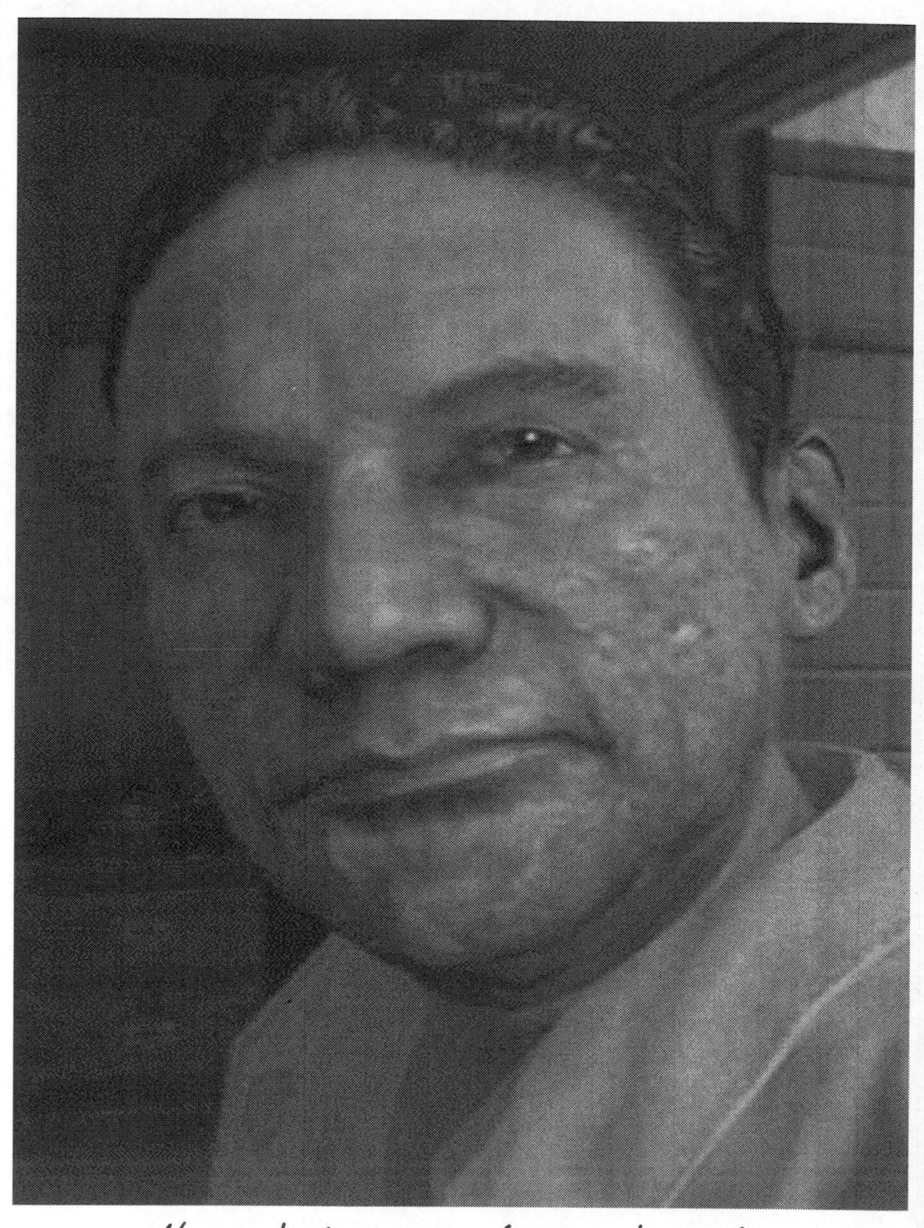

*Noriega's depiction in Activision's popular video game "Call of Duty: Black Ops II"*

# Epilogue

# An Author's Adieu Addressing Who's Real

NOW THAT YOU'VE TAKEN *A RUN TO HELL*, it's time to ask: Where do beloved and despised characters go after the last page? Frankie "No Throat" Cinelli would have told . . .

"The answer is fuckin' obvious, my friend. Some live and others don't."

As an author, I miss the wisest wise guy ever to chomp a Philadelphia cheese steak. He always took them wit'. That's how you order the city signature regalement, where the classic sandwich was born in South Philly. You say wit' or wit' out, meaning Frankie loved them *with* grilled onions.

Anyway, while Jaime manages double duty as Bureau Supervisor and Mother, and as Lee pours through notes preparing tomorrow's evidence lecture, let's hunt down some folks. We'll mostly focus on who's "real" in this fictive account.

## Manuel Antonio Noriega Moreno

Noriega was indicted in 1988 by United States federal grand juries in Miami and Tampa on charges of racketeering, drug smuggling, and money laundering. During "Operation Just Cause," the 1989 U.S. invasion of Panama, Noriega was captured and flown to the United States, where he was imprisoned while awaiting criminal dispositions.

His trial on the Miami indictment lasted six months from September 1991 to April 1992. It ended with Noriega's conviction on most charges. Sentenced to 40 years in prison, he served 17 years, after a sentence reduction for "good behavior." Hmm. How good was he to forgive more than half his lengthy sentence? Must have been lovely.

Noriega was extradited to France, where he was sentenced to seven years imprisonment for money laundering. In 2011, France extradited the former dictator and well-traveled felon to Panama, where he was incarcerated for crimes committed during his rule. Diagnosed with a brain tumor in March 2017, Noriega suffered complications during surgery. Two months later, on May 29, 2017, he died in custody at the age of 83.

While imprisoned, Noriega had sued video game publisher Activision for creating a villainess character based on him without his permission in the hugely popular *Call of Duty: Black Ops II*, a great game for gamers. He complained, among other things, that the shooter game damaged his reputation. Oh, my. Rudy Giuliani served as co-counsel defending Activision. What happened? The judge tossed out the case, essentially agreeing with the game creator that Noriega's portrayal is protected by the Constitution, and that the lawsuit was frivolous and absurd.

Historians group Manuel Noriega with murderous authoritarian rulers: Muammar Gaddafi of Libya, Augusto Pinochet of Chile, and Sadam Hussein of Iraq. Unlike his contemporaries, this SOB's legacy of misery survives worldwide in the form of drug addiction that still ruins and takes lives.

## The Royals of Monaco

The Grimaldi family continues to reign. A treaty between the tiny nation and France provided that if the reigning Prince failed to leave dynastic offspring, the sovereignty terminated, and the realm reverted to France. In 2002, about three years after Lee started teaching law at the University of Miami, an agreement expanded the pool of potential royals to more broadly guarantee Monegasque independence.

Some say the loss of Princess Grace cost the principality a dash of glitter. You *gotta* agree. Following her plunge off the treacherous D37 highway called the Moyenne Corniche, she died on September 14, 1982, at the age of 52. The incident left mysteries abounding in print and on web sites. "Readers Digest," online at rd.com, presents "11 Unanswered Questions About Grace Kelly's Death" that *A Run to Hell* answers. Maybe they owe me a footnote.

Grace's accident scene the day after

Her husband, Prince Rainier Grimaldi, III, never remarried. While smoking sixty cigarettes a day, he puffed and ruled until near death. On April 6, 2005, he died at the age of 81. At that time, he was the world's second longest serving head of state. Rainier is survived by their three children: Princess Stephanie, Princess Caroline, and Prince Albert II, who inherited the throne.

"Drop by the Monte Carlo Casino," Grace no doubt would still beckon us, "next time you cruise the Mediterranean."

Okay. So, we all know that's probably not happening tomorrow.

# The Kelly Clan

Let's turn to Grace's brother, Kell, more formally John B. Kelly, Junior, and Rachel Harlow, two very real and very different folks. Let's just call them a quality couple sure to liven up your dinner party.

*Kell*

First, let me say, mystery always shrouded the untimely dual deaths of Lee's dear friend Kell and his brother-in-law, as evidenced in the actual published newspaper articles displayed and quoted in my tale. The Monday, March 4, 1985, "Philadelphia Inquirer" front-page lead story, which decorates this book with Kell's photo, declared: "Cause of death uncertain," while noting Kell had "a mild heart ailment." His demise was a tragic loss for the City of Brotherly Love. Consider his éclat—the locally acclaimed "gentlemanly lifetime" and his family's attachment to the town.

Kell shared his father's passion for athletics. In the 1920s, Dad won three Olympic sculling medals, including gold, for the United States in rowing events he was declared unfit to enter. At the time, Dad was a brick layer, which rendered him ineligible for Olympic competition because folks, who performed labor, were deemed to have “an unfair muscular advantage” over true gentleman. But Dad persisted until they let him compete and he beat the bastards. Ultimately our questionable gentleman became a multi-millionaire running Philadelphia’s largest construction business.

In 1956, his son Kell won Olympic bronze in the single scull event. A statue of the senior Olympian is situated beside the Schuykill River where both rowed. It’s placed beside a bucolic thoroughfare that Philadelphians posthumously named Kelly Drive in honor of our Kell, the junior sculler.

The home, where siblings Kell, Grace, Margaret, and Elizabeth were raised at 3901 Henry Avenue in the East Falls section of town, was purchased in 2017 by Prince Albert. He announced plans to establish a museum there to his mother’s memory and an office for his own foundation, which is dedicated to protection of the environment.

## Rachel Harlow and Tanya

Harlow deserves recognition. Truly. Generations before “woke culture,” Harlow put herself out there. She often appeared in Philadelphia media, including the nationally syndicated Mike Douglas television show produced there, identifying herself as a transgendered female before there was outspoken LGBTQ community support. She attended the Cannes International Film Festival, where she became a center of attention. David Bowie, then in his "androgynous phase," met her and later cited her influence.

TUESDAY

# DAILY MAGAZINE

PEOPLE • HOME • MOVIES • THE ARTS • TV • STYLE

# Different, yet the same

*Philadelphia's famous transexual started life as Richard Finocchio, but became famous as Rachel Harlow. After years of shunning publicity, she's back in the spotlight. Her restaurant is Harlow's — and she's still Rachel.*

Baby boomers blasted

*"Philadelphia's famous transsexual," declared the press*

The real-life beauty's renown transition and Kell's prominent stature in Philadelphia society lent their 1970s relationship a flavorful air, finding its way into my story because the public perception of Kell is so strongly associated with the pairing. They remain eternally e-linked in web histories, blogs, and biographical accounts.

Harlow's strong presence motivated the creation of transgendered Tanya, who coupled with fictional character DEA agent Dave Tills.

## Drug Enforcement Agency

The DEA deserves a salute for their fine work in taking down drug kingpins, who dealt with Noriega, including Columbian drug lord Pablo Escobar. The narcoterrorist, who founded and was the sole leader of the Medellín Cartel, was killed in a shootout on December 2, 1993, while resisting arrest.

Drug Kingpin Pablo Escobar

## FBI and CIA

Supervisor Martin of the Federal Bureau of Investigation and his Central Intelligence Agency colleague typify dedicated officers of the two agencies. The CIA has no law enforcement authority, focusing on intelligence collection abroad, while the FBI is primarily a domestic agency, maintaining fifty-six field offices in major U.S. cities. In 1980, the United States Joint Terrorism Task Force created a partnership between thirty-five federal agencies, including the FBI, CIA, and DEA, to combat terrorism. The agencies also join in operations where their jurisdictions overlap, and agency conflicts—*as we saw*—can arise.

## Doctor Hugo Spadafora

Now, let's attend a checkup with Hugo. If you're from Latin America, you instantly recognize the physician-revolutionary, who really lived a full, though murderously shortened, lifetime. He died as Jaime described on September 13, 1985, at the age of 45. The

CIA continues to maintain the horrific audio recording that documents his demise.

In 1989, Manual Noriega and his followers were found guilty in a Panamanian court of conspiracy to murder Hugo. Noriega was tried and convicted in abstentia, while in United States custody.

*Revered in Central America*

## Coaches Dooney and Paterno

This vignette is for pigskin fans Don't fear moving ahead to Carmella Ruiz if American football isn't your game. Just understand that Lee's coaches are real and true to life.

Ray Dooney long led the William Penn Charter Little Quakers against archrival Germantown Academy Patriots in what's arguably the nation's oldest continuous schoolboy football rivalry, first played in 1876. The NFL recognizes a New England high school match up as longest running: Norwich Free Academy versus New London High School, dating back to 1875, though not played during World War I. Sissies. Well, it's difficult to substantiate these things, anyway, because none of the participants in those early matchups are alive enough to offer verification.

JoePa: Hero or coward posed CNN

On a sad note, I turn to Lee's college alma mater. As Head Coach of the Penn State Nittany Lions from 1966, Joe Paterno racked up championships until a child sex abuse scandal involving former defensive coordinator, Jerry Sandusky, led to his termination in November 2011. "JoePa," as the campus community knew him, died weeks later, on January 22, 2012, some say of cancer. Others attribute disgrace.

The National Collegiate Athletic Association vacated Penn State's 111 wins from 1998 through 2011, as part of its punishment, which dropped JoePa from first to twelfth on the list of winningest NCAA football coaches. Settlement of a subsequent lawsuit, brought by local politicos, posthumously restored Coach Paterno's full record.

Yet, college administrators never replaced his statue, which was taken down and stored in some undisclosed location. I have mixed feelings because JoePa had long devoted himself to an athletics program that did so much for the players, student body, and university he cherished.

In 2012, Sandusky was found guilty of 45 counts of child sexual abuse and was sentenced to serve 30 to 60 years in prison, effectively a life sentence for the then 68-year old. Prison administrators held him in solitary confinement more than five years for his own safety, while he filed various appeals, including an application for resentencing, which was denied in 2019. I have no uncertainty here. Sandusky received what he deserved: the strongest dose of justice the law allows.

## Carmella Ruiz

Let's return to Panama. Frankie No Throat's love, Carmella, is a composite of folks, opening our eyes to the rich makeup of Central American culture. We last saw her at the Mira Fora locks of the Panama Canal.

Ten years after our trip to Panama, on December 31, 2009, the United States turned over control of the canal to Panama. Annual traffic had risen from about 1,000 ships in 1914, when it opened, to nearly 15,000 annually when the United States let go. How did this affect the populace? Panamanians rejoiced, Carmella among them, filled with nationalistic pride.

*Protesters oppose turning over the canal*

Turnover of the canal didn't come naturally. President Ronald Reagan famously said: "We built it, we paid for it, it's ours, and we are going to keep it." That was true of the canal, but not of the ground under it. Anyway, we turned the thing over fair and square.

Since then, Panamanians demonstrated the ability to operate and maintain the canal, having built a second series of locks permitting larger ships through, which opened in 2016. An era of United States colonialism ended peacefully, while we remain friends with Panamanians in a way that accommodates both nations.

## The Philadelphia Mafia

The Philadelphia Mafia family was founded in 1911 by Salvatore Sabella in South Philadelphia. It remains active to this day in the Greater Philadelphia area, South Jersey, Atlantic City, Wilmington, and Trenton. Over the years, the family earned notoriety for violence, largely due to a succession of violent bosses and multiple mob wars, which the local press covered like it follows the Phillies, Eagles, Flyers, and Sixers. If the organization were a Rotary Club, it would be regarded as a medium-sized and active association of members engaged in racketeering, bookmaking, loansharking, drug trafficking, fraud, corruption, and Frankie No Throat's specialities: money laundering and murder.

Faces on display in this story are molded from the crime family poster children: Crime Boss Angelo Bruno, who reigned from 1959 to 1980 and one of his successors, "Little Nicky" Scarfo, whose reign is sometimes referred to as a "dysfunctional period" due to his hot temper and penchant for violence. And, let's face it, when a Mafia boss is deemed dysfunctional, the "boys from downtown" are all-stars en route to the Mafia Hall of Fame.

*Philly mob boss "Little Nicky" Scarfo after sentencing for murder and racketeering*

## Jaime Calero

Lee's sweetie, if you'll accept a term of endearment that Jaime and Lee privately exchange, retained her surname after they wed. She's proud of her heritage. As for Lee, he remains honored to have been chosen as her husband.

Jaime is as real as these pages make her, a character defined by determined women, who "broke the glass ceiling" of the FBI, so long an all male bastion. Her promotion to Supervisory Special Agent—a senior agent doing field, administrative, and analytical work while leading investigations—was a landmark promotion that didn't come easily to women at that time.

She raises her head high again on the pages of a novel in progress with the working title: *We Took Separate Trails but Stepped in the Same Shit.* Indubitably, editors will trim my title, at least to the extent it fits a book cover. This tale comes from the heart, touching a disorder that causes the suicide of one United States hero every 65 minutes.

## Lee Gunther

As for Lee, we've learned something through him, have we not? Sometimes a run to Hell can be your path to redemption. Find Lee, right now, in *The Boardwalkers*, where the law professor is beseeched to ply his true craft. Allow me to extend your invitation.

Take a seventy-year stroll beside surf, where saints and sinners, loving spouses and their lovers, as well as Mafiosi, lawyers, judges, and street people are tender life mates, eager bed fellows, and deadly foes. You'll catch them in a lethal mystery set at the adult playground called Atlantic City. It's available from the usual booksellers. I strongly recommend selecting the Second Edition Redux.

## And Now for Us

It's time to part and I've considered how best to do so. After all, every book has a last page. I'd like to close the way Lee's guardian angel may have, if given the chance. Frankie No Throat always loved the songs he couldn't sing. He also had an affinity for vintage Hollywood classic films. Remember? After whacking Jackie Toes, Frankie scrubbed himself in a vinegar bath while watching his horse-riding hero, John Wayne, in "Stagecoach."

So, in Frankie's memory I'll close by borrowing words uttered by Rick—played by Humphrey Bogart—in the 1942 Academy Award winner for Best Picture, "Casablanca." In the final scene, Bogie said as I'll say right now:

"Here's looking at you, kid."

I'll look for you again soon on the boardwalk.

Best wishes!

*Schof*

**A LEGAL THRILLER AND WHODUNIT SNARES BOARDWALKERS.** As tide rolls, evidence stacks against a trial lawyer charged with gruesomely slaying his wife. Without an alibi an innocent man faces a death sentence, while a Mafia boss confronts death's open jaws. Either's survival costs the other's life.

Seventy salty years of Atlantic City is exposed from prohibition to the birth of casino glitter palaces. Here you can learn about love from a killer with a heart, search for your soul among the soulless, and hope to snare a murderer before it's too late.

Put on flip-flops. Then join lawyers, judges, cops, hoods, players, preachers, street people–*the good and the gutter snipes*–in a perfect read for any beach, hearth, or comfort zone.

**Reader reviews of *The Boardwalkers* on Amazon:**

*5.0 out of 5 stars* **A compelling murder mystery that you can't put down once you begin!** WOW! Once you begin this book you are pulled in and never let go! With the plot and so many sub-plots...so many threads which all come together in a surprising ending you just can't stop turning pages.

*5.0 out of 5 stars* **An excellent fast paced read!** Both the book and the author are new to me and I can honestly say this was one of the best books I've read! Set in Atlantic City *Boardwalkers* is a fast paced read that will have you turning the pages! A trial lawyer is accused of murdering his wife but swears he is innocent. Wonderfully written characters including judges, prostitutes, dirty cops, the mob and more. It's one of those books that are hard to put down. I definitely recommend this Book!

*5.0 out of 5 stars* **A phenomenal read**. If you are looking for a book with detail, mayhem, and major plots twist, look no further.

*5.0 out of 5 stars* **Exciting and well-written!** I really enjoyed reading *The Boardwalkers* by Frederick Schofield. There was a lot going on in this novel, but the author handled all the different threads and scenarios perfectly, so I was never confused and always eager to see what would happen next.

Schofield is particularly good with characters. There are quite a few, and each is unique, with his/her own distinct personality. No stock, one-dimensional characters here! I look forward to more by this author!

Find full reviews and critical acclaim at Amazon.com. Learn about the "stories behind the stories" in articles videos, music, and more at **Frederick-Schofield.com**

Made in the USA
Middletown, DE
01 October 2020